FORTUNE IS A WOMAN

WINSTON GRAHAM

Fortune Is a Woman

DOUBLEDAY & COMPANY, INC.
Garden City, New York

*The characters in this book are entirely imaginary
and bear no relation to any living person*

LIBRARY OF CONGRESS CATALOG CARD NUMBER: 53–7980

Fortune is a woman.

Machiavelli: Il Principe, Chapter 25

Surely men may be excusable and nevertheless miss happiness, and be tormented in many ways.

Spinoza

FORTUNE IS A WOMAN

chapter 1

You might think that that first time I met her hadn't really a lot of significance. Everything has changed so much since, that sometimes it doesn't seem any longer to have happened to her and to me. Yet the more I think of it the more important it seems to begin there, if anyone is to understand the rest.

I remember I'd been on the move since early morning, slipping out of a shed where they kept the empties behind a country pub, getting away before the maids woke, and making more or less direct south for Salisbury. I'd hoped to see it before the evening; but I'd only picked up one lift all day, a lorry driver with neuralgia who put me on about ten miles. Even that wasn't direct; and when the drizzle started I was sorry I hadn't gone on with him to Andover. I didn't want a night under a hedge.

The car was a bit off the road and she was changing a wheel. At least, she was going through some halfhearted motions with a jack, but when she heard the footsteps she straightened up and looked round. She was only a kid, and there was no one else in the car. I asked her if she'd got a puncture and she said, yes, and murmured something about a broken milk bottle, so I said, did she want any help, and she said: "Thanks. Thank you so much. I was afraid I might not be able to move the screws."

The car was a Daimler with some sort of a sports body. She'd been travelling fast, and it was lucky there was a wide verge. I got the jack under and worked the car up on it. She stood and watched for a bit, and then fetched a torch, because darkness was falling, and held it for me in a black-gloved hand. We didn't talk much, because there wasn't much to say, but once or twice I thought the torch wavered over to include me.

After I'd put the other wheel on I started tightening it, and the brace slipped on the nut. I straightened up and looked at her properly for the first time.

"You've hurt your hand?" she said.

"Look, will you get in and put the brake on?"

"What for?"

"The wheel turns instead of the nut."

"Oh, I see." She handed me the torch and slipped into the car. When the screws were a bit tighter I let the car down and finished the job. I put the hubcap back. She hadn't come out again. I pushed the punctured tyre into the boot with the tools and shut it. Not another car had passed all the time. I wiped my hands on a rag and went round to the door of the car.

"It's O.K. You can drive on now."

She said: "Thank you very much. Can I give you a lift somewhere?"

"I was going to Salisbury."

"I live a mile from there."

I walked round the car and opened the other door. She had switched on the interior light.

I said: "I'll muck your car up."

"Oh, no, it's all right. Get in."

I slid in and she pressed the starter. The car bumped off the verge and accelerated away with a well-bred hum. Nothing coarse or effortful about it. They were both thoroughbreds, she and the car, and I'd no place in either of their lives.

She wasn't more than eighteen, I guessed; tallish and fairly plump, the way some young girls are at that age. She drove very fast. At the time I thought perhaps it was just because she was

10

late or because she wanted to get rid of me as soon as possible.

After a bit, perhaps more to break the silence than from any real interest, she asked me if I lived in Salisbury, and I said I'd never been there before. Then it came out that I was looking for work, and she said, had I been out of work long, and I said, long enough. I think she glanced at me then, maybe wondering how old *I* was, under the dirt.

It was easier really to sit quiet than to talk; it was queer to sink back in this luxury knowing that in a few minutes it would have wafted on, leaving you to the darkness and the rain and the "no hawkers" notices. Now and then a reflected light would show up her face. It caught the gleam of her stockings sometimes, and a sort of paler opalescence to her wrist when her coat sleeve slid back. She'd a lot of dark hair, tied loosely back somehow at the nape of her neck and quite long, and very pale skin, so smooth that her face seemed a bit unreal, like a cameo, except that her mouth was human enough and lovely. The fine bones of her face suggested how she might look in a year or two's time.

Somewhere along the road she had to brake because of a convoy of half a dozen army trucks; and, after she had gone past them like a torpedo, she made some sort of remark about the prospect of war. It was everybody's small-change topic at the time, like the weather, so I didn't answer, feeling the way I did. After a second or two she glanced at me.

"Do you think there'll be a war?"

I said: "If it is, it'll not be my war."

"How do you mean?"

"Well, I think those can do the fighting who've got something to fight for."

She said after a minute: "Do you think a dictatorship would give it you?"

"It couldn't give me less."

"That's something I can't argue about."

I rubbed a streak of blood off my hand. "Perhaps it's easy and straightforward for you, because people like you feel you're fighting for something that belongs to you. I've nothing like that to believe in. The only privilege I've ever had is the privilege of being kicked around." I could see her expression but I couldn't read it. "So if there's a war, I'm getting out of the country. And

11

if I did happen to be caught in England I should try and get by as a pacifist, or a foursquare gospeller, or a Second Adventist. Just so I can keep my hands clean and let other people make heroes of themselves."

I don't know what particularly made me say all that just then. Even in those days, however I felt, I wasn't much of a one for shooting a line. Something in her, I suppose. Anyway, when I'd said it I think perhaps I half expected her to stop and tell me to get out; if she had I should have taken it as the familiar, natural thing, what I was used to; I should have gone, satisfied to walk, knowing I'd asked no favour. But she didn't. Instead after a minute she said:

"I haven't met anyone like you before."

"I expect it's a bad exchange for a mended puncture."

"I didn't say that."

We were coming among houses.

"Is this Salisbury?"

"Not quite."

"You know," I said, "you and me shouldn't talk the same language. That's the trouble."

She said quietly: "I don't think we do."

We cut through the single street and were out in the country again. If I could have seen her foot I think it would have been hard down on the accelerator pedal. Between us we'd summed it all up, and there wasn't anything more to say.

"And what will you do if there's a war?" I asked.

"Give up my work and take another job, I suppose."

"Oh, you—work?"

"Does that surprise you?"

"A bit."

"I thought it might."

"Well, that's all right. I don't mind." After a minute I said: "Are you training for something?"

"I'm studying ballet. I'm taking it up as a profession." After a second she added, a bit defensively: "Perhaps that doesn't sound like work to you—but it is."

"I don't know anything about it," I said. "It doesn't belong where I come from."

"And where *do* you come from?"

"Does it matter?"

"No . . ."

"I'm English."

"Oh, I never had the slightest doubt about that."

I wanted to ask her what she meant, but the car was slowing up.

"This is where I live," she said. "You go straight on for the centre of the town—if you want the centre."

"Thanks."

"But if you've hurt your hand I can have it dressed for you first."

We were turning towards some double gates, and there were lights in a house well back. "No, it's nothing. I'll get down here."

As she stopped, I remember, the headlights whitened all the drive until it curved away towards the house.

I opened the door. "Well, thanks for the lift."

She didn't say anything, but groped about in her bag, and as I got out she put two coins into my hand. I pulled my hand back quickly, and one of the coins rolled on the floor of the car. She began to say something and I began to say something, both at the same time; but before we could get it clear a man came up out of the darkness.

"Is that you, Sarah? Where have you been? Who is this?"

He was about my own height, thin and probably iron grey.

"I was kept late with Valerie, Daddy. I had a puncture. This man changed the wheel for me, so I gave him a lift."

"O.K.," I said. "It wasn't much trouble, and I got a lift."

Her father looked me up and down, from my two-day beard to somebody else's shoes.

"Oh . . . I see," he said stiffly. "Very well. I'm much obliged to you. Good night."

The girl said good night to me a bit more graciously, and they moved off. She was explaining about Valerie. I could see she was going to get a talking to for risking herself with a tough like me.

I stood there for a second looking after them. They'd already almost forgotten me. I was out of their little world—a man with no name who'd served a purpose and passed on. I was a stray bit of a larger world that was expendable for their convenience and comfort. Of course I was used to that sort of thing, but I didn't

13

like it. I began to walk off down the road. I heard the car move into the drive. It was minutes before I knew I was still holding one of the coins she had given me. It was half a crown.

I found a bed at a hostel that had just been opened, and the next day I went to see the man whose name I'd been given; but he was on his holidays so I was back where I started. It was hay-making time but the weather was against it. Perhaps I was against it too. I've thought since that people sheered off not so much from the ragged clothes but from something in my eyes. I couldn't make it easy for them to feel sorry for me. All I collected all morning was ninepence and a pamphlet headed "Thy World Is a Lamp unto My Feet."

In the afternoon I got a job chopping wood. At least it wasn't much of a job because the old woman I did it for couldn't afford to pay me anything, but I thought I might as well do that as nothing. In the middle of it a policeman came up and asked me what my name was and how long I'd been in the town.

I told him and he said: "Were you the man who changed the wheel of Dr. Darnley's car and was given a lift in it afterwards?"

When you're living like I was living you don't look on a police-man as your friend and protector the way comfortable people do. There's a sort of cold war goes on, even when you've done nothing: "Move along there, please," "Now then, can't bed down here, you know." And even when they don't speak they look at you, taking a mental note in case there's a petty theft; and you look back at them, maybe showing what you'd like to say.

This was a very young policeman. I said: "I changed the wheel of a car."

He said: "I'll have to ask you to come along to the station. There's one or two questions we want to ask you."

"What's the game?"

"Miss Darnley has lost her bracelet. We're just checking up. You don't want to make trouble here, do you?"

The old woman I was doing the job for was sticking her head out from one of her upper windows. I guessed she'd suspected all along there was a catch in it somewhere, and now it was going to turn out I was a child murderer or something in disguise.

"So they think I took it, eh?"

"We've just got to check up," the policeman said pacifically.

"You don't want to make trouble here. We can talk it over quietly, like, at the station."

He was bluffing, I knew that much, because he hadn't made a charge, but I'd nothing to hide, so I chucked the axe down and went with him. I was pretty mad about it, and I thought: perhaps she'll be at the station waiting to accuse me.

But when I got there there was nobody but a big sergeant with a bald head and another policeman sitting in a corner by the door—and of course the usual smell of disinfectant.

They asked me my name and where I came from and how I'd been given the lift last night and whether I'd seen anything of a diamond bracelet and where I'd spent the night and who I'd called on this morning. Then they asked me if I was willing to be searched. I said, why should I be? Were they arresting me, and if so, what for?

The sergeant looked at me with a suspicious eye, because I'd shown that I knew the ropes.

"Ever been charged before?"

"Yes."

"What for?"

"Knocking a policeman down."

You could feel the temperature cooling off.

"What did you get?"

"Seven days."

The sergeant got up and walked round his desk and bit the end of his thumb.

He said: "Look, son, we know your kind and we're used to dealing with 'em. If you want trouble you can have it, and believe you me, no one will blame us for arresting you on suspicion. But if you'll answer questions and submit to a search without a charge we'll do the fair thing by you. It's up to you to choose."

I thought it over. But the smell of germ killer was too strong.

"O.K.," I said. "If it makes you feel better . . ."

They searched me. The police aren't very imaginative, but the way they search you shows the imagination of all the crooks who've cheated them in the past.

"Satisfied?" I asked when they'd done.

I must say the sergeant was trying to be fair. He rubbed his bald head and looked at me pretty distastefully and then went back to the outer office to telephone. While he was doing this a policeman came through, and by the snatch of talk that passed while the door was open I could tell that it was a call to Dr. Darnley. As it happened, Darnley was one of their local J.P.s.

When the sergeant came back he said: "All right, son, you can go. We're not going to make a charge."

I said: "Thanks. Shall I leave a forwarding address?"

"If you'll take my tip," said the sergeant, "you'll keep your tongue a bit quieter, or one of these days it'll lead you into trouble."

I didn't answer. There was no point in going on being kiddish and pert. Besides I was too fed up about things. If I'd spoken again I should have done just what he thought. I went down the steps of the police station, shaking the half crown she'd given me up and down in my hand. I thought with the arrogance of a young man: someday . . . maybe . . . But of course I never seriously believed it would happen.

chapter 2

And of course it never did happen in the least like I vaguely imagined then; and it was nine years before it happened at all.

I didn't get out before the war came. I'd gone up to Liverpool with half an idea of finding a ship, but I left it too late, so, soon after Dunkirk, I was called up.

It wasn't that I hadn't meant those things I'd said to the girl. Every word of them had been formed and forged since I was old enough to think. But it's so much easier to talk about getting out than to do it—or even to make the first move to do it. Impulse plays a biggish part in my life, and in this case for some reason the impulse didn't come. I can't put it plainer than that because I don't know myself.

To start with, when I got in the Army, everything went wrong. It wasn't the training but the discipline that got me down, and all the silly routine of it; but after a few months it came easier in spite of my better nature. Then someone gave me a stripe, and so it all began.

I was in the Army six years, and moved around a good bit. I didn't have many friends; but as it happened two of them made suggestions about what I might do when I came out. One of them, Roy Marshall, a New Zealander, gave me such a good account of life out there that it was tempting to emigrate to a new country where I could begin again from scratch. But while I was waiting for my papers a letter came from the other one, Michael Abercrombie, and a month later I went to see him at his offices, in King William Street, and took the job he offered me in the insurance world.

I'd come to like him quite a lot, and I suppose that had something to do with it. He was a tall, dour-looking man with sharply slanting eyebrows that vee'd above his nose whenever he was in trouble or perplexed. He looked determined and a bit of a driver, but in fact he was mild-natured and rather self-doubting when you came to know him.

I remember, after meeting his father that morning, we went out and discussed it over a cup of coffee. I remember he asked me if I was interested, and I thought of the offices I'd just been to on the fourth floor, marked "Abercrombie & Co. Adjusters, Established 1841," and of the little typist with the three-inch heels in the outer office and the other people there taken up with odd, sly businesses of their own. And I couldn't see myself among it.

He tried to explain what they did. When a firm or a private person or a ship suffered loss or damage and made a claim against an insurance company or an underwriter, an adjuster was engaged to examine and assess the loss and adjust the claim so that it was acceptable to both parties.

"Except for a few old established firms like ours, it's not a business that had a lot of standing in the between-war years. But that's changing. The adjuster has formed an association of his own, and qualifications are being brought in to put it on a professional basis like, say, accountancy."

"And where d'you suppose I should get the qualifications?"

"That's not the most important thing in your case. Though I expect they'd come." He frowned at his coffee. "My uncle died about eight years ago, and to be quite frank, Dad's a bit of a freak in this profession. For a certain type of claim he's perfect; but for other work, where one needs a tougher, stronger character, he's no good. And the underwriters recognize it. So a lot of business is beginning to pass us by. As for me, I want to specialize in the marine side of the business. It's the only one I'm really interested in. In any case, I'm too much like Dad in the wrong way. I'm complementary to him, not opposite. And we need an opposite."

"Should I be flattered or damned insulted?"

He didn't laugh. "A bit of both perhaps. But I've been in too much trouble with you to think you need anything wrapped up. I've a terrific respect for you, Oliver."

"Dear heaven," I said.

"We need a man of absolute integrity, pleasant to meet, but able to put over a strong line where it's necessary; a chap who's keen-minded and knows his way about and can sum people up."

"What do you know about my integrity? All you know is that I didn't pinch the mess funds."

"I know what you've told me about yourself."

I said: "When I left school I went to work on an airport. Then I was in a garage for two years. I went to night school for a bit trying to get a slant on journalism—chucked it up when my father died, went on the roads as a tramp, crossed the Atlantic as a stoker, did farm work. How d'you suppose that fits me for your sort of a job? And pleasant to meet! You've got a pretty good imagination, haven't you?"

The waitress came along and Michael paid her.

He said: "My dear chap, I've known you for four years, so I ought to be entitled to my own opinion. I suppose you're still living with the image of the man you were before the war. Perhaps he looks the same to you in the mirror. Well, that's just a delusion. Forget it. Oh, I know you had a raw deal in the old days—but whether you like it or not the war suited you. The old Branwell assault tactics . . . Now you've got to try and make sure that the peace suits you too."

I shifted uncomfortably. "The trouble at the moment is that I feel a phony—neither fish, flesh, nor fowl. At least there was a real person before the war, even though he belonged among the down-and-outs."

"It's a question of reorientating your mind, isn't it? Well, I thought this might be one way." When I didn't speak he said: "Of course, from another angle, you may not be open even to consider the job. It's a big change from being second in command of your battalion to rushing off to see if Mrs. Smith's fur coat really was damaged beyond repair when the water main burst."

We got up and went out. It was raining. The buses were hissing over the wet streets and people crowded the pavements. There was a man selling matches in the entrance to an alley. I bought a box. I thought: well, it's not eight years since you passed the night in Swindon workhouse; it's not much more since you did seven days for hitting that policeman in the eye; it's not twelve since your father turned on the gas and you came in and found him nearly dead and covered in vomit. Mr. Branwell, with his wing collar and his black tie, coming up from Surbiton on the nine-fifteen.

Well, what was I waiting for, hesitating for? Because farming in New Zealand made a prettier picture?

"I'd let you down in six months. By the time I knew anything about it I'd be sick of it and want a change."

"It's possible. But I shouldn't think so. Anyway, don't decide now. Think it over for a few days. There's no hurry."

We crossed the road and turned into Cannon Street.

"I've got to call on a chap here," Michael said. "I'll walk with you. What bus do you want?"

I said: "Look, there's not much need for me to say more now. But I don't want to think it over for a few days. Just tonight; and then I'll see you again tomorrow. O.K.?"

I expect he knew then that I was going to accept. For so easy-going a man he smiled very rarely, but he smiled now and touched my arm.

"All right, Oliver," he said.

I suppose a war has done that sort of thing for plenty of other people. I'm not unique. But it used to turn in me sometimes like laughter to think that the result of all the blood, tears, and sweat had been to turn at least one rather mangy stray tomcat into a house pet living fatly and comfortably off the society he'd been so much up against.

19

I used to remind myself deliberately sometimes, because human nature has only so much capacity for surprise, and before you know where you are the extraordinary has become the commonplace, and you're behaving as if you've never known what the other side is like. Personality isn't static; it's like a skin or the bark of a tree, constantly growing and shedding.

Not, if the truth be known, that it's easy to live either fatly or comfortably as a claims adjuster, when you're likely to be rung up any hour and sent to Sherborne or Southampton or Sheerness.

I took two rooms over a woman's-dress shop in George Street. I could have got something cheaper further out, but it pleased me to be in the West End. And it pleased something in me to play out the joke. I hadn't got any roots and never had had, so it was right somehow to live where none would grow. When it came to being thrown out of the job—or I tired of it myself—there'd be nothing to drop but the key in the door.

For six months, Michael nursed me and we went most places together. After a time I began to find an interest in the things I had to do. I began to see it wasn't just another job, filling in a corner and doing the same routine things. You had to be quick on the uptake; you had to know the value of things—and people—and often enough you had to be a bit of a detective as well.

I also began to see what Michael meant when he said the firm needed stiffening. Both he and his father were liked everywhere they went, but there was some short measure in them for this work. Perhaps, though they'd have denied this, it was because they thought everyone was as honest as themselves. I'm not at all sure it was anything so unsubtle, but that it didn't come from some sort of fundamental pride which wouldn't *let* them make concessions to a certain attitude of mind in others. Because, when you come down to it, every suspicion that a man holds is a tiny encroachment on his own integrity.

Presently they began to send me out on simple assignments where it was just a question of making a routine report. Then, when these were approved by Lloyd's without wrecking the city, they began to turn over the other minor stuff, which sometimes was as easy as pie and sometimes wasn't. Once I had to go out to Salisbury about some cars, and I thought: I wonder what happened to that kid who gave me the lift, and if she's still living here with her father and if she ever got her bracelet back; but I wasn't interested enough to inquire.

In the first two and a half years while I worked there, I didn't make many friends. Michael did his best, insisting on me being best man at his wedding, and doing all he could to get me known in the insurance world, but I suppose there was still something in me that didn't make me a very likable companion, in spite of what Michael said. It was all very well for him to talk about "trying to belong;" but I still didn't, or couldn't—at least, not in the important things.

The one friendship that did grow up between me and another man came unstuck because of a girl. Fred McDonald was the claims manager of a firm of brokers called McBurton & Hicks, and after we'd met once or twice in the course of business he invited me to his house in Harrow. McDonald was a stoutish bald man in the late forties with a good-looking face that had grown an extra layer of fat all round it. When I went down there I found he had an unmarried daughter of twenty-two called Joan, and we soon grew pretty friendly. I took her out a good bit, and I suppose they all began to think the thing was as good as settled. Then one morning I woke up and realized it didn't mean anything to me at all, and I cut it off short. I believe she was a good deal upset about it—though if she but knew it she hadn't missed much.

One day a report came through of a fire in a house in Kent. The Old Man was away with a chill and Michael was busy, so I went down. The people were called Moreton and the address was Lowis Manor, Sladen, near Tonbridge. It took a bit of finding and in the end it was seven or eight miles from Tonbridge and almost as near Sevenoaks. I left my fifteen-year-old two-seater M.G. at a timbered gatehouse and walked up the drive to the house.

I don't know much about architecture, but something must have registered because I remember stopping before I got to the door, and that wasn't just to look for a burnt-out roof or an eye-glass window. It was a biggish, mellow, timbered place that looked as if it had been there so long that the countryside had accepted it as a part of itself. You got the feeling it had grown there and never merely been built. The centre with the front door was set back between two wings, and the drive broke into a gravel courtyard with flower beds against the walls of the house and steps down to a lawn and formal gardens.

A plump man in tweeds answered the door, and when I explained what I came for, he said he was Mr. Tracey Moreton and would I come in.

"We've nothing dramatic to show you," he said abruptly, as if he might be apologizing. "The smoke woke us and we were able to keep the fire under until the brigade came. The damage is chiefly in one room."

He led me into a low room at the back of the hall, and there was the usual sort of mess: blackened furniture, curtains hanging in shreds, a partly collapsed wall that looked as if it had been hacked away.

"Apparently there was a fault in this chimney," he said. "The firemen say one of the beams has probably been smouldering for weeks, but last night it reached the store cupboard that backs on to this room from the kitchens, and the jams caught alight." He coughed. "That's why there's this stink. My mother noticed it first and roused us. If you'll excuse me I'll wait outside. The smoke gets on my chest."

I had a good look round. The curtains and some of the other flimsy things had been burnt, and the furniture had been rather badly charred; but there was no real structural damage except what the firemen had done breaking away the wall round the cupboard. I squeezed through the cupboard into the kitchen and surprised an old girl peeling potatoes, who looked at me as if I'd just popped out of her vinegar bottle. When I found Mr. Tracey Moreton again, he led me in a bored way across to a big drawing room at the other side of the house and poured me out a whisky-and-soda.

I said: "It's been a lucky escape. If there'd been more draught you'd have been without a home today."

He nodded and coughed and put a glass down beside me on a little curve-legged eighteenth-century table. Everything in the room was old and valuable. "I'll get an architect round to examine the other chimneys. It's locking the stable door, of course."

"I wouldn't say that. Was there anything of special value in the room: furniture or rugs?" After drinking, I moved the tumbler around in my hand; it was old Bristol glass.

He said: "Luckily there was nothing particular except the Foster, but it's a bitter blow to lose that."

In the previous two years I'd learned enough to guess what he was talking about.

"I noticed two pictures. One was a sea scene, but they were both too badly burnt——"

"The sea scene was a cheap print. The Foster was of the mill and spinney which used to be at the back of this house. It was specially commissioned by my grandfather." He lit a cigarette but didn't offer me one. After a minute the whiff of some herbal mixture told me why. He peered at me through the smoke with his small incurious rust-coloured eyes.

"Have you any idea of its value?"

"I think it was put at five hundred when the insurance was taken out, but its sentimental value's a lot more to me." He got up. "I have the policy somewhere here . . . but, no—of course, it's at my solicitors."

"Doesn't matter. I'll check when I get back to town. About the damage to the floor . . ."

I didn't finish because a young woman came in carrying a bunch of yellow chrysanthemums. She began to say something but stopped when she saw me.

"Oh, sorry, I thought——"

He said casually: "This is Mr.—er—oh, yes, Branwell, who's come about the insurance. My wife."

We muttered the usual sort of polite words, and she went across to the grand piano and began sticking the flowers into a tall green vase. She didn't recognize me. She obviously hadn't an idea. But I knew her at once. It was queer. I thought I'd forgotten her. But it was just as if somewhere in my mind, in my memory, all the details had been stored and shut away and the sight of her opened them up.

chapter 3

When she went out, as she did two or three minutes later, I took a lot more notice of him while we finished our business together.

He was forty or a bit more, with sparse fair hair climbing at the temples, and a thin moustache that he couldn't leave alone, so that his signet ring glinted in the latticed light from the windows. All his movements were irritable and impatient, like a man who's just missed a train. The herbal stuff didn't seem to be doing his breathing any good.

By now I was getting over the surprise of seeing her again. What did surprise me was that it seemed to mean something to me.

After I'd finished my drink I went back to the study and took a detailed inventory of the damage. With Birket Foster's "Mill and Spinney" to be reckoned in, my first estimate was going to be a lot wide of the mark. Before I left, I saw Tracey Moreton again, and after a minute he said: "Were you in the Eighth Army?"

"Yes. . . . Why?"

He shrugged. "Some expression you used. It sounded like the lingo."

"Were you?"

"More or less. I was shot down over Tobruk in '42."

"What month?"

"June."

"I didn't go out until the end of 1941. I was in Haifa in June. Were you there later?"

"No, I was living at the expense of the Italian government."

It's always the same when that sort of thing crops up. He'd been polite before, but bored. Now he had a more friendly tone. He came with me to the door—I hadn't seen any servants except

24

the old woman with the screwed-up hair in the kitchen—and I left him there.

I crossed the gravel square and looked across the grounds. On either side of the tall holly hedge that flanked the drive were formal gardens, with box hedgings, a sundial, a lily pond. Tracey Moreton had gone in. I walked round the house, past an older stone wing and an arched doorway that led to a cobbled courtyard where a man in shirt sleeves was brushing out a stable. He didn't bother to look up as I went past the doorway. At the west side the ground fell away gradually and had been made into a series of terraced lawns divided by yew hedges. At the foot of them was a tennis court which was rapidly going back into meadow, and apparently no attempt was being made to prevent the solitary pony from grazing wherever the fancy took him. Behind the house were two greenhouses and some potting sheds. I saw someone moving in one of the greenhouses. It was Mrs. Tracey Moreton.

Looking back on the moment, it does seem to me that I got a feeling of the importance of what I did next. I could turn and go out to my M.G. and drive away, and that would be the end. Or I could walk up to the greenhouse, and after that it would be too late. There'd be a sort of expenditure of action that wasn't recoverable.

I went up to the greenhouse.

She was picking tomatoes. The plants were nearly done and looked shrivelled and a bit spotty; but there was still a fair crop. On a bench were some plant pots, and a fern standing in water. For a few seconds she didn't see me, and I looked at her.

Although the recognition had been instant there were many differences. She'd fined off to slimness; narrow-waisted, dark-lashed, that lovely mouth; her hair was shorter and done differently, was slightly ruffled and shining. I hadn't ever known before what colour her eyes were.

She turned quickly and saw me. She looked faintly surprised, the way I suppose most people would look if they found a chance caller wandering where he'd no business to be.

"Are you looking for my husband?"

"No. . . . I saw you in here. I came to pay an old debt."

"A debt? To me?"

"Yes." I put my hand in my pocket and took out a half

crown. She looked at it but didn't make any move to take it.

"I don't know what you mean."

I said: "Before you were married your name was Darnley, wasn't it? Sarah Darnley?"

That evidently decided her she hadn't got a lunatic to deal with.

"I'm sorry—I don't remember you. What did you say your name was?"

"You never knew it." I put the half crown on the wooden bench. "You gave me this in '39. Or one like it. D'you remember a puncture on a lonely road?"

Her eyes were slightly less dark than her hair and lashes, intelligent and warm, but a bit secret, as if she'd learned to play it that way.

"I do remember one that happened to me; but I don't think . . ." She hesitated. "You aren't . . . *Heavens,* yes."

We stared at each other for a second. Water from a tap in the corner was dripping as regularly as a metronome.

I said: "Did you ever find the bracelet?"

She must have been remembering.

"I can't tell you how sorry we were about that—afterwards—when it was too late. It was found—the bracelet was found near where I'd had the puncture." She was still holding her basket and she put two more tomatoes in it before lowering it onto the bench in front of her. "The thing must have dropped off when I was struggling with the wheel before you came. The clasp was always a bit unreliable."

"So are tramps," I said.

She flushed. "I'm *very* sorry. I wasn't to know—we weren't to know that you were not just an ordinary man of the road."

"But I was."

"You couldn't have been, or you wouldn't be so much changed."

I said: "The war came. I got pitched into things. It could have happened just the same to anyone."

"But I thought . . ." She stopped herself there. "Anyway . . ."

I waited for her to go on. But she didn't. I stared at the half crown. "I think maybe it brought me luck. Perhaps now it'll do the same for you."

"What makes you think I need it?"

"Don't we all? Anyway, thanks for the loan." I turned to go, but at the door she said:

"Wait."

I stopped. She said: "I—don't know your name."

"Oliver Branwell."

Her eyes went quietly over me.

"I'm very sorry you were put in that position over the bracelet. I've said so."

"Forget it."

"Then will you forget this money too? You must see . . ."

She picked up the coin and held it out to me. Her fingers were a bit stained with handling the tomato plants.

"No." I smiled briefly. "I don't see. It's yours now, Mrs. Moreton. I like to pay my debts."

The next week I went down again, to see the local builder and get the thing settled up.

As before, Tracey Moreton let me in, and she didn't seem to be anywhere about. We talked business for a time. There was one further complication, in that the sticky smoke from the jams had, in his opinion, damaged the polish on certain pieces of furniture in the hall, and he wanted these put right. One Queen Anne walnut cabinet, he said, he had only just paid £60 to have restored. It seemed a reasonable enough attitude, but it meant further delay before a settlement was agreed.

After we'd done all we could, Moreton offered me a cigarette —not from his own case but from an antique carved satinwood box—and said in his indifferent way:

"I believe you'd met my wife once before."

Somehow I hadn't expected her to bother to tell him.

"Yes. She didn't remember me."

"It's not surprising, is it? Were you actually—on the road, when she met you before?"

"It wasn't just a stunt with a genteel background, if that's what you mean."

He rubbed his middle finger along the line of his moustache. "War's a crucible, isn't it? Everything gets thrown into the pot. Some come out finer-tempered. Others have been badly handled and flawed. Were you in the rifle brigade?"

"No, the K.R.R.C."

"I know a man called Brigadier Waterton. And a Major Morris-Scott."

"I've seen Brigadier Waterton; I never met him. My O.C. was Lieutenant-Colonel Eden."

"Eden . . . I rather think my brother knows him. Wasn't he at Charterhouse?"

"I don't know," I said dryly.

"No." He coughed as we went towards the door. "I've not been in circulation since the war. Exposure brought on asthma. Can't shake the damned thing off. My grandfather had it. Come and lunch with us sometime."

I couldn't have been more surprised. Before I could think it out my voice said: "Thanks. I'd like to."

We were at the door, and his eyes travelled incuriously over my face.

"Sunday?"

"Thank you very much."

I'd left my car outside again, and I walked down the drive among the holly bushes, which were speckled with red berries this year. There was a gardener brushing up leaves, and he nodded and touched his hat. Over in the fields a cow was lowing, and the autumn sun cast long shadows from the trees. What must it be like, I thought, to be born in a place like this? In spite of his offhand manner he was likable—and he seemed to like me. The invitation to lunch could only have come from our being in the Middle East together—unless his wife had suggested it.

As I got to my car I heard another car somewhere and could tell from the high-pitched hum—I knew before it came in sight round the bend.

She slowed up to turn in through the gatehouse, and I put my hand up to stop her. She was driving a Bentley, a good bit prewar but still sleek. She was wearing no hat, but a loose grey coat with the collar high about her neck like a ruff. She'd a disconcerting face—one of those that are never quite the same two days together; one of those in which the mood seems to transcend the features. There was a cocker spaniel in the car beside her.

I said: "Good morning. No punctures today?"

"No." She smiled, but her voice was cool, not specially friendly. "Are you just arriving?"

"Leaving. I stopped you to apologize."

"What for?"

"Bothering to pay off old debts on my last visit."

"You'd a perfect right to."

"It's an arguable point. But don't let's argue it. The grievance wasn't all I remembered."

"I'm glad."

"Did you get into trouble that evening for encouraging a dangerous character?"

She smiled. "More or less. As it happens—this is the bracelet."

She'd pulled her coat sleeve back. I stared at the thing on her wrist.

"It's very lovely."

Perhaps something in my voice gave away more than it should. She slowly pulled her sleeve back over her wrist. At her movement, the spaniel put its forepaws on her knee and wagged its tail. Its bloodshot eyes were mournful and friendly.

I said: "May I ask you a question?"

"Of course."

"Do you always drive so fast?"

She gave a soft laugh. "I'm often in a hurry. I left some things in the oven today."

I stepped back. "You're losing time on me. I hope to see you on Sunday, thank you very much."

"Sunday?"

"Yes. . . . Your husband invited me then."

She pressed in the gear. "Oh, of course. I'd forgotten."

We separated and I watched her car disappear up the drive. I got in my own midget and drove away. She'd covered up, but I knew now that the invitation hadn't come from her.

chapter 4

*I*t had been a good October, and Sunday was the best day of the month. I drove down through south London, through the deserts of brick, bumping and wobbling over ten miles of more or less empty tramlines.

When you turned in at Lowis Manor, you couldn't help but reflect that there was enough space in this house for eight families if you took as a guide the space they were occupying thirty miles back. It straggled all over the place like a miniature town, with all its additions and afterthoughts. But, unlike any town, it was all good to look on. It squatted there in the sun with its timbered walls and its panes of leaded glass, its old bow windows supported on carved wooden brackets, and its clusters of slender chimneys.

I took my car up the drive this time, and Elliott, the chap I'd seen brushing out a stable, opened the door. He was a man of about sixty in a collar too big for him and with a face shrivelled to match his neck. As I was looking at a small French picture in the living room, Tracey Moreton came in with an older woman.

"Glad to see you, Branwell. Admiring my Watteau?" He stopped to get his breath. "May I introduce you to my mother. This is Major Branwell, Mother."

So he'd got to know that somewhere. Mrs. Moreton was tall and finely lined and rather papery; but all the same she gave you the impression of alertness and vigour. You felt she'd never be slow to make up her mind or doubtful once she'd made it up.

"My son's spoken of you, Major Branwell. I believe you were in North Africa together."

I said: "Well, in the same area. But I'm afraid my army rank's two years out of date."

"I don't think that sort of thing is ever out of date," she replied.

At that moment, Sarah came in, and there was the usual conversation while Moreton poured out the drinks. We had lunch in a long half-panelled room at the back of the house with a patterned plaster ceiling and an oval Chippendale table. A door behind a screen led into the kitchen, and the old man with the collar served the meal. They showed a polite interest in my job, and I tried to explain what an adjuster was; how, though he represented the insurance company, it was his duty to be completely fair and impartial to both parties in the settlement of a claim, especially so if the claimant did not employ an assessor to act for him. I'm still not too good at talking and eating at the same time —not easily, that is. Halfway through the meal, Tracey excused

30

himself and, refusing Sarah's offer to get him something, went out. There was a minute or two's silence.

"It's been the same all this month," Sarah said to Mrs. Moreton. "The adrenalin wears off quicker each time."

"Autumn has always been difficult. But I wish he wouldn't give way so quickly now. Sometimes it used to pass off with the inhaler."

I didn't say anything, but I suppose they thought I had to have it explained to me.

Mrs. Moreton said: "He was in the water nine hours. That began it. The long internment, too, had an effect—but not only on his health. . . ."

"You've another son, Mrs. Moreton?"

She smiled at me. "Yes. The barrister. He served in the Guards, like his father before him. But he was luckier than his father."

I looked at her inquiringly.

She said: "My husband lost a leg on the Somme."

The old chap came in and took Tracey's plate away to keep it warm.

Mrs. Moreton said: "I often think how much more fortunate I was than women who went before me. They could only stay at home. Inactivity is the worst thing—the corroding thing. . . ." For a second or so she looked pained and angry. "There was a Moreton at Crécy and two brothers at Blenheim. The head of the house was killed at Marston Moor."

"You've been a warlike family."

"In six hundred years? No. . . . There were long periods when whole generations. . . . They were content to live in peace here. This is our place. The wars have not been of our seeking. But when they came—we did our share."

I glanced at the room. "You had so much to fight for."

"Yes," she said. "And so much to lose."

When Tracey came back in five minutes he seemed a lot better, and after lunch he insisted on showing me the rest of the house. There was a fourteenth-century hall built of stone, but this backed on to the stables and was no longer used. The present hall, he explained, had originally been the courtyard; and it was therefore a good bit more lofty than the other rooms. It had a high beamed roof, which rose in an arch to two small windows; and a

31

wide irregular staircase led up to a gallery with a heavily moulded handrail carried by squat twisted balusters. The lower windows had deep wooden window seats, and the light that came in was palely green because of the flowering shrubs outside.

"In the old days people used to go out of doors to bed and cross the courtyard to eat their meals. But in the early eighteen century that sort of tough living went out of fashion, and they enclosed it."

Halfway up the stairs I stopped to look at another picture: it was of the three wise men bringing their gifts at the Nativity. He stopped rather impatiently. "There are only three or four pictures in the house worth anything. My father thought nothing of that, but I've just had it restored. It's by Filippino Lippi, about 1500. The one over there on the other side is an early Constable."

Upstairs was more of a warren than down. There were only a few obvious signs of neglect, stained ceilings or swollen doors; but he seemed to take a certain pleasure in pointing them out.

"It's a burden round my neck and I damn it daily. But if it came to the point I wouldn't part with it. Not even now when I earn nothing for its upkeep."

"Before the war . . . ?"

He made his usual face, as if he'd tasted something nasty. "Before the war I didn't need to work—at least not in the way most people do: signing on each morning under a boss. During and since the war a grateful government has made it necessary. But now I can't. Shall we go down?"

For all his casual and modest way, he walked with a sense of style, a slight arrogance. On a railway platform you wouldn't possibly mistake him for a gentleman farmer, even though he dressed like one. Perhaps that was how it came after six hundred years of squirehood. Perhaps that was how it should be. I thought: poverty's relative. He considers himself poor with three servants and a Bentley, because he can't afford hunters and a flat in town.

While we were upstairs two visitors had come, and one of them was standing with his back to the fire drinking coffee. He was a big, handsome rather popeyed man of about thirty in a grey check suit and a thick yellow silk tie. The other was a dark quite pretty girl with a chiffon scarf round her long arching neck and an attitude. The man was telling a story in a high tenor voice; he cocked an eye at us but went on to the bitter end. Lady Caroline

Stockholme, who apparently had *the* most appalling taste in loose covers, had either willfully or accidentally misunderstood some advice on the matter given her by the speaker, with the result that she'd gone to the wrong shop and been *bullied* by some awful man into buying an entire new suite of furniture.

Everybody laughed. The chap in the grey suit was killing himself to get in a postscript, but, seeing me, he put it off until after the introductions. His name was Clive Fisher and we shook hands and he grinned amiably enough as he plunged on with the story. The girl was his sister Ambrosine, and she inclined her head at me without putting any strain on herself.

I said it was time I was going, but Tracey Moreton waved me to a seat.

"Clive is the uncrowned commissar of good taste in the county of Kent. Nothing ever really goes without his sanction. When my Lippi came back I knew that only his approval would make it possible for me to hang it again."

"Not merely *my* approval," said Clive, who had been listening since his name was mentioned, and appeared to take Tracey's remarks without batting an eyelid. "There are standards that *anyone* can apply. Any *reasonable* person, that is. For instance, if one applies such standards to the El Greco which has been restored in the National Gallery—if one applies *any* standards at all —one knows that the iconoclasts who did it ought to be hanged in Trafalgar Square."

"It isn't only the El Greco," said Ambrosine languidly. "They all look like picture postcards."

I listened to the discussion that raged over this, but didn't join in. Culture, for what it was worth, was coming to me late and piecemeal. These people talked a language they'd known since they were kids. Tracey Moreton had an air of having been everywhere and done everything. Probably he had.

Sarah had gone to the side table for more coffee, and I suddenly knew that her eyes were on me. I turned and looked but then her eyes had slipped away. All day we'd hardly spoken. Yet to speak to her was what I'd come for. Not that I'd anything special to say—except that for some reason I wanted more than anything to remove the impression I felt I'd given her, that the old grudges still rankled.

I waited, biding my time. Mrs. Moreton went out, tall and a bit angular, and the company lost a lot of its dignity for her going. Fisher seemed very much at home, and I gathered that he was some sort of an artist himself. If you could judge from his clothes, he did pretty well out of it.

Then Mrs. Moreton came back, and I realized I'd lost my chance. Suddenly I'd no wish to stay any longer, and I got up, almost in disgust at myself, to go. I thought Sarah would stay with the Fishers, but instead she walked with Tracey and me to the door.

I said: "Do you often come to London?"

"Monthly to Harley Street." Tracey's breathing was getting noisy again. "But Sarah is up twice a week. She designs dresses for Delahaye."

"Perhaps you'll have a meal with me—one or both of you." I turned to Sarah. "What days are you up?"

The sun shone across her face as she looked at the heavy studded door. A muscle moved in her cheek.

She said: "Tracey's due to go again in about a fortnight, but really he doesn't stay very late. Why don't you come and see us here again?"

So that was that.

"Thanks," I said. "I should like it very much. And thank you for today."

I left them standing there together at the door, and got into my car, fingered the self-starter, and put in the gear. Sarah was the same height as her husband. As I swung the car round she lifted her hand, but it was only to shield her eyes from the glare of the sun.

chapter 5

I was in the office when a report came through of a burglary in Prentiss Street, which is only just round the corner from

George Street, so I told Michael I would look in there on the way home. The Lloyd's claims slip was as laconic as usual.

Assured: Mr. Gerald Litchen, 13 Prentiss Street, W.1.
Policy: Comprehensive No. 70647. £5,000.
Nature of Claim: Burglary £930 os. od.
Date of Occurrence: Second of November.
Period of Policy: 12 months from August 7th last.

When I got to Prentiss Street, which runs down through Wigmore Street and ends in a cul-de-sac behind Selfridge's, I found No. 13 was a house, and not a flat as I'd expected. A maid with slant eyes and plucked eyebrows answered my ring and looked as if she expected me to be selling something. When I told her my business she said Mr. Litchen was away and Mrs. Litchen was in bed ill with the shock of the burglary and would I call again sometime. I said, no, I wouldn't, so she let me grudgingly into the hall and went upstairs to see her mistress.

After a minute she came down and said Mrs. Litchen wanted me to be shown the scene of the burglary, and after that Madame would see me herself. I went into a living room which had gold walls decorated with surrealist masks, and white furniture like a doll's house. The long curtains were primrose yellow with red pelmets, and the carpet was royal blue.

"You can see the windows for yourself; and I was told to show you this cupboard where all the things has gone from."

The window had been broken open and was easily reached from the area outside. The cupboard was bare, but the maid said it had been full of Georgian silver which Mr. Litchen had collected. Then she left me to finish my inspection.

The police had been and gone earlier in the day, and all I could do was make detailed notes of the way the window had been forced and the accessibility of the room. Tomorrow I would call on the police and check up.

The house was very quiet, and when I'd climbed back out of the area I lit a cigarette and waited for the girl to return. When it was half smoked I squeezed it out and threw it through the window. The masks grimaced at me. Why did anyone want to live with nightmares?

I was looking round for a bell to push when the maid came.

She took me upstairs and into a bedroom with peach-coloured walls and ivory satin curtains. The woman in bed said:

"That will be all, Dolores. You can go now."

"Very well, Ma'am."

"Mrs. Litchen?" I said.

"Yes. Do sit down. The room's in *turmoil* but I know you'll excuse it. I've had a hell of a headache ever since first thing this morning. You know what it's like when you're wakened two hours before your usual time."

I heard the door close on Dolores. Mrs. Litchen was a blonde of about twenty-seven with heavy eyes, a nice nose, and a sulky mouth. Her hair was long, to her shoulders, and shone as if there was never anything else to do but brush it. She wore an ivory satin nightdress, to match the curtains, and inch-long peach-coloured fingernails.

We talked.

She said Gerald was away, and she hadn't wired him because she knew how *frantic* he'd be when he heard about the loss of his silver. She had vague ideas, she admitted they were vague, of trying to get duplicates and saying nothing to Gerald at all. Often it was weeks together and he never even looked at the stuff.

The front door closed and I thought: that's the last of Dolores.

I asked if anything else had been taken besides the silver, and she said no. Personally, if she had only herself to consider, she wouldn't waste any tears over the loss; one didn't have a lot of room in these modern houses; would I be good enough to mix her a drink?

I was good enough, and was told to take one myself. She tasted it and nodded her shiny page-boy head.

"You mix a good gin, Mr. Oliver Branwell. I'm sorry to seem such a frantic invalid, but *could* you pass me a cigarette?"

I lit her cigarette. She thanked me through her lashes. I didn't sit down again but said I had all the data and would try to get the claim through as quickly as possible. She stretched her long legs under the coverlet and said:

"Well, I'm glad you came. Thanks for putting things straight in my mind. But don't hurry away on my account. There's all the evening to kill."

I said: "A good bit of it's dead already."

36

"I expect you're aching to get back to the wife and kiddies."

"No wife."

"No wife?" She eyed me up and down. "How very clever of you. What's the recipe?"

I said: "Never having an evening to kill."

"I don't think that follows." She shut her eyes and leaned back against the head of the bed, the cigarette dropping between her lips. The smoke escaped slowly.

As I made a move, she asked me how the police would go about recovering the stuff; but when I told her, she looked bored and put a slim lazy arm behind her head. There was a television set at the other side of the bed, and a futurist picture framed in coffee-coloured wood, and a recess with black mirror glass that didn't quite reflect the crystal race horse standing in it. It was nice to be able to recognize something.

I said: "What's that picture?"

"That? It's one of Bredanski's early pieces. Eels swimming in a bowl."

I said: "I thought it was Hampton Court maze seen from the air."

"I suppose you altogether despise modern art."

"You can't altogether despise what you don't understand."

"Oh, can't you? I know plenty who do."

There was a pause.

"Well, thanks for the drink. I——"

"Pour me another, will you? I can't very well—get out of bed with you here."

I didn't rise to that; and when I came back with the glass in my hand she was watching me.

"Tell me," she said. "Do all insurance men come like you?"

"What way?"

"Well—thirteen stone, nice hair, cold grey eyes."

"You're overweight. And they don't."

"Not as good-looking?"

"Oh, much better-looking."

"All the same," she said, "I bet you could be fun if you really let up on that expression."

I said: "I might say the same about you."

She sipped her drink. "What are we waiting for, then?"

I went back for my own drink. "Your husband, probably."

I gave her time, but when I turned again, her eyes had gone like little brown stones.

She said: "My husband's in Scotland."

"I shouldn't bank on it. You know how these tiresome men get around."

There was a minute's silence. A dog was yapping monotonously in the street outside.

"Anyway he'd beat the life out of you if he even found you here in my room," she said vindictively.

"Don't scare me any more. I'm a bundle of nerves as it is."

She put her glass down carefully on the table beside her. "When you've finished your drink you can find your own way out."

I thought it better to say nothing to that. I'd said enough. There was a perceptible pause.

"Good night, Mrs. Litchen."

She didn't answer, and I went out. I had a job to find the front-door catch, which was hidden so that it shouldn't spoil the line of the paint.

Ten more days passed before I rang up Delahaye's. I'd thought about it from the beginning. It was weak to give way now—especially when it probably only meant a snub at the end of it —but sometimes you can't reason with yourself.

A well-bred voice answered at the other end, and I said:

"Can you tell me which days Mrs. Tracey Moreton is in London?"

"Tuesdays and Fridays, sir."

"Oh, thanks. Then I'll ring tomorrow."

But I didn't ring tomorrow. I'd been working pretty hard ever since the visit to Lowis Manor to try to get the thing out of my system; so there seemed no harm in postponing a couple of appointments for the following afternoon, and by three-thirty I was walking down Bruton Street. Delahaye's is in Clare Street, and, after passing it once and deciding there probably wasn't a back entrance, I settled to wait. It wasn't too difficult, because there was a shop selling art reproductions nearly opposite, and I spent the best part of an hour in there, to the refined annoyance of the assistants.

At a quarter to five, Sarah came out and headed away from me towards Bond Street. She walked with the quick ease of flat-heeled shoes, taking rather long strides for a girl, and she steered among people so expertly that we were near the end of Bond Street when I caught up.

"So it *is* you," I said. "I thought I recognized your walk."

She glanced up at me in surprise, half smiled.

"I was just leaving. How are you, Mr. Branwell?"

"I was off to get a cup of tea—somewhere. I . . . Perhaps you'd join me."

"Well, thank you. But I rather wanted to get a train before the rush began."

"It's starting," I said. "Look around. It—won't be any worse in half an hour."

She seemed as if she was going to object, but instead she gave in, and I led her across Piccadilly to a café on the other side. She was wearing a sort of Burgundy-red coat with wide sleeves and a little round hat of the same colour with a shiny black pin in it. It made her look older, sophisticated.

As we sat down I said: "As a matter of fact I'd been waiting outside Delahaye's for you."

She put down her bag, took off her gloves, folded them, picked up the menu and stared at it.

"Does that amuse you?" I said.

"Why should it?" She had flushed a little but she didn't look up.

The waitress came and I ordered toasted scones. They hadn't got any, only plain toast or bread and butter. When she'd gone I said:

"I'm sorry I brought you in here. I intended taking you to the Berkeley, but when I saw you—when I caught you up—the thing went right out of my head."

"Was it you who rang yesterday?"

"Yes."

She met my eyes. "I often come in here for lunch. I haven't been in the Berkeley for five years."

Alone with her like this, I was as unsure of myself as I'd ever been in my life.

"You've been at Delahaye's for some time?"

"About eighteen months."

"I suppose it's a nice sort of hobby."

"Oh, it's more than that. We need what I earn."

"As a sort of—additional pocket money."

"Heavens, no. Have you any idea how much it costs to live at Lowis Manor?"

I shook my head. "I'm sorry. Your concerns . . ."

"There's nothing to hide. Tracey's father died in 1940, and the death duties then meant sacrificing his investments. Taxes have gone up and up ever since."

"What about the ballet? Didn't you intend to take it up?"

"That went when the war came. In any case, I think it was too late. I hadn't started early enough. Daddy let me go into it to keep me quiet."

The waitress brought the tea, clacking the crockery upon the glass surface of the table, then found she had no sugar, so went off for it. I watched Sarah's hands as she poured out the tea.

"And your father?"

"He sold our house and lives in London now."

"Perhaps that's what you should do."

"What, sell Lowis Manor? Would you?"

"Maybe," I said. "I don't know. Perhaps not."

We drank our tea. Something in our talk had helped; I don't know what it was. At least it had helped me. I had stopped sweating, feeling uncouth.

She said: "Why particularly did you want to see me?"

A chasm there. "Old times' sake. . . . I wanted to. Isn't that a good enough reason?"

"Not for waiting."

"I think so."

She smiled slightly but didn't speak.

I said: "When I met you that night you were like something out of a different world. Now our worlds are at least on speaking terms. That pleases me where it hurt most. . . . When did you marry?"

"In 1940. Tracey was a squadron leader."

"He's a good lot older than you."

"Yes."

"And then?"

She fumbled in her bag, took out a bit of handkerchief, and dabbed one corner of her mouth.

"Oh . . . that's all there is, really. And you?"

"More toast?"

"No, thanks."

I took out cigarettes, passed her one, lit it. For a second as she leaned across the table, her face was close to my hand, her eyes a dark amber in the match light.

She said: "And you?"

"Oh, I get along."

"I wish you'd tell me how it happened, this change in you."

"Is there such a change?"

"Yes. . . . Oh, yes. At least, as I remember you, you were bitter then, angry in a sort of resentful way—and yet not unlikable, really."

"And now?"

Her lips moved suddenly, as if she hadn't quite got control of them. "I still think your bark's worse than your bite."

I said in surprise: "Have I ever barked at you?"

"Not at me . . . yet."

"D'you think I might?"

"Not at me . . . no."

I was silent for a bit. "There really isn't anything to tell. You know how I felt. It wasn't that that changed. But things happened by accident. After the retreat from El Agheila, I got chivvied into taking a commission. I felt badly about it for a long time—as if I'd let myself down. . . . Something *I* believed in. Queer, I suppose. Then afterwards, when it was over, Michael Abercrombie offered me this job."

"Who's he?"

"Well, my boss, in a way, and my friend."

"Is he nice?"

"Oh, very. He's all the things that I'm not."

"And what are you not?"

I met her eyes and smiled. "Cultured . . . charming . . . understandable . . . good . . ."

"Don't you find it hard work being none of those things?"

"No. . . . I just sit back and let it come."

"A sort of—wolf in sheep's clothing?"

"Or a sheep pretending to be a wolf. Since I took this job I haven't been able to decide."

She said more soberly:

"Perhaps there aren't any wolves or sheep really—only people."

There was a short silence.

"I must go, Oliver."

The name seemed to slip out.

With a feeling of warmth I said: "I'll drive you down."

"No, of course not—thank you. I expect Tracey will meet me at the station."

"Do you think, if I phoned, you would have lunch with me one day? You and Tracey?"

"Thank you."

"How's Clive Fisher?"

"All right. We don't see a lot of him. It was he who found me the job with Delahaye."

I got the bill and waited while she stubbed out her cigarette and pulled on her thin suède gloves. Gloves like that seem to fit as closely as a skin. As I looked at her I knew I felt about her as I'd never remotely felt about any woman before. I wondered if she knew it, the way women are supposed to know.

If this was falling in love, then I'd done something for which my talents were very ill-suited. But I knew that the choice was no longer mine.

chapter 6

I saw Sarah several times that winter and the following spring, sometimes in town but sometimes at Lowis Manor. It wasn't at her invitation that I went to see them again but at his. I never could quite understand his liking for me; I wasn't his type at all; but in spite of trying not to I felt a bit flattered by his friendship. I still wasn't used to having my company sought. The fact that so far as he was concerned I was constantly breaking the tenth commandment made me uncomfortable, but at least the coveting was decently disguised. I got to like old Mrs. Moreton, too, who was unvaryingly nice to me.

In the late spring I was made a junior partner in Abercrombie

& Co. It was too early but there was no arguing with Michael and his father. They told me what I already knew—that more underwriters were putting their business through Abercrombie's; and also that brokers—and sometimes even claimants—who had had a claim settled by me asked for me by name when another claim came along. I knew it and was glad to have made the grade. But that was what I was paid for. The rest only followed because they were the sort of generous people they were.

It was on a serious case of fraud that I met Henry Dane—in the March of that year. Dane was a solicitor who specialized in insurance business and had made a big name for himself as an investigator. Just before the war, he'd successfully broken up a ring of crooks who had been defrauding the insurance companies for years,.and as a result he had a lot of influence with the companies and at Lloyd's.

We met at first as rivals, and that was often the way; but we soon grew to respect each other and became friends. He was a queer chap, a rough diamond at heart, and perhaps that was a link; a man who looked forty-five and was ten years older; a man who went at everything with his teeth set, whether it was a job of work or a game of golf. I met his wife, Gwyneth, who was much younger than he was, and pretty. They both lived twice as energetically as most people.

A fortnight after the partnership was settled I bumped into Roy Marshall, who was over in England for a few weeks, and he told me that the opportunity in New Zealand was still open. If things had been different, he might have been an unsettling influence. But now it was too late. I tried to believe that the partnership was the important factor; but in fact it was Sarah.

Of course that didn't make sense any way. The infatuation should have sent me away instead of binding me closer. There wasn't a chance of its leading anywhere but to futility and useless heartburning. There wasn't a chance even if Tracey had never existed.

In July, I was invited down to Lowis Manor for the weekend. It was the first and only time.

I arrived for dinner on Saturday, and we had it fairly late in the long dining room where the light faded early. Candles were lit to match the glowing evening outside.

Mrs. Moreton had just come back from a holiday. It appeared that she went to the Isle of Wight to stay with her sister for the months of May and June every year. Towards the end of the meal she said: "I'm afraid I'll have to ask you to excuse me. I promised to be down at the Bancrofts' by half past nine."

"What is it this time?" Tracey asked.

"The old lady's worse. The district nurse can't stay, and Mr. Bancroft must get some sleep."

"My mother's still living in the squirearchy age," Tracey said to me. "She won't grow up. She still imagines herself as the lady of the manor with responsibilities towards her flock."

Mrs. Moreton flushed slightly. "So I have. So we all have, one to another. In any case, I've known Mrs. Bancroft for forty-four years. I suppose one may still be allowed to profess friendship."

When she'd gone and we'd sat down again, Sarah said: "You shouldn't have said that to her, Tracey."

"Well, it astonishes me that within twenty-four hours of her return she should plunge back up to her neck in the life of the countryside. She'll stay that way for the next ten months. I often wonder what the village does without her in May and June."

"It misses her very much. As everyone does. You don't alter people by altering the rules, do you, Oliver?"

"Oliver doesn't know," said Tracey. "Or if he does he'll keep it to himself, as he keeps all his feelings to himself. I often used to wonder what a strong silent man was like."

"Don't talk rot," I said.

Sarah picked a broken carnation out of the low bowl of flowers on the table, sniffed it casually, delicately. "I remember Tracey's mother when Tracey was first reported missing. I was on leave here, as it happened. When we got the news she called the servants together—there were more of them then. Elliott was the only man in the house, and she made him read the twenty-third Psalm. Then she said some prayers herself, and there wasn't a tremor in her voice. . . . Whatever you think of that, it shows courage—and pride. Perhaps in a few years, if there's another war, there'll be nobody left who would do that. It's—something that's being lost. . . ."

"And all I thought when I was struggling in the water," Tracey said, "was: well, if this is the temperature of the Mediterranean

I'm damned if I'm going to bathe here any more. It shows how the stock has deteriorated in one generation."

Over the carnation, Sarah made a little expressive face at me, and Tracey caught the glance.

"It's all very well for Oliver," he said. "He's one of the up-and-coming. We're the down-and-going. Heroic gestures, like Mother's, are out of fashion, and we haven't yet learned the proper motions of the proletariat." He lit one of his herbal cigarettes and waved it at me. "I know what you're thinking. You think I'm a reactionary. Well, that's just where you're mistaken. Mother's a reactionary—I'm a progressive. I want progress but I don't want uniformity and stagnation. I don't want bread and skilly for every-one—in a concentration camp."

The pungent smell of the herbal cigarette reached me. Sarah got up and went to the sideboard. Her spaniel, Trixie, who had been watching her carefully from a corner, rose at once and shook herself and was ready to be off. "I believe Tracey thinks you need converting, Oliver. Though if you asked him I don't suppose he'd be sure what he was trying to convert you to."

"I'm not converting anyone," her husband said, running a finger along his moustache. "I'm stating what's slowly becoming self-evident to everyone—only everyone won't admit it yet. Even Oliver won't admit it."

"I don't know what you want me to admit," I said. "Anyway, it's all relative, isn't it? What looks like bread and skilly to one man may seem like milk and honey to another."

Sarah straightened her brows at me and smiled. "Well, I'm sorry this is where I leave the argument. Another outdated convention, don't you think? And I haven't even a good deed to go to."

Elliott must have heard us stirring, because he came in then. After Sarah had left, Tracey said:

"D'you remember the character in one of Meredith's novels who allowed his daughter to be pressed into a distasteful marriage because he couldn't resist his future son-in-law's port? We've only nine bottles of this left, so I restrict myself to two a year. Gently, Elliott, gently."

"Yes, sir." Elliott expertly poured out two glasses; then he went off to the kitchen with his head bent and a squeak in one shoe.

"If it's so good," I said, "I wonder you waste it on me."

He looked at me with a sort of mischievous irony. "When the tumbrils start rolling, your friendship will be useful to me."

"I'll get my secretary to make a note of that."

There was a thrush or a blackbird chattering just outside the window.

"Just sip it," he said. "It's better that way. Seriously, I sometimes think that the methods of the French Revolution might be preferable to the methods used here. Who was it—a woman—said to some Americans a year or so ago: 'We don't cut off their heads in this country, we cut off their incomes.' It's a pretty admission, isn't it? Or do you agree with her? I might if I'd been in your shoes. But don't you think the French way is the more logical— as always—and perhaps in the end the kinder? I *bitterly* resent being an anachronism. How many people in England are there like me, still clinging to the very remnants of their belongings— still keeping up a pretence. . . ." He gestured impatiently.

The port glowed in my glass a rich plum purple. "These—er— remnants . . ."

"Oh, I know. We carry the surface sheen. But it can't last. There are many for whom it hasn't lasted—*old* people, living servantless in corners of big houses, watching their gardens overgrow and their floors rot. And others who've had to get out in the last years of their lives to finish up in rooms or tiny villas with what they were able to save from the wreck. I'm not up against the reasonable redistribution of wealth. I'm up against the unreasonable *destruction* of property and all that goes with it; because once the family life has gone out of a house, it's as good as destroyed, dead, like the socket of an eye. And the country's the poorer for it—nationally and spiritually the poorer. Only a fool deliberately squanders his assets."

I lit a cigarette. "I used to think I knew some of the answers. I don't any more. I confess I think your hardships easier to bear than some I've seen. But perhaps that's ignorance and prejudice. Anyway, I wouldn't wish you to suffer them."

I don't think Tracey was listening. He had slumped a bit further into his chair, his eyes fixed on his glass. The spark of vitality had gone.

He said: "In Victorian days they used to write bad melodramas about the death of the breadwinner, because when the father died

46

it could mean the breakup of the family. Well, the same sort of thing is happening today, only it's happening in a different circle of society. When the head of a big house dies it often means the home has to go too."

I didn't answer, and I don't think he wanted an answer.

"Wasn't it Bacon or somebody who said: 'No people over-charged with tribute is fit for empire.' The question is, what are we fit for? All the other things I care about, the wider things, are being dissipated as well. As the houses come under the hammer the pictures will go—and the libraries—and the furniture—it's true it's to America, which isn't so bad; *they're* not being destroyed; it's one of our dollar exports. But it's bad enough, and the worst of that's only just beginning, because capital takes time to disperse. And who are the artists of tomorrow to sell to? And what are the architects to design? It's like the breakup in Italy after the Renaissance."

There was silence for a bit. Then he poured me another glass of port.

He said: " 'Thrush, sing clear, for the spring is here; Sing for the summer is near, is near.' My father used to sit in this chair, until he died, with his stiff leg stuck out under the table. He was an old devil, really, but I liked him. We agreed on nothing, and he played me a dirty trick in the end. . . . And yet . . . I'm not a sentimental man, but I've a strong sense of heredity. More than I let my mother see, because I'm not willing to accept the conventional poses she expects. It's no good putting on a suit of mail armour to go and stand in the fish queue."

I slept in one of the four bedrooms which led out on to the gallery overlooking the hall, a big room with a four-poster bed and two lattice windows looking over the lawns which ran to the trees of a side lane about two hundred yards away. Elliott was already out cutting the lawn when I woke. A bee droned against one of the panes, and just in front of the windows was an over-grown Irish yew with two starlings chattering in it.

Tracey wasn't down to breakfast, but Mrs. Moreton was there before me, as pleasant and as dignified as ever in spite of the fact that she hadn't got to bed till three. I thought: it would have been queer if my own mother had been like that, or did the cor-rosions of real poverty make all the difference? The constant striving after minimum decencies, the constant failure. The floor-cloth and the sacking and the oilcloth table, the bare communal stairs, the back yard of rubble and ash . . .

Mrs. Moreton said: "How many to lunch?"

"Eleven," Sarah said. "Victor, of course—and Clive Fisher is bringing some girl friend. But Mrs. Antrim has her sister in to help, so we can leave it to them."

"You haven't met my second son, have you, Mr. Branwell? Tracey—well, Tracey, I think, has the better brain, but all the success has come to Victor. Very—unfair; but it's the way things happen. Tracey's illness, of course. . . . But in any case Victor gives one the impression of being more capable of meeting life on its own terms. I think you'll like him."

Objective about her own children. That, at least, my mother could never have been. For her, existence had meant being in the arena *all* the time—and for those who were with her. That was the crux. Always, she had blocked the mind of its fair and rational escape. Or was I being unjust?

"Do you ride?" Sarah was asking me.

"I've been on a horse twice. Why?"

"I thought you might like to see a bit of the countryside."

"With you and Tracey?"

"Or with me. I don't think he . . . We usually get hacks from the village. They're very docile. The poor things have had all the life knocked out of them."

Carefully casual, I said: "I should like that very much."

chapter 7

*I*t was nearly an hour before we really started. I was in a fever to get off in case Tracey should come down unexpectedly and decide to go with us, or lest one of the other guests should arrive.

Elliott found a pair of Mr. Victor's breeches for me, and these fitted fairly well if a bit slack round the waist. All the same I felt very odd, and when I saw the horses they both looked as high as churches, with thin stilts of legs. I realized that Sarah's idea of a hack was quite different from mine.

The man who'd brought the horses from the stables held Sarah's brown horse while she got on, and then waited wooden-faced for me to do the same. Fortunately, just at the right moment, Elliott came out of the house and took his attention, and the first the man knew was the grey horse nearly stepping on him as I lunged onto its back. I grabbed the reins and said, "Sorry," and followed Sarah through the gate.

We went out of the main gates and turned left, and left again up the narrow lane that ran along the east boundary of the house. After a few yards, Sarah held in her horse until I came wobbling abreast of her.

"All right?" she asked, smiling.

"I feel like a country gentleman in the opening scene of a pantomime."

"All we need is the big bad wolf."

"Will Trixie do? Don't encourage her to bark, will you, or my damned horse will bolt."

"No, he's a pet really. You're holding the reins a bit tight. And try to grip more with your knees. When we get through the farm I'll show you; that's if you'll let me."

We followed the lane about a quarter of a mile. Once the grounds of the house were left behind, we passed through wheat fields, and then came to the farm she had spoken of, a low timbered house in a hollow beside a pond. She called a greeting to a red-faced man of fifty-odd who was carrying a bucket across the cobbled yard.

"That's the Home Farm," she said. "Lowis Farm. The Spooners have rented it from the Moretons for a hundred and fifty years. It's the last farm that belongs to us. There used to be eight—and part of the village, of course. It was wretched luck—most of it had to be sold at the worst time, just before property shot up in value. Some of it has been resold since at four times more than we were paid."

Over in the distance you could hear the church bells. It was a peaceful scene. But the next hour wasn't peaceful for me at all.

She seemed to enjoy teaching me and apparently didn't find anything silly in my clutchings and joltings. The horse was the most perverse devil I've ever known, and wanted to do everything the way he thought of it and not the way I did. Yet it didn't matter. It was queer. I felt different from what I'd ever done in my life—a sense of freedom that ten times outweighed any bumps or bruises. It isn't until something comes straight that you realize it's been twisted inside you: a tension goes; you know a new kind of experience, a letup, a feeling of happiness. I shall never forget that morning because it was the first time it came.

At length we turned for home and after walking together for a bit, she said: "D'you mind if I go on, just as far as that wood? I think Firefly would enjoy the gallop. I'll wait for you there."

I said, no, of course I didn't mind; and watched her go off across the fields, her blouse rippling and her hair streaming, and Trixie scuttling behind. My grey brute of course wanted to follow, but after checking him twice I thought, hooray, why should I be left behind, and gave him his head.

I don't think my hair is long enough to stream, otherwise it certainly would have done. Victor Moreton's breeches, which had been too slack, now seemed to be straining at every seam. I went through all the symptoms of diving and crash-landing twenty times a minute, and the ground thundered away below like someone trying to rip a carpet from under the horse's hooves. The trees got nearer. Bits of mud and foam flicked up on to my shirt and I thought, thank God I was in a mechanized war.

I pulled on the reins and the brute's wicked head came half up, and we made a semicircle round Sarah and plunged into the wood.

Sarah found me among the foxgloves. She got off quickly and said: "*Oliver!* are you all right?"

I was trying to rub a daub of green lichen off the shoulder of my shirt.

I said: "That horse had its intention in its eyes from the minute I got on."

We stared at each other intently for a moment, then I lay back

50

and laughed with her. I hadn't found anything so funny for a long time.

"Are you hurt?" she asked, sobering up.

I got up and felt myself in various places. "I'm hurt. But not injured. Let's go and find him."

We found him grazing peacefully enough at the far side of the copse. He cocked a wary eye, but Sarah caught him all right while I held her horse. We tethered them both and sat on the grass for a rest and a smoke. Trixie came and settled down near us, her nose on her paws.

From this higher ground you could see Lowis Manor and most of the gardens. Half a mile to the west was the village, with its church and its pub and its cluster of cottages, and beyond that were the telegraph poles of the road that ran to Tonbridge.

I moved myself carefully, to avoid the sore places. "Is this wood yours?"

"Yes. Our land ends at the gate. Down there—you can't see the stream but there is one, where the bushes grow in a line— down there was the old mill and the spinney that Foster painted. You can still see a bit of the wheel and the stonework. This wood was full of bluebells six weeks ago. I used to come up every year and pick them."

"Used to?"

"Well, until this year. This year the weather was so bad and— somehow one slips into a habit or slips out of one for no particular reason."

She was lying against the trunk of a fallen tree, her cream silk blouse open at the neck. Her hair was ruffled, and the ride had brought a flush of colour to her cheeks. She didn't look as unapproachable as usual—or as I imagined her usually to be.

I said suddenly, on the impulse: "Are you happy, Sarah?"

Her eyes flickered up to my face, then she looked away again over the fields. She sat up and rubbed a finger along her boot.

"Well, that certainly changes the conversation, doesn't it?"

"Drastically."

"What d'you mean by happy? Consciously, permanently feeling good about myself? No. . . . Who does? There are times when I'm happy, times when I'm not. Doesn't that happen to everyone? I've been like that all my life."

I said: "But doesn't one ever strike a balance?"

She straightened her brows. "Look down there. You can see them coming out of church. I hadn't realized you could from here. A balance?" She drew at her cigarette and then seemed to dislike the taste and threw it away. "It sounds like the text for a sermon. Prepare to meet your Auditor face to face. Very solemn."

"Very suitable."

"My accounts," she said, "would be untidy—as usual. I've an untidy mind, Oliver; it doesn't always know whether to put an item on the debit or credit side—and often changes the entry after it's been made. There'd be a lot of spilt milk—sorry, ink— on the book. Blots and crossings out. Red ink, too—and purple. Horrible! A tidy person like you—expecting a balance—would be quite dismayed."

I let my cigarette smoulder.

After a minute she added: "Well?"

"Well, it's a nice enough answer, as answers go."

"It was a nice enough question—as questions go. Look at that hawk. See him hovering over the hedge. After a field mouse, I expect."

"As a man who at one time was suspected of pinching your bracelet . . ."

She looked at me quickly and smiled, but didn't speak.

"You were my mascot during the war, weren't you? Sort of. That half crown. You brought me luck." I hesitated, and then decided to go on playing with fire. "It entitles me, don't you think?"

"To what?"

"To take a few liberties."

"I haven't noticed any. Are they to come?"

I stared at her profile. "Well, that question . . . But sometimes one wonders. . . ."

"Wonders?"

Her eyelids were half closed. I wasn't sure if she was peering more closely at the remote figures near the church.

"If there isn't a sort of frustration in some people's lives—who seem to have so much that isn't used, that doesn't have a chance to express itself. . . . That's why I asked."

"Was it?" she said in a small cool voice.

"Perhaps I'm wrong but—— The way you ride, the way you drive a car. Sometimes even the way you walk . . ."

"Shows what?" she said, turning her eyes full on me. "I've always wanted to know how a frustrated woman walks."

There was no going back now. It was fight or go down. "A frustrated woman walks with funny little steps, usually with her heels a bit inward and a good deal of weight on each step. It's aggressive and nervy—like everything she does——"

"Well, I'm sorry to get aggressive and nervy about those people coming to lunch——"

"*You* walk," I said, "with a long vigorous sort of stride. If a stranger sees you he probably thinks: that girl's got that walk because she's a swimmer, or a runner—or a ballet dancer. . . . And when you drive a car a man would think the same sort of thing. He'd think a girl who drives like that must have an unusual ability for it. Perhaps she's been trained or perhaps it comes natural, but either way it's an expression of her temperament, and either way she'll do. Because of that——"

Sarah got up. After a second she said: "But will she do, Oliver, will she do? Hasn't she compromised in the good old-fashioned way by getting married and sticking to her contract and living comfortably with her husband in the country, just as she was brought up to do? . . . And d'you seriously think"—she turned on me rather angrily—"d'you seriously think the other way would have been the better way? By now I should have been a prima ballerina earning four pounds a week in the back row of the *corps de ballet*. Is that the sort of fulfilment you'd have prescribed?"

I got up beside her. "You couldn't have been."

"That's all you know. Have you ever even been to the ballet in your life?"

"No. Not ever. I'd like to go with you sometime."

"It's so easy to criticize, to give advice, to sit back and talk about frustration and fulfilment and—things. But nobody's life works out to a pattern; we don't slip into ready-made slots. There's always wastage. . . . Isn't there? We make the best, not the worst, of our lives—and use what we can. D'you suppose if you put the same test to any woman . . . Or most men. Everybody's life is in some sort of a rut—if it wasn't it wouldn't be a life at all. And the things that we don't do, can't do, because of the pattern we've chosen, seem important if we brood on them, magnify them. . . ." She stopped for breath, and I waited, wanting so much to touch her, not daring to. "Anyway, why should you care; why should you question me?"

I said: "I wasn't criticizing—or giving advice. God forbid. All I asked you was, are you happy?"

"The answer's no," she said. "Do you propose to do anything about it?"

"If you'll tell me something I can do . . ."

She bent and picked up her crop, rather slowly straightened up, turning it round in her fingers. Then she raised her hand to push back her hair. It was a suddenly young gesture.

She said: "That's Victor arriving now. I must hurry."

The first I saw of Victor was coming down the stairs after having changed. He was standing halfway down discussing with Tracey whether Barber & Curry had made a good job of the Constable, and whether Clive Fisher approved of the new place for hanging it. Victor was a bigger man than Tracey and might well have been the elder. On the surface he was an altogether more distinguished-looking man: a sleek well-shaven face, tweeds of a newer cut, put on, one felt, for the country visit, a prosperous good-tempered voice, a physical ease about him.

But all the people who came to lunch that day, with one exception, were of the same breed—comfortable, confident, well groomed, *healthy*-looking. They'd never been alone in a strange town with tenpence in their pockets or packed their shoes with paper to keep out the wet; or suffered from anaemia or pimples or rheumatism.

Nor, I thought, seeing myself suddenly in the glass, had they ever—probably—accepted a man's food and drink and then made a pass at his wife. Even an ex-jailbird might have some standards. Not that there seemed much risk of my stealing Sarah's affections —it was only my own which had gone further overboard. Tracey was safe.

Before I could resolve the unresolvable, Sarah came in with Clive Fisher and Ambrosine and Clive's girl friend. This latter was a tall blonde with a good figure, and I hadn't realized how tall she was because I'd only seen her once before and that was in bed.

54

chapter 8

She sat opposite me at lunch. We'd been duly introduced, but neither of us said a thing about having met before.

When I looked at them together I knew it was no great coincidence that Clive Fisher should be a friend of Vere Litchen, the girl whose husband had lost his Georgian silver. They were the sort of people who would move in the same circles and who would attract each other: artistic in a fashionable way, amoral rather than immoral; good-timers living on their nerves.

Mrs. Moreton sat next to her younger son. She might be able to take a detached view of Victor, but she doted on him just the same. He had that week been adopted as prospective candidate for a Sussex division at the next election; and talk centred round this for a time. But Clive in his usual assertive way began a rival topic by talking ballet across the table to Sarah. He had, he said, two tickets for Covent Garden next week but he was too *deadly* sick of these sentimental nineteenth-century fairy tales; would she and Tracey like to use the tickets?

Sarah said: "Sometime when you have a spare ticket I think you should give it to Oliver. He boasts that he's never been to the ballet, and I think he should be made to go."

"Never been to the *ballet?*"

The whole table suddenly seemed to be listening, and everyone immediately stared goggle-eyed at me. It was mean of Sarah to let it out that way.

I said: "Rare animal from the South American jungle. Self-raised on raw meat. Do not touch."

Vere Litchen yawned behind five scarlet fingernails. "Does not breed in captivity," she added.

"Well, choosy at any rate," I agreed.

After a minute, Tracey said: "What are they doing, Clive?"

" 'Sylphides,' 'Swan Lake,' 'Façade.' "

"You'd better take Oliver yourself then, Sarah," Tracey said, fingering his signet ring. "There was a time when I could face Chopin, but every time I hear him now I have to come home and play records of Bach to get the flavour out of my mouth."

After a long second I said stiffly: "Thanks, but I can't manage next week. Thank you all the same."

Clive was still looking at me with his prominent blue eyes. For the first time I was an object of genuine interest to him. "You should make the *effort*, old boy. It won't *debauch* you."

I was already halfway to regretting the refusal. "I'll make the effort when I can. May I hold you to that, Sarah?"

"All right," she said, but her smile was cool.

"I'm out in any case because I get my monthly injection on Wednesday," said Tracey wearily. "I couldn't face London two days together."

"Do they do you any good, those things?" Victor asked, frowning.

"No. But they keep me alive."

There was a laugh. I wondered if Tracey's wit was one of the things which had counted with Sarah when she married him. Perhaps still did count. I really hadn't an idea what they felt for each other. I only knew that she and I had moved towards a new intimacy this morning but that my blundering had spoiled it at the start.

One loophole I'd left for myself; and the following day I went along to Covent Garden to do the thing in my own way. But to my disgust I found the season was ending on Saturday and no tickets were left. So the opportunity to repair the damage was gone, and I had thrown the chance away.

Looking back on the autumn and winter that followed, I seem to have spent the time in a sort of fitful dream, often restless and discontented but not having the initiative or the opportunity to do anything about it. I saw Sarah three or four times, but never alone, and she kept me at a distance, there was no doubt about that. Once I met Tracey and had a meal with him at his club.

So it was April again—a pretty fateful spring for us all—and I saw that a season of ballet was opening next week and that one night they were doing exactly the programme I'd missed. I dropped everything and went along and stood in a queue for an hour and got the tickets. Then I phoned Tracey and told him what I'd done and did he mind if I took up that invitation from last year? Would he let Sarah come and initiate me? He sounded amused and said he'd no objections; he'd call her. This was the point, and I chipped my pencil all round with teeth marks before he returned to say Sarah had her hands floured but sent a message she'd be pleased to come.

Then there was a week to wait.

That week a rather unusual case came in and took up a good bit of my time. Charles Highbury, the film star, was taken ill in the middle of a film and the whole production was held up.

As it happened the underwriters who instructed us hadn't put any business in our way since the war, but Michael had heard they were dissatisfied with the people they usually employed, whose fees were a good bit less than ours.

It wasn't the sort of case I'd had much experience of, nor did it seem likely to be one where we should have a decent chance to justify our higher charges. However, after a conversation with the producer, I went straight up to the Dorchester, where Highbury was staying, and saw him there along with the studio doctor and another doctor, who called himself Mr. Highbury's personal physician.

Highbury was the heartthrob of two continents, a handsome powerfully built chap in the late thirties who usually played the tough hero in adventure films; but a good bit of the glamour had been switched off when I saw him. He'd refused to be shaved that morning, and had a very sizable black eye where he'd fallen down in a faint after getting back from the studios the night before. He was feeling ill and peevish and he took a poor view of me, so I slid out of his ice-blue satin bedroom and sat down in a corner of his sitting room to make a few notes. It was fairly obvious that he'd have to have a few days off, at least until the black eye mended, but when the two doctors came out there seemed to be a good bit of dissension between them as to what was really the matter with him. His personal physician said he'd had a nervous breakdown and needed at least three weeks' rest; the studio doctor couldn't find anything the matter with him and was pretty unsympathetic, I thought. It was the same only more so with Victor Dorrington, the producer of the film, though you could understand his feelings, with the production already £10,000 over budget and his leading lady under contract to go to Hollywood in six weeks' time.

The following day I went to the studios to see what was being done to minimize the loss in the way of a rearranged shooting schedule, but the trouble was the script had been written round Highbury, and there was hardly a scene in which he didn't appear. One or two remarks that were dropped I filed away for reference. In time one gets into the habit of remembering small things just in case they should come in useful later on.

On the way back I called at the Dorchester again but got no further than the private sitting room. While his secretary was in with the Presence, I admired the photo of Janet Vale, Highbury's film-star wife—who, I gathered, was in Edinburgh at the moment, making a personal appearance with her new film—and then, certainly with no intention of snooping, went over to the handsome Louis the Something escritoire by the window. Open on it was Highbury's engagement book and I saw that on the night he was taken ill he had had an appointment to dine with a Mr. W. Croft, at Monk's Court, N.W.8, and that the appointment was ticked. If he had kept the appointment it made nonsense of his story that he'd collapsed as soon as he got home from the studio.

That afternoon I happened to meet an underwriter called Charles Robinson, a good-looking youngish man with dark eyes, who said his own firm had been approached when the film was being mounted but that they had refused to write the risk because they had insured Charles Highbury's last film and he had been ill in the middle of that and run them in for a large claim.

I decided to let the thing simmer over the weekend. Highbury might suddenly go back, and there wasn't a lot we could do about it even if he didn't. If a man says he's ill you can't force him to work. You can only hope that he'll have some thought for his own reputation.

It was Monday I was meeting Sarah, and I was grateful in a way to this case for taking my mind off her for a bit. It would be the first time I had been with her alone since we went riding together; and things hadn't ever been quite the same since then.

I was at Covent Garden well ahead of time, watching the crowding faces carefully in case I should miss her. There was a beggar selling shoelaces, and I bought a pair although I didn't need them. It had been warm all day, and heavy clouds had hung over the city. Big spots of rain were splashing now and then on the stonework of the Opera House.

I caught sight of her long before she saw me. She was getting out of a taxi, and she glanced at her watch as I pushed down towards her.

"Hullo!" I said. "You made it all right?"

"Yes. I was afraid I should be late." She smiled at me, more with her eyes than her mouth, and that meant a lot. It meant that it was going to be all right.

We got to our seats as the orchestra was tuning up. The seats were at the extreme side of the lowest circle. She was wearing a scarlet frock I hadn't seen before, buttoned to the throat, made of some silk stuff, waisted, with a skirt as wide as a gypsy's.

I said: "I hope these seats are all right. I—remember you saying once . . ."

"D'you remember that? You don't get the full depth of the stage but it's like being in the wings, part of the company."

"Ever since last July . . ."

She looked at me when I stopped. "What?"

"I've been trying to fix this evening. Ballet companies are capricious——"

"You mean since we talked of it at Lowis?"

"Yes. . . . I turned it down then. Galloping insanity."

She looked down at her programme, flicked through the pages. "I think there's been a change in 'Façade.' Oh, no. I must have misunderstood Tracey. He said something this morning——"

"How is he?"

"Fairly well. Mrs. Moreton's away and we're having some repairs done, and that always makes him cross because they are never done the way he wants them. We may go away ourselves next week."

"Oh? Where?"

"Only to Scarborough for a bit. Victor is there, and it will be a good thing for Tracey to be away while the dust is about. And the servants need a holiday. We're closing the house. Have you been away?"

"No. . . . No, I've been in London most of the time. Busy, you know. Not riding . . ."

She smiled, put her hand on the balcony edge, as if to look down into the orchestra, where all the fiddles tuning up were making a rather exciting sound.

"I suppose—that other time it was because Clive Fisher was giving us the tickets. Was that why you wouldn't go?"

"Partly. Mostly."

"You don't like him, do you?"

"Well, he's not my favourite type."

"Sometimes—about some things that you must feel most deeply you say so little, Oliver. Are you very intolerant underneath?"

"Very intolerant."

There was a moment's silence.

"But possibly rather nice," she said as the conductor came up the steps to his rostrum.

chapter 9

You couldn't expect my first feelings about ballet to be anything but good—though I suppose if you'd asked me afterwards I should hardly have been able to describe a thing. It was one of those queer experiences, seeing something in absence of mind. The dancing and the music and the colour didn't create an emotion for me; they commented on an emotion already in me. They were a foreground fulfilling the purpose of a background.

Sarah, of course, never took her eyes off the stage while the curtain was up, except once or twice to whisper a word of comment or explanation. Her look was of someone deep and lost—and at the end she seemed to find it hard to come back to ordinary things. She didn't raise any objection when I got my car from a side street and took her to a place for supper. There was lightning flickering in the sky as we went in.

In the restaurant we talked about ballets and the people who danced them. If there had been a certain amount of constraint in her attitude this winter it wasn't there tonight. She'd been in a dream; that made the difference. Unfortunately it wasn't the same dream as mine.

When I had passed her something she said: "Your finger's been hurt at some time. That one. Was it in the war?"

"No. . . . When I was eighteen I wanted to get away from home—at *any* price; so I went as a stoker, crossed the Atlantic. Coming home, I got the finger crushed. The surgeon wanted to hack it off, but in fact it mended pretty well."

Sarah said quietly: "I think Tracey's right in a way, Oliver: you don't talk enough about yourself. You don't even talk about the war."

"We're too near another to make light conversation about the last."

"And there's your work. What have you been doing today?"

Of course I didn't mention the Highbury business; but instead I told her about a case last week when a man had tried to defraud the insurance company on the theft of some motorcars.

"Do you get many false claims?"

"Quite a few. More often in fires than in burglary, because it's easier to cover up." I tried to go on talking, as she seemed interested. "People like to get rid of bad stock. But even then we often catch them out. It isn't really easy to start a fire without paraffin cans or a stack of plywood boxes. Often the floor gives way, and part of the preparations falls through to the cellar or into the foundations and isn't burnt."

She picked up her glass and stared at the wine. "Moral to that, I should think, is start your fire in the cellar."

"And near a lift or any part of your warehouse where there's a good upward draught. Of course, these days people try to be too smart."

"How?"

"Well, they're not content with the old ways: they try something new, with electricity or gas. The simplest props are still the best: candle in a wastepaper basket; that sort of thing."

61

"Why a candle in a wastepaper basket?"

"Well, you set your fire, drapes, stock, piled chairs, whatever it is, soaked in turpentine; and under it you put a candle, standing on hemp or something, inside a wastepaper basket. Then you light the candle and leave, and the fire breaks out when you're asleep in bed sixty miles away."

"Very ingenious. Has that often been done?"

"We don't know how often."

There was a crack and a rumble outside. She looked up startled, then looked at her watch. "I hope it isn't going to break now. I must keep an eye on the last train."

"I'll drive you down, of course. That goes without saying."

"Is that a new car you have?"

"New to me."

It was warm in the restaurant, and the hum of noise made a sort of privacy: you could talk within a small personal orbit; the waiters and the diners and the vague ordinary faces were out of focus. There was no more thunder, and when at length we came out we were surprised to see the streets fairly streaming with water, as if they'd just been hosed. There was no rain then, so we ducked hurriedly into the car.

"I'm not too late for the last train."

"No, nonsense. But will you be all right in that thin coat?"

She said she'd be all right.

I started up the engine, and then a silly thing happened. I'd only had the car a month, and as it had been fine all the time I didn't know the sliding roof leaked. While we were having supper a lot of rain had come through and lodged in the upturned sun visors. As soon as I moved the car the water spilled out in a cascade. I got most of it directly on my head, as if someone had tipped a cup of water over me. Sarah got nearly as much in her lap.

It was one of those things that sometimes happen as if specially arranged by a malignant joker. I got out a handkerchief and a piece of clean cheesecloth and gave them to her and apologized and laughed and fumed, while the water trickled down my neck. It was a job to see what we were doing, and because I'd moved out of my parking place, a taxi was angrily hooting behind. By the time I'd drawn in again and made sure that most of the spare water was mopped up, it was raining again.

I said: "I can't tell you what I feel about this. I'll drive round to my flat and pick up a mack and a rug."

Her frock rustling, she curled her legs underneath her and sat on them. "I'm all right. I'm too used to the country to be afraid of a bit of water."

"Your frock isn't. We're only five minutes away."

I manoeuvred the car out and turned it north, across Piccadilly and up Regent Street and along Wigmore Street. Just for a minute when we reached the flat I couldn't get out, the rain was so heavy. It bubbled and blistered on the windscreen, and the street lights glimmered on a canal with cars ploughing through it tyre-deep.

I glanced at Sarah and saw her pull her coat round her. I thought she shivered.

"You'd better come in and dry yourself in front of the fire," I said. "It's a good hour's run and you'll be frozen."

She didn't speak.

I said: "This is giving me hell."

"It needn't. No one would expect such rain."

We waited three or four minutes, until the next break. Then I ran round and opened the door. She got out and we crossed to the shelter of the dress-shop porch before I let myself in.

I've never been proud of my flat, but it never looked shabbier than when she went into it. Things look more faded when there is something like her to compare them with.

The gas fire popped, and I pulled a chair up a bit. "Sit here. I'll get the rug. It's in my room."

When I came back she was standing with her skirt held out like a fan and her hair a bit ruffled with the rain. She was looking curiously about her, in a strange element, sizing it up.

I said: " 'She stood in her scarlet gown. If anyone touched her the gown rustled; She stood in her scarlet gown, Her face like a rose and her mouth like a flower.' "

Sarah had half turned, but she didn't speak for some time. I'd only switched on one table lamp—to try to disguise the worst—and the light showed her pale eyelids.

She said: "What's that?"

"Something I read the other night."

"I didn't know you read poetry."

"I don't, much."

"Or quoted it."

"A dog's allowed two bites. After that you can shoot him."

"I wouldn't want to—for that."

I went across and took a newish raincoat out of a cupboard. It was sizes too big for her.

She said: "I think we should go. Tracey may be getting anxious."

"Ring him if you like."

"Well, I can't—from here."

"No. . . . I suppose not." I chucked the raincoat on a chair. "Tracey's a very generous man, isn't he?"

"In what way?"

"He doesn't seem to mind your coming out with me."

"He thinks—he says I don't get enough . . . change."

"All the same, it isn't every husband . . ."

"Oh, I know. We have—a perfect understanding and trust."

At the time I wouldn't admit how those words made me feel. "So any cavalier . . ."

"In the last two years I've been out three times without Tracey."

"*Sorry.* . . . Forget I spoke."

I lit a cigarette for her, and there was silence for a while. The gas fire was hissing like an angry audience.

She said: "I'm dry now. Let's go."

Perhaps it was the wine I'd drunk.

I said: "You know I love you, don't you?"

She got up so that her face was in the shadow. The cigarette between her fingers was quite steady.

"Yes."

"How long have you known?"

"Since that Sunday we went riding."

"Not before then?"

"Yes. . . . I think before then."

"And what of Tracey's—understanding and trust?"

She said: "I'm afraid it doesn't cover this."

She put her cigarette to her lips and drew on it. The glow lit up her face.

"Why did you come out with me, then?"

Her eyes flickered over me for a second, then she moved slowly to pick up her coat.

"There were reasons. . . . It's stopped raining, Oliver."

"Carry your own coat. Put this on," I said, holding out the raincoat.

She hesitated and then came back.

"Why did you come out with me, Sarah?"

"Should I not have done? Perhaps it's because I wanted to. Perhaps it's because I'm a bitch. I don't know. I'm very sorry I can't answer. I shouldn't have come." She laughed, under her breath, without humour. "That's obvious, isn't it? Sorry."

"There's nothing to be sorry for—or to blame yourself for. Nothing in the world. I hope you'll come again."

"Pity you didn't—go on pretending. . . . So much easier to cheat when nothing's been said."

I helped her into the raincoat. In the coat there seemed nothing of her. She turned with a sort of wry smile to thank me, but instead she said: "Oh, Oliver, don't look like that."

Then the step that couldn't be taken was taken. For a second she looked up at me not resisting the pressure of my hands on her arms; and I bent and kissed her cheek and then her mouth. It was queer. It was as if suddenly something had happened so that experience was two seconds old and racing downhill.

I felt her pushing me away, and at once I let her go. The shabby room grew its four walls, shadows made the same geometry on the ceiling; I took a deep breath; she and the coat were gone.

I caught her at the door. "Sarah . . ."

"Let's not say anything more now. We'd better go."

"Sarah . . ."

She turned then—in a sort of anger that wasn't quite anger.

"Don't say anything, Oliver. Not now. . . . You see you were right, weren't you? It just doesn't work out. I shouldn't have come."

I drove her back to Lowis. There were no speed cops or I should have been run in. It wasn't that I drove so fast but that I couldn't pay the job any attention. Not surprising, I suppose. It was the first time in all this time I'd ever so much as touched her except once or twice to shake hands. Perhaps that first meeting was partly to blame; but she'd always seemed so very far away. Nor, looking back even ten minutes, could I decide how

65

much give way there had been on her side, what *her* thought and *her* feeling had been. And she didn't help me, she wouldn't talk about it.

The house was in darkness when we got there except for a light in the main hall. I stopped well back, hoping no one would hear the car, and got out to open the door for her. But as I did so Trixie began to bark, and I saw the gleam of a cigarette. Tracey was standing on the top step.

"That you, Sarah?" he called. "Bring Oliver in for a drink. I want to talk to him."

chapter 10

I suppose we'd had the whole drive to recover. Anyway, he seemed to notice nothing peculiar in our manner. All the same it was an ordeal, standing there in the light blinking and drinking, pulses going faster, imagining one's face was stretched and shiny and unreal, or perhaps smeared with lipstick.

I think he only wanted an excuse for getting me inside. Alone in the house except for the two old servants, he was probably glad of someone to talk to—and I had a pretty sharp twinge of conscience at the thought. Part of the hall was in dust sheets and there were builder's ladders beside the stairs. Woodworm had been found in the heavy oak balustrade running round the gallery, and they were not quite sure yet how far it had spread. He was full of a scheme for improving the lighting in the hall by putting two fresh windows in the roof but doubtful whether he could afford the thing as he really wanted it.

Presently Sarah excused herself and went off to bed, but I stayed there until nearly two, sipping his brandy and trying to take an intelligent interest in his concerns, feeling by turns depressed and elated, and by turns a fine fellow and the cheapest of hypocrites.

When I looked back three months after, I felt I ought to have seen and understood far more without any sudden happening to point it from outside. I wasn't just out of my shell. But there it was. I didn't, not an inkling, not the breath of an idea. It took the Highbury case to set off the fuse.

I'd talked the case over at length with Michael and his father; and we'd had a conference at the studios on the Monday. When Charles Highbury was still off on the Tuesday morning, I phoned Dorrington and suggested we should get another opinion; so arrangements were made for Sir Roger Fetter to call on Mr. Highbury on the Wednesday morning. On Wednesday afternoon I called on Sir Roger. He was of the opinion that there was nothing seriously wrong with Mr. Highbury except a bruised eye, which was rapidly mending. When I got back to the office I sat and thought the thing over pretty closely for about an hour. I wondered again about the night before his collapse, the date he'd had with a Mr. W. Court in north London, that I'd seen marked in his appointment book. Had he kept it, and did it hold the solution? Mr. W. Court, Monk's Croft, N.W.8. About six I got my car and went to see.

My map didn't show Monk's Croft; and north London is a warren if you don't know your way about. It took me the best part of an hour up and down residential byways before a policeman told me it was Monk's *Court* I wanted, and that was the big new block of flats on the right. By then I'd got the thing straight, and the janitor told me a Mr. William *Croft* lived on the eighth floor. He also told me that Mr. Croft was an American and worked at the Embassy.

Mr. Croft himself let me in; a pleasant, well-dressed, quiet-spoken chap in his thirties. I'd met one or two such in the last years of the war, and they mostly seemed to come from the neighbourhood of Boston.

It was a big flat, with white walls and reseda-green curtains and a lot of built-in bookshelves. After he'd shown me in and stared at my card a minute he said:

"Can I help you?"

"I hope so, Mr. Croft. I'm very sorry to trouble you, but I'm an insurance investigator and I'm trying to clear up an incident that occurred last Thursday evening, to Mr. Charles Highbury, the film star. I gather he had dinner with you that evening."

"He certainly did."

"And got himself rather knocked about . . ."

"Well, not at the dinner table."

I laughed. "Naturally not. But . . ."

I stopped there and eyed him and hoped for the best. I wondered if the bluff would work, or if it was the wrong bluff.

Croft looked a bit troubled. He fiddled with his tie and stared out of the window. "I think this calls for a drink," he said. "Will you have a Scotch-and-soda?"

I knew then that my hunch had been a good one. He was a time clinking glasses at a cocktail cabinet and when he came back he said:

"Can we get this straight? Just what interests do you represent, Mr. Branwell, and just what trouble am I laying up for myself or for anybody else if I talk to you?"

"None at all. I can promise you that. I'm working for the underwriters who have to meet a claim put in by Mr. Highbury's producer, because Highbury is ill. Well, they'll settle the claim in any case, but they want to check up on exactly what happened. There's no question whatever of wanting to make a charge against you—or anyone else, for that matter."

"Well, I should hope not!" he said, and laughed. He raised his glass and drank, and as he did so he caught my eye. He put his glass down. "You don't suppose *I* hit him, do you?"

I said cautiously: "Mr. Highbury *is* a bit vague as to what exactly happened."

"There's no reason why he should be! It was clear enough to everyone else, I guess."

I sipped my drink. "Could you tell me how it all started, Mr. Croft?"

He said: "D'you mind if I ring Highbury first—just to make sure he's no objection to my telling you?"

"Not in the least."

He put his glass down and looked at me. "No. . . . Maybe I shouldn't. I think you're O.K. I think I can trust you. . . . There were just the four of us: Charles and Janet—that's his wife, Janet Vale, you know—and Joy—that's mine—and we had them in for the evening. I'd met them in Hollywood last year. We had them in to drinks and a meal, and afterwards we played canasta. You know it?"

I said I did.

"Of course we gambled a bit—nothing to get excited about—and Charles and Janet lost a few pounds; I think nine or ten pounds between them. The last game or two they began to pick on each other, the way husbands and wives do. I winked at Joy, as much as to say: the screen lovers aren't above that. Then we finished and had a few more drinks and they got more and more kind of fretful with each other. And they were just going—Janet had put on her coat and they were in the hall—that little hall you came in by—and suddenly they started in to fight. There wasn't room to do the thing properly, but he bit her hand and kicked her ankle, and she suddenly connected with a beautiful straight right to the eye. I remember when he went down she said: 'Take that, you great big canary,' and walked out. He was with us till two o'clock, and then we got him in a taxi and sent him home."

I finished my drink. "Thank you very much, Mr. Croft. That more or less confirms . . . I'm much obliged to you."

"It was mighty embarrassing for us. We'd never entertained them before. After she'd gone he told us *all* his matrimonial troubles for the past twelve years. And there were plenty of them. I suppose it happens to us all, one time or another, but I've never actually gone in for that sort of thing with my wife, have you?"

"No," I said.

He seemed a nice fellow, and, now that the first fence was over, anxious to talk. So I sat over a second drink, chatting with him and wondering whether this new angle was really going to help in any way. It wasn't till I got up to go that I saw the picture.

It was at the end of the room and I'd glanced at it absent-mindedly once before, feeling there was something about it that I knew. This time I saw it was a water colour of Lowis Manor. I moved a bit nearer now, still chatting. The thing was painted very much from where Sarah and I had rested after the horse ride, except that it was lower down. The rear of the house was in the left background, and the foreground was taken up by a mill and a wood. That seemed wrong because I knew the mill had been gone a good many years.

"Admiring my water colour?" He'd followed my eyes and broken off what he was saying.

"Yes. . . . I know the house."

"Do you? That's interesting. I'm very proud of it because I never owned anything like a genuine Birket Foster before."

There was a good cube of ice left in my glass; and just for a moment I felt as if a piece of it had gone down my collar.

"A Foster? Genuine?"

"Yes. I picked it up about twenty months ago. It's called 'The Mill and Spinney,' but that's not very illuminating. Where did you say it was located?"

"I'm not certain. I may be mistaken. Is it signed?"

"Oh, surely. You see there in the corner. My dealer in Bond Street told me there were a good many fakes about so I was specially careful."

"You bought it from him?"

"No. . . . No, I didn't. Why?"

"It's—there's a man I know. Makes a study of Foster. I thought he'd be interested."

"No. . . . I had it through a dealer in Chelsea. He put me in touch with a young woman—who had it to sell. At the time, I was going to take it home with me to the States; but then I got this appointment so I thought I'd keep it right here. I guess I'm very proud of it."

"Yes," I said. "But what——"

"Apparently she was acting for the owners, who wanted to sell it privately: they were short of cash, hit by the war, wanted to realize on it without publicity—that sort of setup. Of course I didn't fancy parting with fifteen hundred dollars for a fake, so I had it verified before I paid the money. I've often wondered about it, because she asked for the money in cash." He looked at me sharply. "Don't tell me the thing was stolen."

"Oh, no. . . . At least, not as far as I know." I swallowed something. "What was the woman like?"

At that moment the telephone rang, and for about five nasty-tasting minutes I stood and stared at the picture and listened to him talking to his wife. The whole business of Charles Highbury and his troubles had been knocked right out of my mind. They might never have existed.

He came back at last. "You'll pardon me, I hope. My wife is in Essex. You see——"

I said: "What was the woman like?"

"What woman?" He looked at me. "Oh, the one who sold me

70

the picture. . . . Young. About twenty-five or six. Quite a looker."

"Was she tall and dark, slight but not thin, curly dark hair with a touch of bronze, and a very clear fine skin. Eyes nearly black in some lights, but in others a sort of deep hazel."

"That's the girl." He smiled. "So you know her well. She seemed pretty much of a lady. Don't tell me she's a crook."

I forced out some sort of an answering smile. "No. You're safe enough. The story she told you was more than half true."

I drove back to the garage and parked the car, but then instead of going home I walked through Hyde Park and Kensington Gardens. I suppose I must have walked seven or eight miles. I got in about eleven and went up and switched on the light and looked round. It all looked just the same: the faded green carpet and the two green plush easy chairs; the gas fire with a bit chipped out of one tier; some magazines and books I'd been reading, which had been piled carelessly and had spilled on the floor; a half-empty packet of cigarettes half open on the sham antique writing-desk that I was always intending to change and never did. I went over and opened a drawer and then aimlessly shut it again. It wasn't only desks that were sham.

Two days since Sarah had been in here—like a coloured bird making all the drab things drabber. It was only two days since all that had happened.

I sat on the divan-cum-bed and lit a cigarette and then went into the kitchen and fished out a bottle of whisky. I don't drink whisky often because I don't much like the taste, but I'd been started on that tonight. I flipped off the top and slopped a good lot in a glass. One bad taste and another.

I thought: take it quietly; there are degrees of enormity, aren't there? Insurance companies are fair game, and they know it. Is that what it is? Is that *all* it is?

I sat for a long time, until Big Ben sounded faintly on somebody's radio nearby. Then I got up and pulled back the coverlet of the divan and undressed and got into bed. Suspicion is a queer thing. So long as your mind is full proof against it you don't feel it at all. You don't know it exists. But let the smallest puncture be made. . . . About three I got up again and lit the fire and sat by it in my pyjamas chain-smoking.

After a bit I must have dozed off in the chair because when I woke it was coming light and there was the first murmur outside of the morning traffic.

The weather had been unsettled since Monday, but today looked fair enough. The sky was a pale-primrose colour with windy streaks between the jutting wings of the building opposite. It was going to be a bright day for some people, but I didn't feel it would be a good one for me.

Because of the fire claim, I knew that Tracey insured through Burton & Hicks, the brokers, of whom Fred McDonald was the claims manager. I'd not seen a lot of McDonald since I stopped going out with his daughter, but I made an excuse to call in and see him about a fire claim on a Southampton wharf. As I was leaving I said: "Oh, I suppose you still handle Tracey Moreton's business, don't you? D'you know if he's increased the insurance on Lowis Manor recently?"

McDonald rubbed his second chin with a fat thumb. "Moreton? Isn't he—— Oh, I remember. There was a small claim on it, wasn't there, a year or so ago. I think he has. Why d'you ask?"

"It's not important, but when I saw him a few months ago I told him I thought he wasn't covered on present-day prices."

McDonald pressed a bell. "Yes . . . when the policies came up for renewal—about last October. I'm not sure of the exact terms. Can soon let you know, if you like."

I made noises not quite strong enough to discourage him, and when his typist came back with the file, he said rather unamiably:

"Contents cover he increased from £25,000 to £30,000. I suggested that he increased the cover on the house but he didn't seem to think that necessary."

With a feeling of sudden relief I said: "What is it? I don't remember offhand."

"Twelve thousand pounds. I've never been down but it's quite a gem, I suppose."

"Yes. . . . If I see him again I'll suggest that he brings it up by fifty per cent."

"All right. Goodbye, Branwell."

I went out of the office into the shadow and sun of Gracechurch Street. So suspicion had got out of hand. It wasn't as bad as the bogies of the early hours had whispered.

All the same there was enough to be going on with.

When I got to Abercrombie's, the typist said: "Mr. Lawrence, of Haskell's, has been phoning. He wanted to know what the latest information was on the Highbury case. I've also put some papers from Berkeley Reckitt on your desk."

I went in and read the papers from Reckitt and picked up the phone to get Haskell's, at Lloyd's. Then I put it back. My mind wouldn't run to sick film stars. I knew I ought to do something about what I'd learned last night, but the tailpiece had knocked me over.

I picked up the phone again, and asked the girl to get me Sladen 35. While I was waiting I took out a pencil and put some figures down, but after a minute or two I made squares round them and began jabbing at the paper.

Sarah answered the phone. When she knew who it was her voice seemed to change. Perhaps it was my fancy.

"I thought I'd ring," I said. "How are you?"

"I'm fine, thank you."

"And Tracey?"

"Not awfully well."

I stared at the phone. "I'd like to see you again sometime pretty soon. I—want to see you both. Would it be convenient if I came down tomorrow?"

There was a pause. "We're just getting ready to go away. We leave on Saturday morning, you know."

"Oh. . . . I'd forgotten. . . . What about tomorrow evening?"

There was a sound of a muffled conversation. "We're only going for a week," she said. "Is it urgent?"

Was it urgent? "No," I said. "I suppose not. Will you phone me as soon as you get back?"

"Of course." Her voice was very guarded today.

"There's one thing I wanted to ask Tracey," I said. "Where is it he has his pictures cleaned—the Constable and the Lippi, for instance. I was talking to an American last night. I said I'd get the name."

I heard her ask Tracey and heard Tracey say: "What does he want to know for?" and Sarah's explanation. "It's Barber & Curry. They're in Bond Street, halfway up on the right-hand side, Tracey says."

"Right. Thank you. Enjoy your holiday. Goodbye."

"Goodbye."

I looked at the receiver as if it had done me an injury and then slowly put it back on its rest. It was nearly lunchtime and I'd done nothing useful all morning. I sat thinking for about ten minutes, then pulled a sheet of the firm's notepaper towards me and wrote, "Messrs. Griggs Agency, Private and Confidential. Dear Sirs, We should consider it a favour if you would give us information as to the business record, if any, and financial stability of Mr. Tracey Moreton, of Lowis Manor, Sladen, Kent. Yours faithfully, for and on behalf of Abercrombie & Co. O. Branwell."

I stuck it in an envelope and slid out of the office without being accosted. I caught a No. 23 bus and dropped off at the top of Bond Street and walked down. Barber & Curry is one of those shops which show a solitary discreet Old Master on an easel in the corner of their window with a tapestry curtain for a background.

The manager was at lunch, but another man in a white coat seemed to know everything, so I said I'd called about a picture I wanted restored. He said vaguely, oh, yes, what was my picture? I said, an early Foster, but first could he possibly give me some idea of the work they had carried out for Mr. Tracey Moreton, of Lowis Manor, who had recommended me, and the cost of the work to him.

The man in the white coat said: "What name was it? And what were the pictures?"

"T. Moreton," I said. "One picture was a Constable and another was a Lippi. Possibly a Watteau as well."

"I don't remember them personally, but I'll check that up."

He went away, and then came back to say that the only client he could trace was a Viscountess Morecambe. *What* was the year? Last year, I told him, knowing now all I could know but having to make a tactful exit.

So in five minutes he was back again, with a wooden face this time, as if he suspected there was a confidence trick in it somewhere but couldn't quite see where. They'd done no work for Mr. Moreton—nor had they handled a Lippi in recent years. If I would care to wait until the manager came back. . . . I said, no, I'd see Mr. Moreton before going further, and a minute later I found myself out on the pavement again.

chapter 11

I knew I had to get the Highbury thing off my chest before the weekend, and I knew now what I wanted to do, but I could no longer bring any interest to it. I felt sick to the depths of my stomach.

I went round to the Dorchester and asked to see him on urgent business. Fortunately his secretary was out, and a typist who was deputizing wasn't so tough to get by. Charles Highbury was up but still in his bedroom, in a magnificent black silk dressing gown with gold lapels.

When he saw me, he smiled faintly. "Oh, the insurance gentleman. Do come in. I'm afraid I was rude to you last Friday, but my nerves were all to pieces at the time. These agents and producers simply give one no moment's peace. Cigarette?"

I said: "I thought nothing of it. Glad to see you looking so much better." The black eye had completely mended.

"I'm far from well yet, but Dr. Aymar thinks another ten days will see me fit to go back to work. They're filthy little studios anyhow. One is choked with dust, and the cameramen have no idea."

We chatted for a bit. He was turning on the charm this evening. It flowed from him as easily as warm water from a tap. You could see he loved himself for being so nice.

But I couldn't meet him halfway. This time it was I who wasn't feeling so good.

I said: "Up to now, Mr. Highbury, we've simply made out short interim reports to the underwriters on the progress of this case, but it's time they got a fuller account. That's really what I came to see you about. I'd rather hoped I'd be able to give them a definite date for your return."

"Well, you can, old boy. A week on Monday. Aymar says it will be all right by then."

"But what do *you* say? It's very hard on Dorrington with what's-her-name off to the States and . . . I was wondering if you thought you could possibly manage this coming Monday?"

"Dorrington will get over it. He's had worse headaches. You don't realize what a complete collapse I had."

"That's just the point," I said. "I do."

He smoothed a crease in his dressing gown. "Just what is that remark in aid of?"

"Do I need to go into details?"

"By all means if you have something more to say." The charm supply was drying to a trickle.

I said: "When a famous film star is suddenly taken ill it's natural to make inquiries. That's all. And when his wife overstays her time in Edinburgh . . ."

"And what good will this—this vulgar prying into my private life do you?"

I said: "If there's been a fire in a warehouse, it's my job to say, if I can, how the fire started. If a man goes sick, and the sickness costs someone a lot of money, it's just as much my job to find out how things got that way."

He stood up slowly. He'd the shoulders of a prize fighter and the waist of a professional dancer.

"Run away, Mr. Snooper. You don't amuse me."

I got up too. "Isn't it true that you're known as the he-man of pictures?"

"So what?"

"If I have to make an interim report at this stage I shall be forced to say that Mr. Highbury is still suffering from the effects of a blow received from his wife on the second of May last, which knocked him out and has so far kept him in bed a week. These reports are confidential, of course, but they have to pass through the hands of quite a number of people, and it's not impossible that somebody should talk to the press——"

"Go to hell," he said.

"All right. I'll not be making out the report till tomorrow. Let me know if there's any change in your plans."

He had had his finger on the bell for some time. He looked white and rather savage.

"Miss Grey, show this gentleman out. And see that he isn't admitted again—under any circumstances."

76

I went out and down, and out of the hotel and walked slowly up Park Lane. I'd done what I could now. It was up to him to capitulate or to call my bluff. I was relieved that I'd done what I could because now I could forget it. I was relieved to the depths that now I could concentrate on the only important thing on my mind. It nagged at me like a raw toothache that wouldn't let me alone a minute of the day or night.

Henry Dane got up from his desk and went to the window and rubbed his forefinger along his furrowed cheek.

"Well, go on. I'm all attention now."

I said: "It seems to *me* to be an insurance fraud, but I've no real proof of it yet; and so far it's a very modest one. In any case, there are reasons at present why I don't want to come out into the open. I thought if anyone could advise me . . . Nobody's had more experience than you, as the solicitor with the sort of record——"

"All right. Skip the compliments."

I told him then what I knew and what I suspected. I changed one or two of the facts about and gave no names, so that he couldn't have any idea who I was really talking of.

He sat on the window sill and filled his pipe, ramming down the tobacco with the cap end of a .303 bullet that he always carried.

"Man in any sort of financial trouble?"

"It's hard to find out. Griggs Agency have nothing to report on him. He's always lived as a private gentleman. He was badly hit by death duties a few years ago."

"Wife in the fraud, d'you think?"

"Yes."

"Mother?"

"No, I'm almost certain not."

"Can you lay your hands on this first picture?"

"Yes. But I've asked about the artist, and I don't think it would be possible to prove that he didn't paint two pictures of the same scene. I'm told it was done sometimes."

"Then you may be mistaken about the fraud."

"No. . . . There are other things."

"You assessed the damage after the first fire?"

"Yes."

"And you think they're planning to do the same sort of thing again?"

"Sooner or later. I'm pretty certain of it."

"And that they've made a friend of you . . ."

"Yes, to make things easier for them when the time comes. I remember the man, only the second or third time we met, asking who chose the adjuster to be employed on a case. In fact often we've talked about insurance, and I've told him what I knew. The wife as well . . ."

"These other pictures . . ."

"That's what I was wondering about. This next week I could lay my hands on them, more or less at leisure. D'you know any way of telling an Old Master from a cheap copy—any, so to speak, general rules?"

He blew out a smoky breath. "Some fakes are so good they cheat the experts."

"But I don't think these would be all that good. They're hung in a hall well out of reach."

"Yet you could get to them?"

"I could get to them."

After a bit he said: "The man you should see is Lewison. He's got a little shop in the West End, not far from you. What he doesn't know about fake pictures nobody knows—unless it's that Dutchman. Lewison served two terms in prison before the war, but it's all forgiven and forgotten now. He was a great help to me in the Killarney case. But you'd better mention my name or you won't get a word out of him. And you'll have to *pay*. He doesn't talk for nothing."

"This man," I said. "Might he know something about fake antique furniture too?"

Dane smiled a slow sardonic smile. "He should do. He makes it."

There was no tactful arrangement of a solitary oil painting in the window of Mr. Lewison's place. A Reynolds-type small boy in a heavy frame leaned against a lacquer secretaire cabinet. Some odd pieces of Doulton were grouped anyhow on a cane-bottomed stool. Chippendale—or pseudo-Chippendale—chairs were being used to prop up a panel of a sort of evening party painted in the Spanish style. When you got inside you realized that all the best

78

stuff was in the window. It was the shop of a man who never said no to a reasonable proposition, whether it was a pianola or a jemmy. I wondered who insured him.

A tall chap with a big nose and a stoop came out from behind a Jacobean bookcase and sniffed suspiciously, as if he thought I'd brought in a bad smell.

"Mr. Lewison?"

He didn't answer for a minute but turned back for his glasses. When he'd got them fixed, he stared at me through the wrong part of the bifocals and said:

"This shop, as you can see over the door, belongs to Martha Goodman."

"Are you Mr. Lewison?"

"What is that to you?"

"Mr. Henry Dane, the solicitor, sent me. He thought you could help me, give me some advice. I'm an insurance investigator."

He tried the smell of that, and didn't altogether like it. "I am not an informer."

"I'm not asking you to be. It's some advice on two pictures that I want—how I might be able to detect whether they were genuine."

He stared at me and fiddled with his glasses.

"What are the pictures?"

"Two oil paintings. A Constable and a Lippi."

"Lippi never painted in oils. Where are the paintings?"

"I can't produce them. It's some general advice I want."

"General advice is useless. There is only one way of coming to detect whether a painting is a fake or genuine, and that is by studying a thousand pictures—in great detail. Then, in a few years perhaps, it is a *feeling* that one gets. Rule-of-thumb methods can only help sometimes—if the copy is a poor one."

"I should be prepared to pay for your opinion," I said.

He frowned and then slopped off behind the bookcase again. I thought I heard a door shut. A stuffed ferret kept a pretty sharp watch on me.

When I was beginning to think I'd have to make a noise to attract attention, the old man came back. With him was a woman about half his size, hurriedly wiping her arms on her apron.

"This is Martha Goodman," said Lewison, as if he'd produced something I was searching for. And then, evidently seeing I was a bit slow, he added: "There has to be someone to look after the shop. Now we can go inside."

By the time I got back to my flat it was well after six, and it was even chances that I might have left any further move until the Sunday. I might have let things slide and gone to a cinema—and in that case everything would have been different. But I knew well enough that in my present state of mind no film would be a strong enough dope.

So I had a snack meal and started about eight. There was no point in getting there before dusk; and although Tracey and Sarah would probably have left in the morning, the old servants might potter about for hours afterwards. I didn't know what the exact arrangements were, and it might be that a caretaker would be left in the house, in which case my journey would be wasted.

It was a windy evening, even in the West End, with a good lot of cloud and a few patches of coldish blue sky. I got my car off the fourth floor of the garage, and drove slowly down Park Lane and Grosvenor Place to Victoria, along Victoria Street and across Westminster Bridge to St. George's Road and the round-about at the Elephant and Castle. I didn't hurry.

My mind was full of stuff about age cracks and varnishes and the mesh of canvases and manufacturer's marks and whether the stretcher was glued or tacked and if the priming varied. My mind was full of that but I didn't think about that. I thought about Sarah. I thought about our last meeting. "There are reasons," she had said when I asked her why she came out with me.

I took the main road for Rochester, and at Dartford turned sharp south along the valley of the Darent, through Farningham and Sevenoaks. I hadn't been that way before. As the light began to fade I saw that there was a three-quarter moon rising among the clouds. You could feel the wind more out here; it was a half gale and all the warmth and summer had been blown away by it. I passed a good many orchards and the trees were shaking their blossom like nautch dancers.

About a couple of miles away from the house, I stopped for a smoke. In spite of the clouds it wasn't dark. I wasn't too happy about the gatehouse. Sarah had told me it was empty; normally they let it, but the man had died and the new people hadn't

80

come in yet. But that was some time ago. I didn't want to spend the night in jail.

I threw the cigarette end out of the car and started up. I was still able to drive on side lights, and I went past the gatehouse. It was in darkness. I parked a couple of hundred yards beyond, on a grass verge under some trees, and switched off the lights and slid out.

I didn't go back that way, but shinned over the wall into Tracey's property.

The back of the gatehouse also showed dark, so I walked up the drive, keeping well in to the holly trees. There was still a good deal of light over in the west, and every now and then the moon would flood out like an arc lamp, making sudden black shadows under the trees. When you looked up, the great clouds were racing so quickly that you got a sense of the world turning over.

Lowis Manor was unlit, as I'd expected; but there was one obvious thing to do as a precaution. I walked straight up to the front door and pulled the bell. If Elliott was still here, or some caretaker, it would be easy to fake a story.

It looked a big place in the half dark, silent and squat. I rang again. It was one of the old-type bells, not electric, and you could picture the bell wagging and tinkling in the very depths of the house, in the kitchen where nobody stirred now.

I stepped on a flower bed and tried to peer in at the window of the hall, but it was too dark inside. A circuit of the house first, just as a further precaution. There was all night if necessary.

I started off anticlockwise, meaning to take in the stables last. But I never even got as far as the kitchens. On the southeast side of the house, just past the big Irish yew tree, were the bow windows of the dining room. The gravel path ran close to the house here and almost level with the windows. Sarah had told me once that this was because the ground had risen through the centuries. I was just going to peer in when I saw that the last window was ajar.

If anything would have amused me in the mood I was in, that would have. Probably old Elliott had slipped up. Or perhaps Tracey himself had left it open, in the hope that there *would* be a burglary.

The latch was on the first hole. There was just room for me

to put my knife in and knock it up. Then I put a leg through onto the window seat and stepped into the room. It was as easy as that.

I brushed the window seat to take off any dirt, and then flicked my torch about for a second or two. The room was unfamiliar in dust sheets. The fine Chippendale table—which might also be only an imitation—had something lumpy on it. In the corner behind the screen was the door leading to the kitchen. Perhaps old Elliott hadn't gone but had fallen asleep in his chair. More likely that he was getting quietly sozzled in his favourite pub.

I went into the hall.

I didn't want to use my torch much at the front of the house; and, in any case, just when I opened the door, the moon was full out. It all looked most odd. The decorators were still very much in charge here, and had left two pairs of stepladders standing in the middle of the floor with a plank between. The furniture was draped in white and in unfamiliar places, and there was a great pile of dust sheets near the foot of the stairs.

The moon went behind a cloud, and the room suddenly frowned at me. The wind was buffeting against the house, and I thought for a minute I heard a footstep on the stairs. I peered up through the darkness but there was nothing there. A noise, though: *tap-tap . . . tap-tap-tap* somewhere upstairs. You couldn't expect a house of this age to be silent in a half gale.

"Tracey and I have a perfect understanding and trust," she had said. . . . Forget that. First the pictures. That was what I'd come for. Proof. Take them down, into some room with heavy curtains and a north window.

I'm a fairly quiet walker, and the old stairs only creaked once as I went up them. And then I saw that the pictures were not there.

I stared at the blank spaces, feeling thoroughly annoyed and frustrated, as if the things had been hidden away specially to thwart me. Then I realized that no one in their right senses left pictures up when the decorators were in.

As I came down the stairs again, I thought I could see a promising shape covered with a dust sheet beside the door leading to the old hall; and when I went across, I found it was in fact the two pictures I wanted.

I'd never seen them at close quarters before and they were bigger, heavier than I thought. The faces of the magi in the

Lippi were life-size. In the shaded light of the torch, they seemed to be half alive; you could fancy the contorted features ready to move, ready to break into a whisper. What had Lewison said? Wooden panel, coated with glue size. All sorts of details that I couldn't follow: gesso . . . yolk of egg and water . . . green earth . . .

I leaned the picture over on its face and fished out my penknife. I struck the blade into the back of the panel. It went in. I put the knife away and picked up the pictures, one in each hand.

The moon was still behind the clouds, but my eyes were getting more used to the dark, and it was reasonably possible to move about without bumping into things. I made for the living room, avoiding the ladder on the way, and was almost at the door when I stepped on something. It was like a thick piece of rubber and I kicked it but it didn't move far.

I put one picture down and took out my torch and switched it on. The thing I'd stepped on was a man's hand. I jerked the torch back and it caught the edge of the picture frame and slipped out of my hand. As it hit the floor, it went out.

Of course the hand was not unattached—the rest of the man was there, somewhere about two feet away from me, a thicker shadow than the others. I'd dropped my torch—that was the first thing: light. I leaned the pictures shakily against a table and trod across the hall towards the switch by the door, not caring now who knew I was here.

Get to the switch and fumble with it and flick it down. Nothing. The light had been turned off at the main board.

I stood there against the door. One of two things to do: go out through the door behind me, leaving it to somebody else to ask the questions; or stay and face it out.

The first shock was passing. I'd seen plenty of dead and injured men; it wasn't that.

Then the moon came out brilliantly, and with the light behind me I could see it all, the white peaks of the furniture, the piled dust sheets, the ladders, the two pictures leaning, and the lumpy shadow of the man just in front of the door of the living room. It was all motionless, waiting for me. I felt gutless and weak. I went back.

He was lying on his side with one arm flung out. His face was

83

in the shadow but I thought I knew the clothes. There were two or three bits of wood on the floor around him. I picked up the torch but the bulb had smashed. After a minute I pulled the man over. It was Tracey Moreton.

His eyes stared past me, over my shoulder, as if he was looking at someone there. Only he wasn't looking. He seemed thinner and smaller than usual. I couldn't tell how long he'd been dead.

I pawed over him for a minute and then stood up. I still felt shaky, and seeing who it was hadn't helped. I needed a drink. I needed a drink and I needed company.

Something made me look up; and then I saw that the moulded balustrade of the gallery just above was broken. That was where the wood had come from. And my foot was crunching on bits of wood that crumbled like old biscuits.

The wind gusted against the house again, and the thing upstairs went *tap-tap-tap*. There was a funny smell somewhere. My brain was still working in fits and starts, but it seemed to be a good idea to get a better view of the broken balustrade. As I passed the pile of linen at the bottom of the stairs, my foot caught in a tangle of it and I lifted it away. The thing wasn't a dust sheet—it was what appeared to be a good lace curtain.

The top of the stairs was darker, and just before I got to the broken balustrade the moon went in again. The break was almost opposite the door of Tracey's bedroom and two doors from the one I'd had. The door of Tracey's bedroom was open, and through it I could just make out the grey oblong of the windows. I tried to see what had caused the break. It wasn't merely the handrail; one of the big twisted supporting balusters had given way. Of course, this was where there had been woodworm.

Another curtain on the floor. Perhaps he'd tripped, fallen. But why the curtains—unless my first suspicion, before I went to the brokers and was reassured, was actually true. An embittered man intent to seize the opportunity he'd rarely have: his mother away, the servants gone, alone except for his wife. . . . Not this time the small claim, but the big one—setting him free from the incubus of a rambling expensive house, setting him on his feet again, enough capital to live comfortably. Perhaps Sarah was not in this major fraud, perhaps he'd sent her away too.

Somehow, by mischance, he had leaned against the balustrade

and it had given way. In the middle of his preparations, before he'd been able to destroy it, the house had destroyed him.

I turned to go down again. And then a terrible thing happened. There'd been a lull in the wind for two or three minutes, and as I straightened up I heard Tracey breathing close beside me.

chapter 12

*T*he moon brightened and quickened, and then died again. In the room behind me, a French clock began to strike the hour. Nothing touched me. Nothing stirred. The wind was roaring away among the distant trees.

I couldn't move. Then I gripped the broken balustrade and slowly forced my head round, stared into the darkness.

"Tracey!"

No one answered. The house was empty except for myself and a dead man on the floor below.

I swallowed a dry lump and walked into the bedroom. There were blankets on the floor and the curtains were crooked at the window. The smell of Tracey's herbal cigarettes was strong. Perhaps that had suggested the other. I cursed my nerves, found I was still clutching a piece of wood off the balustrade, didn't throw it away. The feel of it gave me a silly sort of comfort.

And then I heard it again—or thought I heard it again—out in the passage behind me.

I wheeled and ran out.

"Tracey!"

The clouds were heavy and I couldn't see if the body was still there. The sound had seemed to come from further along, at the corner where the passage branched towards the back of the house. Bump against a chair, push it away, on to the corner.

The corridor was narrow, but there were two good windows in it. I blundered along it to the next turn; another corner and two steps up. When I got there I couldn't hear anything.

After a bit, I held my breath, and a second or so later imagined I heard the creak of a floor board beyond the steps.

"Who's there!" I said. "Is it you, Tracey?"

Tracey was dead; I'd seen him; are you mad shouting like that? But his breathing, unmistakable. I went on. This part of the house, the shabby part, I knew less well. Not far away now was the *tap-tap-tap . . . tap-tap.*

Stop and take a grip. I'd come out on another landing beside the servants' staircase. That queer smell again. Five doors here, and the moon squinted through an open fanlight. There was dust in the moonbeams. A deflated-looking vacuum cleaner stood beside a cane chair.

The wind leaned against the house, and the old wood creaked. After the wind had gone, the *rat-a-tat* sounded behind the nearest door. I went in.

A box room of some sort. Between me and the window was a forest of lumber, and in the middle of it all sat two men. I pushed my way in, treading on fishing tackle and knocking over skis. I hit at the nearest man and he fell off the table and broke. Busts that had been relegated here by someone with modern tastes. The window was banging. Struggle through to it, but the catch had rusted off. Outside the trees were waving wildly. Looking back from here, I thought the landing seemed dark. I had a sudden desire not to go back there.

I got out somehow, tried the next door. Locked. The third was a bedroom, smelt occupied, fusty. The fourth had trunks and suitcases on the bed. The fifth—with a window facing the moon— was a sort of sitting room, with a radio by the door and an electric fire flanked by a couple of down-at-heel easy chairs. There was nobody in it; but on a side table was a small glass-bowled paraffin lamp.

I went in and fumbled with a box of matches. The things were like straws; three broke before I could hold one to the wick. Then a slow warm yellow light squeezed out the moon.

Comforting. It would show me all I wanted to see. I went back into the passage and stared and listened. There was nothing now —no breathing, no cigarette smell; even the window had temporarily stopped. Only that other smell. I looked at the moon-beams in which the dust was still floating. It was too thick for dust. It was smoke.

I ran down the servants' staircase to the ground floor, came out in a passage with doors, pushing through one, found myself in the butler's pantry. Wrong. Back into the passage and try the end door. A maid's sitting room or something. Beyond that was a room with a Welsh dresser, an open fireplace, bulbs spread on trays. More smoke here; I took the door where most of it was coming from—and found myself again in the butler's pantry.

I coughed and waved away the smoke. Desperately urgent not to be lost in this house any more. I got back into the passage where the stairs were, took the third door. A place for hats and coats; a telephone on a table. Backing out, I nearly knocked the glass of the lamp off. I turned back into the butler's pantry. There were two ways out of it, and I'd only tried—no, the other way led into the room with the bulbs.

Stop and think. Must go back there. Smoke was thicker now, and as soon as I got into the next room, I saw where I had gone wrong. A green baize door. I pushed through it and into the central kitchen.

Smoke in a wave—and heat for the first time. But no fire. A pile of old net curtains on the table, and a smell of paraffin. Coughing, I pushed through the door into the stillroom. Less smoke here. Try the larder. No. Another door led to yet another passage and a lower sort of door that fairly obviously opened on cellar steps. Before I reached it I knew. You could hear the noise, a murmuring sort of noise.

The door jammed, but when it came open the heat struck in my face. No need for the lamp. I shoved it on a ledge and went down three or four steps. I'd seen the results of a good many fires these last two years but I'd never seen one at this stage before.

They were big cellars, and this one was supported by two groups of wooden pillars fairly close together and probably under the main stairs. It looked as if two great fires had been built, one within each group of four pillars; but one only was ablaze so far. You could guess what materials had been used to create this furnace of white flames by seeing the other not yet alight: a candle guttering to its last inch amid a mass of shavings and a big precarious pile of plywood boxes and flimsy furnishings, reaching to the floor boards above.

At the bottom of the steps you weren't choked so much with

smoke, it was the light and the heat that were intolerable. I put a handkerchief over my eyes and reached forward into the middle of the second fire and snuffed the candle out. That wouldn't help much because the whole pile would catch alight any moment from the other. I grabbed an iron rod to smash it out of harm's way, but something slipped at that moment in the first fire and a great mass of loose flames scattered over the cellar. This was no one-man job, if it could be got under at all.

I dodged a piece of blazing rag that was floating down and retreated up the steps. At the top I wiped the tears, took up the lamp, ran back, trying to remember. Passage, kitchen, room with bulbs, butler's pantry, coat cupboard. No mistake this time. Lift the receiver and dial.

It seemed to take a long time; as I waited I saw a cylinder partly hidden by coats. Fire extinguisher.

"I'm speaking from Lowis Manor," I said, "near Sladen. A very bad fire's broken out. In half an hour it'll be too late to save the house. You'll need more than one engine. Tell them to hurry."

"Lowis Manor, near Sladen," said the voice patiently. "Yes. What is the name, please?"

"Mr. Tracey Moreton," I said. "Hurry."

I slammed down the receiver and unhooked the extinguisher from the wall. Prewar and a bit rusty, but it might work. In the butler's pantry was a sink and I turned the water on, pulled open half a dozen drawers, grabbed a towel, soaked it. Then I wound it into a sort of turban-cum-yashmak. The thing wouldn't stick in place until I found a pin in an apron behind the door. In the silver drawer were an old pair of gloves Elliott probably used; I put them on. I was about to go when I saw a spectacle case in a corner of the shelves; I opened this, put on the spectacles. The room blurred at me but they would protect my eyes.

The extinguisher under my arm, I ran back to the cellar.

The second fire hadn't caught, and the first didn't look any worse, but perhaps that was my distorted sight. The protection now was enormous; I could get close to the blaze. I dropped the extinguisher on its end and the thing worked. I directed the jet at the flames. Wood that had been incandescent became suddenly black and charred. One pillar was put out completely; then I turned the jet upward.

Here the effect wasn't good. Fighting a losing battle but I

couldn't see why. Spectacles off; at once I saw that the extinguisher wasn't killing all the flames because most of them were already out of its reach. And the second pile *had* caught—at the top.

I think it was then that I pretty well gave the house up for lost. The way the fire had been started under the well of the stairs, the wind that was blowing, the great amount of timber. . . . As the extinguisher gave out, a piece of blazing wood fell across it and nearly knocked it out of my hand. I let it drop. Sparks caught on my sleeve; my coat came suddenly alight. I backed away, rubbed the flames out against a wall. There was nothing more to do. By now, if I wasn't mistaken, the fire would already have reached the main stairs.

Then I thought of Tracey still lying in the hall, lying there in spite of my imaginings. I wondered if it would be his wish to go with the house, making it a funeral pyre. Whether he would or not, I couldn't let him.

Crawl up the steps and sit for a minute in the passage, feeling pretty nearly all in. Pull off the towel, the gloves. My coat had lost part of its sleeve; one trouser leg was burned. Not so much smoke was coming out of here now. It meant that the fire had made a new exit.

I got up, spat, tried to set my bearings right. Back through the kitchen.

The house was blazing now. In the kitchen you could hear the roar of it, just as if someone had turned up the draught on the kitchen range. This wasn't the room I'd come out into when examining the first fire damage. But if I made straight through . . .

I soon found the other kitchen. A grandfather's clock was ticking away in it, measuring out the last minutes. This was where the rocking chair was and the bells on the wall. And one of those black wool rugs . . .

I opened the further door, and the heat leapt at me like a wolf. My estimate had been underweight. The hall and the stairs were blazing. There was no way through.

I backed out and shut it. There might be other ways from the kitchen quarters to the front of the house, but if so I didn't know of them. The only other way was to get out of the house, go round.

It was silly fumbling with the catch of the windows, but

respectable habits still clung. I pushed the thing open and slid through. It was pitch dark where I got out, and I nearly fell down some area steps. I drew away from the house, skirting the greenhouses where I'd met Sarah that first day, rounded a potting shed, the wind putting out cool fingers. Clouds were heavier than ever, the house nearly as black. The window I'd left glimmered, where the paraffin lamp still burned, and, as I looked, there was a sort of flicker at another window further along, a pretty golden flicker like the winking of an eye. That was all.

I began the circuit of the house.

At the dining room where I'd broken in, I stopped and looked. You couldn't of course see the front of the house from here, but you could see part of the front lawns and the trees at the end. They weren't quite dark any longer, and it wasn't the moon that was lighting them.

I put my leg over the sill to climb in again, but there I stopped, listening. An unmistakable bell. It was half a mile away yet.

I had to make up my mind quickly. Meet the brigade and tell them lies. Meet the brigade and tell them the truth. Or go. Nothing more I could do. The firemen would get Tracey's body out. Better to go. No questions asked. None to answer. Sarah could do that. I had to see what Sarah would do.

I brought my leg out, and as the fire engine came in under the gatehouse and stopped—they had to take off their ladders to get through—I slid silently back through the herb garden towards the muddy lane and the car.

It wasn't quite as easy as that. The clamour of the bell had already caught people's attention; as I was going to drop into the lane, I saw two figures coming from the direction of Lowis Farm. They stopped quite close to me, peering over the hedge; then, when they saw the fire engine come slowly in, they scrambled over the wall, pushed their way towards the house. One passed me within a yard; I thought he must see me. That sort of thing makes you feel more like a felon than anything else.

I slid down, getting muck on my trousers, made for the car. As soon as I was in the road, the moon came full out; you could see two or three other people hurrying towards the fire. One looked like a policeman on a bicycle. I kept in the shadow as much as I could, until I came to the car. Just as I was getting in I saw some-one coming along the road towards me.

I shut the door quickly and shoved in the ignition key. As he came up I switched on the side lights.

He stopped, stared in at the car.

"Somethin' wrong, Mister?" he shouted.

He was a tall red-faced chap with a bright-red neckcloth, and he was wearing a sack round his shoulders. I pretended not to hear, shouted something back at him. I started the engine.

"What's amiss up at the manor?" he asked. "What's all the com-motion?"

"Fire engine," I shouted. "Just turned in there. Don't know what's wrong."

I put in the gear and swung the car off the grass verge. He stepped back in a hurry, as if he thought I might run him over.

I didn't know where this road led southwards, but I couldn't turn and repass the gatehouse. The sooner I got clear of this scene and changed my clothes the better.

After about half a mile I slowed down and turned my head, but the trees blocked the view. I don't know if it was imagination that the clouds just there seemed to be tinged with yellow.

chapter 13

I didn't sleep that night or try to. As soon as I got back I stripped off my clothes and climbed into a bath and lay there trying to relax, trying to get calm. I had a burn about eight inches long on my right forearm, but apart from that there was nothing to show. My eyelashes would soon grow again.

I lay there till the water began to grow cold and then towelled myself down, put on clean linen and a dressing gown. The burnt suit I wrapped in a brown paper parcel and put on top of the cupboard in my bedroom. The night air was chilly, and I lit the fire and chain-smoked till dawn. I smoked a packet of twenty and five over.

The call was later coming than I expected. I'd made myself some tea and was trying to drink it when the phone bell began to trill.

I waited a good half minute before I took the thing up.

"Oliver Branwell speaking."

"This is Michael, Oliver. Rather an early call for you, I'm afraid."

So they'd got through to him first. "I don't think I'm going to be very helpful, but what's on the books today?"

"Rather a nasty shock for you, I think. It's Lowis Manor. The Moretons' place."

"What's wrong?"

"Practically burnt to the ground. At least that's what the police say, but they're always pessimistic. And there's another thing——"

"It's a good job the Moretons were away," I said. "Were the servants all right?"

"Oh, you knew that. . . . Well, I'm sorry to say it wasn't quite like that. Apparently the servants *were* away—but Moreton hadn't left. He'd been delayed over something, and it was he who gave the alarm. The brigade was there pretty quickly but . . . Moreton himself . . ."

"Good God," I said.

"Yes. . . . They found his body."

"Good *God*," I said again. It really wasn't hard to say the thing I'd been saying to myself all through the night.

"I'm sorry because I know they're particular friends of yours. I think it's a good reason to go down pretty soon. I should——"

I stared at the receiver. "And Mrs. Moreton?"

"I believe she was in Yorkshire or somewhere. Anyway there was no one else in the house. It's probably better to go this morning."

"I *can't*," I said, "I ricked my ankle last night. I haven't slept all night."

There was a pause. "Oh, hell," he said. "Bad luck. I suppose that means I must go. Hell. And I had a date for a foursome. I suppose I'd better go straight down. How do you get there?"

I told him.

"Is this thing likely to lay you up for a long time?"

"I'm not sure yet. The doctor said he'd know this morning."

Michael grunted into the phone. "I hope it won't put you out for the dinner on Friday."

I said: "Will you ring me when you get back from Lowis? I'll be very anxious to have the news."

"All right, Oliver. I'll do that. Bye."

He rang off, and I put down the receiver.

Well, it was a good act in one way, and a pretty cheap act in another. But what else could I do? The choice had been made last night.

What I hadn't counted on was Michael calling in to see me on the way home. It was after one, and I was still smoking, when the bell rang. I dragged a chair across for my foot, slid off the slipper, and covered my foot with a towel.

"Come in! The door isn't locked."

Michael came in, stooping from instinct, looked at me rather resentfully.

"Oh, you are up. How does it feel?"

"Could be worse. Well?"

He took off his motoring gloves. "Not too good, old boy. The place is a ruin. They saved the oldest part, that stone-built hall with the barrel roof. Otherwise it's gone. It was the worst possible night, of course."

"And Moreton?"

He sat down and shrugged. "Apparently he was caught in the house and fell trying to get out. His wife went up to Yorkshire in the morning and he said he'd follow later in the day. The police had just got her address from a servant when she phoned the police station to ask if they knew where her husband was."

"What time would that be?"

"What? I don't know. Early hours of the morning, I imagine. Why?"

"You saw her?"

"Yes." He vee'd his eyebrows at me. "She was at the local pub at Sladen with her brother-in-law. She was pretty upset, of course. She asked where you were. The brother's Victor Moreton, the K.C. Didn't know that. He'd just been in and identified the body."

I said: "Was Mrs. Moreton there? Tracey's mother, I mean."

"I think she was just arriving as I left. There was another tallish chap there who seemed to be a friend of the family. Fresh complexion—rather bossy type."

"Fisher," I said, and a sharp stab of jealousy went through me. It was that, whether I liked it or not.

"There's no way of telling how the fire started," Michael said, swinging his gloves by the fingers. "I imagine it must have begun in the cellar from the way the whole centre of the place collapsed. Of course I couldn't get near enough—the firemen were still working and there was a dangerous wall; but in a day or two . . . One instinctively thinks of short circuits in a timbered place, but young Mrs. Moreton said they'd had decorators in and seemed to think some of the men had been down in the cellars on Friday evening. I expect some damn fool chucked away a cigarette end."

"Thanks very much for calling in."

"It was almost on my way. I won't stop; I'd better push off." He slowly got up and looked round. "Are you all right? What are you going to do for food?"

"I shall manage all right, thanks."

"Have you hurt your arm as well?"

"Yes, I caught it as I fell."

"I'd take you down to my place but you know what it's like with Evelyn as she is, and one false alarm already."

"I wouldn't think of it. I'll ring you tomorrow."

"O.K. And let me know as soon as you can about Friday. Oh, one bit of good news. Charles Highbury has reported he'll be fit to go back to the studios tomorrow."

"Good," I said, trying to sound interested.

"I understand he's made some sort of a complaint to Dorrington about something you said or did."

"Nothing I *did*."

"Anyway, it won't affect us, because Dorrington's delighted. It was a good shot on my part, you know, when I got you into the insurance world. I often think so."

That stung. "Do you know if Moreton was badly burnt?"

"Um?" He stared at me, his thoughts gone from it. "Oh, I don't really know. I don't know at all. He wasn't burnt to death anyway. If I'd the choice I'd certainly prefer to jump myself."

That night I dreamed I was standing by the broken balustrade of the gallery and Tracey was breathing over my shoulder. I said to him: "Why did you light the fires and then not leave the house at once? How did you come to fall from your own gallery?" And he said: "I didn't light the fires. I didn't fall. It was Sarah." And I looked down and there was Sarah lying twisted on the floor with her black hair like a stain. I ran round to the head of the stairs, but the stairs had collapsed in flames. Tracey put his hand on my arm and pointed down again, and the whole of the hall was wreathed in smoke. Through it I could just see the picture of the magi, and Sarah's dark head. She seemed to have become a part of the picture, a graven image, age-old and ageless. Then Tracey's hand on my arm began to hurt, and I looked and saw it had turned into a flame.

I woke up in a sweat, and the pain from the burn was throbbing. I switched on the light and lay staring up at it, trying to think.

Whatever happened about the insurance, I should go to the police about Tracey's death. I knew now what I'd thought was his breathing was a natural freak of the high wind, that there had been no one alive in the house except me. But that did not in any way relieve me of the responsibility of letting them know that he had died long before the fire reached him.

All Monday I stayed in. The newspapers made as much of it as their space would let them. Some ran pictures of Lowis Manor and two included inset photographs of Tracey and Sarah. The inquest was Tuesday; but I phoned Michael in the morning saying my ankle wasn't good enough. I kept hoping for a phone call, some word from her. But it didn't come.

I'd never been to an inquest since the one on my father, and I'd always sworn I'd never see another; but as the time for this one came near I got more and more restless.

An hour before I knew he was due to start, I phoned Michael and said: "I've just seen the doctor and he thinks I'll come to no harm. If you called for me I could come along and drop in at the inquest while you were actually going over the ground."

"Good," he said. "I'll be round about a quarter to eleven."

I went out and bought myself a stick, and when he came I was ready with a tied-up ankle and a slipper.

He dropped me off at the village schoolroom about ten minutes before the inquest was due to open. There were a few sightseers and a fair number waiting patiently on the back benches; but I squeezed in among them on the very back bench. It was all too light and too small to offer any cover; but at least I was out of the direct line of fire.

After a bit, one or two of the officials drifted in and a policeman or two, and then Victor Moreton. He was wearing the black coat and striped trousers of his profession, and you could see he was perfectly at home in these surroundings. I wasn't sure whether he saw me, but if so he made no sign. Then after a minute he went out again and came back with his mother. She looked pretty well all in. She walked as if she'd suddenly become ten years older. Then Clive Fisher came in with his sister, and following them was Sarah with a limping elderly thin-faced chap.

She was in grey, with a black hat and black gloves. It didn't suit her the way colours did; but that didn't seem to matter. There's a point in attraction when you're so deep in that appearance no longer counts for much. It wasn't until they had sat down that I realized the man with her was probably her father.

Then the coroner came in and things began. There was no jury, as there had been when my father died.

I was glad now I'd come, even though it was suddenly all reminiscent. It had all been so shabby that other time, and me a clumsy kid of seventeen, and the mean hungry inquisitive faces peering, and the coroner with some sort of a distorted eye behind a coloured lens; and outside the rumble of traffic. I'd been bitter that day, up against it, ready to fight the world. The coroner had asked me something and I'd said: "D'you begrudge him even the gas? It was his own shilling, wasn't it?"

Different today. A different bitterness. Yet somehow it was the same sort of personal letdown. The two people I'd most loved and trusted . . .

Victor Moreton was giving evidence of identification. He got a great deal of deference. The coroner was a fat man who blew through his fists, and kept clasping them as if he was going to pray. After Victor, a fireman described the call coming through and said they were only twelve minutes from receiving the call to reaching the manor; but by that time all the centre of the house was ablaze. He told how they broke in the window of the

96

hall and put in hose pipes and how they saw the body of Mr. Moreton lying among the flames. It was lying just below the gallery in the hall, and this also was in flames. They were only just able to drag him out before part of the roof collapsed.

A police sergeant went into the stand and said much the same thing in different words, and then the pathologist from the local hospital was called. He said he'd examined the body at 1 A.M. on Sunday morning, and he estimated that the deceased had then been dead three or four hours. There were very extensive burns, but these had occurred after death. Cause of death was a ragged split in the scalp two to three inches long. The bone underneath showed a stellate fracture extending round to the base of the skull, and the brain was bruised underneath the fracture and bruised and lacerated at a point opposite. In answer to the coroner, he said it was the sort of injury which would be sustained by falling backwards upon the head.

The coroner clasped his hands for a minute and said: "This bruising, these lacerations on the opposite side of the brain—are they what you'd expect?"

"Yes. They're characteristic. It's known medically as the *contra coup*."

"And could these injuries be attributable to any other cause?"

"It's never possible to be absolutely certain. But to me they very strongly suggest a fall—especially as one elbow is badly bruised and there is also a bruise on the hip."

The coroner said: "Is it the sort of thing you'd expect to find in a man who has jumped down some ten feet, say, from a gallery?"

"It's a reasonable supposition. Some people, of course, can jump thirty feet and get off with a sprained ankle. Others slip on a frozen pavement and die without falling any distance at all. If, as I understand, the floor of the hall where he was found was a polished one with rugs, it is reasonable to suppose that he may have jumped, landed on his heels on a mat, and the mat slipped from under him."

The coroner blew on his knuckles and thought it out. "Is there anyone else who wishes to question the witness?"

There was a minute's fidgeting. Victor Moreton got up.

"I think you said, Doctor, that the burns all took place after death."

"That is so. There would have been an inflammatory reaction if he had been alive at the time."

"D'you think it likely that he may have fallen, not jumped, from the gallery, having been overcome by smoke?"

"No. There was only about one per cent of carbon monoxide in his blood. If he had been overcome by smoke, there would have been a great deal more than that."

"But the heat alone, I suppose, might have overcome him. Rising through the centre of the house, and my brother not being in normal health."

"Yes, he might have fainted. It's not impossible."

The pathologist went, and then I saw Sarah get up and go into the witness box. I had the usual queer reaction, as if I'd got thrombosis or something.

You could see when she stood there how taut she was; but there was no give-way about it. The coroner was very sympathetic and said a little prayer between each question. This part, they thought, was really only a matter of form.

She said in a low but perfectly clear voice: "My husband had been an asthmatic since the war and was very susceptible to dust. The repairs that were being done made a lot of dust and we decided to go away for a week while they were finished. As our two servants hadn't had a holiday for some time, we thought we should release them too. Mrs. Hanbury, from the village, was going to come in each day while the workmen were there. I left for Yorkshire on Saturday morning, and my husband said he would follow by car later in the day. When he didn't come I began to get worried and tried to telephone him. There was no reply, so after waiting some time I phoned the police station, and they told me . . ."

The coroner said: "Did your husband have an attack of asthma on the Saturday before you left?"

"He doesn't—didn't—often have *attacks* of asthma, because he had things he could take to ward them off. But he was always more or less asthmatic in a chronic way, had difficulty with his breathing; and this had been getting worse for two or three days before Saturday."

"What was the purpose of your going on before him on the Saturday? I mean, why did you not travel up together?"

She hesitated for the first time. "He thought—he's been having injections from a specialist in Harley Street—and he thought if he could get an extra one that afternoon it might put him right for the week's holiday."

"Can you think of any reason why in fact he didn't go up to London but stayed on in the house?"

"I'm afraid I can't—unless he was ill. . . . We were expecting him in Scarborough about nine."

"I see. Thank you very much. I think that will be all, Mrs. Moreton."

As she came down from the stand, I knew her answer about the specialist had been a lie. I knew it as if she'd shouted it. I thought I hardly heard the next witness, the foreman of the firm of builders, but afterwards I could remember his saying that part of the balustrade had been removed on the previous Thursday. It had been intended to renew the whole of that side. There was some sort of an argument between him and the coroner on the possibility that the fire had been started by a careless workman. Then Elliott, the butler, was called but he didn't have much to contribute. He had left the house at three-thirty and had understood Mr. Moreton was leaving shortly afterwards. He had carried Mr. Moreton's bag out to the car, which was ready in the yard.

Anyway I didn't want to hear any more.

chapter 14

It was raining when we drove back.

Michael said: "What was the verdict?"

"Oh, what you'd expect; death from misadventure."

"Anything special emerge?"

"No. Part of the balustrade of the gallery was taken down on the Thursday. Nobody seems to know if he fell or jumped."

"Did you see any of the Moretons afterwards?"

"Not to speak to."

We drove on for a bit.

Michael said: "The loss isn't quite so total as I thought. The old hall is intact because, except for the roof, it was entirely of stone; the stables were too far away and in the wrong direction, and part of the kitchens were saved by the wind. You could make a small house of the kitchens if they were restored."

"And the gatehouse?"

"Oh, that's all right, of course."

"Was it occupied?"

"No, unfortunately they were just changing tenants. The new people were due in last week, but young Mrs. Moreton put them off until they came back from their holiday."

Did she. "What about the contents of the house?"

"Everything of value is gone. A few sticks of furniture, nothing more. These timbered places, if they once catch on fire, go up like a bunch of sticks. I think in your report you should say——"

"Look, Michael," I said. "I'd like this to be your report. D'you mind?"

Michael looked at me.

I said: "You've done the work so far. And in a way it's better that you should go on with it. I've been friendly with them and I wouldn't want anyone to think the report was unduly favourable to them."

"Damn it, they're not claiming for a new hearthrug on the strength of a cigarette burn. The damage isn't exactly unapparent. But I should have said *our* report, meaning of course the firm's report. It doesn't matter two pins who draws it up. What I was going to say was . . ."

He went into some matter of insurance policy that I didn't listen to. Now was the time to say, "Look, Michael, I've something to say to you." By shamming ill, I'd got away from the responsibility of a snap decision. But there was no excuse for any more delay.

But Sarah might still make some move. . . . Even though she'd lied today. Even though she had lied to me.

Michael broke off. "I don't believe you've been listening, have you?"

"No. Sorry."

"Well, it's not important."

100

"Yes, go on."

But he wouldn't. As we halted at the first traffic block, I said: "Michael . . ."

"Yes?"

And there I stopped. Because at the last minute I knew it was no good. On Saturday night I'd postponed a decision without realizing that the postponement *was* in fact the decision and there could be no going back on it.

"What were you going to say?"

I said: "I wonder what they'll do now."

"Who? The Mrs. Moretons? Pay through the nose for a villa in Tunbridge Wells, I suppose. It's not much fun being deprived of your home these days. Anyway, I imagine they'd be a good deal better off for the change, if it was only the house they had lost."

"I suppose it all goes to his wife," I said.

Michael frowned at a motorcar which was misbehaving itself in front. "No, in this case the house was entailed—by the father. In his will he left it to Tracey in trust for his children; failing issue, to his younger son, Victor. The insurance will go to the trustees, who will invest it and pay the interest to Victor."

"You mean Tracey couldn't have sold the house if he'd wanted to?"

"No, he couldn't have sold it. Of course the insurance on the contents will be the wife's absolutely, in this case much the larger part of the settlement."

"Yes," I agreed quietly. "Much the larger part . . . Who would pay the premium on the insurance of the building?"

"Oh, the occupier has to. That's his doubtful privilege."

We drove on without speaking. That seemed to explain most things. After a long time, Michael said:

"Anyway, I shouldn't think young Mrs. Moreton will stay a widow for long."

"What makes you say that?"

He looked a bit surprised at my tone. "That's unless she chooses to, I mean. I don't know if Moreton was a wealthy man, but he must have been comfortably off. What with her looks and a tidy fortune . . ."

"Yes, I expect you're right," I agreed, turning the knife.

That evening I wrote a letter to Tracey's mother. I wrote to her because I could do it honestly: everything I said to her I meant. A couple of days later the reply came thanking me; not a printed card but a letter. For a minute when I saw the postmark, I thought it might have been from Sarah. Now I was beginning to give it up.

The dinner Michael had mentioned was the annual one of the association. It was the first I'd been to, and, feeling as I did feel, I'd have been glad to slide out of it. The thing was held at a Park Lane hotel, and the Abercrombies had taken a table for twelve, our guests being two brokers and an underwriter and their wives and the general manager of an insurance company. The idea was that each firm of adjusters made up a table and invited their best clients as guests. At the head of the room a long table had been arranged where the big pots sat, such as the Chairman of Lloyd's, the Chairman of the British Insurance Association, and the Chief of the London Salvage Corps.

Charles Robinson, the young good-looking underwriter whom I'd consulted on the Highbury case, was at our table, and Fred McDonald was one of the brokers. I could have done without McDonald for a few weeks.

The President of the Adjusters made a speech about Insurance being founded on Trust; without trust the whole edifice would crumble like a pack of cards. Our motto, he said, was Truth and Equity. We were the youngest and smallest professional body in the United Kingdom, but this nucleus of two hundred members must be looked on as a *corps élite* from whom would spring the spirit and leadership of the future. For this reason every member, he knew, was keen to set a standard of professional integrity which would be recognized as a hallmark of the association.

I looked at Mr. Abercrombie while this was going on and saw how much he was "hear, hearing" in his throat. It didn't need a lot of imagination to see how closely this sort of thing touched him, how it must have irked him in the between-war years to find upstart and opportunist firms claiming the same privileges as himself and sometimes leaving bad reputations behind them. You could see how he would welcome a move to rename the profession and ring it round with safeguards. (Only the safeguards weren't enough. If he but knew it a snake had got in under the fences of his own firm.)

Fred McDonald had been at the other end of the table from me and we hadn't exchanged more than a word; but afterwards he came across and said:

"Been doing any more crystal-gazing lately?"

"Why?" I said. "D'you want six away winners?"

Charles Robinson was beside me, and McDonald turned to him quietly: "The dear boy came into my office a week ago and asked me how much Lowis Manor, in Kent, was insured for. A couple of days later it's burned to the ground. Can you wonder at my question?"

"That's not crystal-gazing," said Charles. "It sounds more like fire-raising."

"Yes," I said. "You only need to put a match to one of those places and up they go. Anyway, you wouldn't begrudge me turning a dishonest penny, would you?"

"I wouldn't begrudge it if you told me how you did it," said McDonald.

"There you are," Charles said to me; "it *is* those six away winners he's interested in."

On Charles's part, of course, it was all light and good-humoured and didn't mean a thing. But there'd been a taint of spite in McDonald's voice.

Dancing followed; but I made the excuse of my ankle and left early. I slept heavily, and when I woke there was an envelope on the mat. I knew that this was it.

Dear Oliver [it ran],

Tracey's mother has shown me the letter you wrote her. It is kind of you to think of her at this time. I saw you at the inquest but wonder you did not come to speak to us afterwards. Victor is being wonderful about it all, but your help and company would not be unwelcome when you have time or inclination to give it.

I hope your ankle is better.

Sarah.

It was a queer letter and a bitter disappointment. It was not the letter of a completely innocent woman. In any case she could not be that. It *could* be the letter of a completely guilty one, inviting me down so that I could still be of some use to her in helping her to get by.

Well, I wasn't going. I didn't reply. I didn't go down to the funeral.

Days passed. There were of course the two claims to be settled on this fire, under separate policies, one for the house and one for its contents. Victor Moreton, who was handling the thing, engaged a separate assessor to represent them. The days became weeks. The claim on the building was settled. I went about my ordinary work and insisted that Michael should deal with it himself. Then eventually the figure for the contents was agreed and settled. That was the last point at which she could have drawn back. Even up to that last minute I'd been hoping.

Towards the end of the summer, Michael began to complain.

"Listen, man," he said; "there are three of us in this firm. One may be pretty elderly and the other trying to specialize, but you haven't any need to take on all the work there is or sweat at it twenty-four hours a day. The Branwell assault tactics can be overdone. Ease up. Take a day off. You've got to last next year as well."

"I'm all right," I said.

"But you're not all right. Look at yourself in the mirror. You look as if you work in artificial light all day and spend the weekends at the coal face."

"Did I leave some behind my ears last week? I take care to wash well on Monday mornings."

"Let me tell you something," he said. "You're still comparatively new to this work. Don't let it get you down. It pays us all to be conscientious, but there is a limit. You go at a thing that's going to bring us in ten guineas as if your life depended on it. Discriminate. . . . Why won't you take your holidays?"

"I'll have a week in October. Any time will do."

"Well, come down with us next weekend. We'd love to have you."

"Thanks," I said, "but . . . Oh, all right. If you're sure Evelyn can manage."

He stared at me broodingly. "There's nothing wrong, I suppose, outside your work? Often you've looked really ill. People have asked. But you're such a close devil."

"I'm not close. And there's nothing wrong."

"Well, you know what I mean. If there was anything—if I could help in any way . . ." I didn't answer, and he ended:

104

"You should take up golf or something. It would get you out into the country for a bit."

So I went down. I found they were without help, and Evelyn was busy with her young baby, so I felt more of a misfit than ever; but I stayed Saturday night and we played bridge, the fourth being John Graves, who had been in our battalion and who lived near. We talked a bit about old times, and having something in common with them helped me. I felt rather better than I'd done for some time, until John spoiled it by saying:

"By the way, I believe you know Sarah Moreton, don't you, Oliver? I met her last week at a party, and your name came up. What an attractive creature she is."

"Oh," I said. "Yes. She's all right."

"Oliver's magnificent capacity for understatement," said Michael. "We've rather lost touch with them since June. You know her husband died in a fire?"

"Someone told me," John said. "It was tough luck. I think she's living in London now, isn't she?"

"I haven't heard," I said.

"She was with a man called Fisher, who does murals and things. How long is it since her husband died? June?"

"May. Why?"

"Oh, somebody told me she was engaged to this Fisher bloke. I don't know if it's true. She was asking about you."

"I was Tracey's friend," I said.

"Yes, that's what Fisher implied. It's queer how it came out that we knew you. I mentioned Michael as being one of my best friends, and the name Abercrombie did the rest."

After that no more was said, but of course it didn't end it for me. You go on for months laboriously covering over the raw spot, one thin skin on another, until you think the thing is partly healed; but at the very first touch it comes away leaving the place as raw and angry as ever. I didn't know what to do about it, and there seemed no cure.

Perhaps Michael felt the weekend had been a failure, because he made no objection when I said I ought to get back on the Sunday afternoon. I left about three, glad enough to be on my own again yet grateful for their effort to give me a change and rest. Leaving them, I felt I was leaving normality: my life never seemed to run on ordinary lines. Not for me the Sunday dinner and the comfortable pipe, the preoccupied wife and the gurgling baby, the gardening and the golf, the weekend visitors and the annual motoring holiday.

I was more restless than I'd ever been in the past—and now miserable as well. The friends I'd made in this new life were only friendly acquaintances. Something in me put them off when they tried to make it more. The only friends I'd ever really made—or *thought* I'd made—had only been using my friendship for their own ends. It was unlikely I should be invited to Michael's house again except in the course of what they conceived to be their duty. I hadn't the frankness, the openness that you needed for real friendship. It was easy to call it shyness, reserve, but it was something much deeper. I made people uncomfortable because I made them think I didn't like them.

And this flat I was coming back to. I could afford something better now but hadn't the initiative to find it. It was as soulless as I was. Two drab bare rooms without taste or personality. A sleeping box and a cooking box.

Perhaps the solution was to throw up this work and get right away. If it was my fate to gather no moss I might as well have the privilege of being a rolling stone. There was nothing to hold me now except the money, the partnership, the satisfaction of the job. And the satisfaction had gone since I had let myself down over the Moretons.

You came to an end. You weren't master of your fate, the way that silly poem said; your life was decided and divided for you. I was coming to the end of another phase. The first had ended with my father's death. The second with the outbreak of war. The next with peace. Part five was due to begin any day.

London was dead that afternoon when I got home. Baker Street was thinly peopled with Sunday-newspaper posters flapping lightly and a skeleton service of buses; but George Street was empty, and almost the only car on the left-hand side was parked outside the little dress shop.

I didn't suppose it was anyone for me and drew up behind it. I thought I'd go in for a smoke before I put the car away. I went in and up the first flight and saw a woman coming down. It was Sarah.

chapter 15

She said: "Oliver, I . . ."

I went up the next three steps, so that I was only one below her. She hadn't changed. Except that she was so much more lovely than my dead memory of her. She was wearing a light flowered summery frock and no hat, and a wide silver bracelet on her wrist, and flat-heeled sandals of green linen.

I said: "Were you looking for me?"

She said coolly: "D'you mind?"

"Not a bit."

I went past her and threw open the door and then stood aside for her. Her frock brushed against my hand as she went in; there was a light perfume to it.

The room looked its worst, but now I didn't care. Turn all the sun on and show it up. She was standing there in the middle of the room, waiting for me to speak, hostile herself.

I said: "Won't you sit down? It isn't Lowis Manor, but the chairs are clean."

"Thanks."

I felt in my pocket but the cigarette packet was empty and I went across to the bureau to see if there were more.

I said: "You're living in London now?"

"Yes. With my father. It seemed—the obvious thing to do."

I shut the drawers. There were no cigarettes. She was sitting in one of the easy chairs, and the sun caught a corner of her hair, making all the darkness into copper. She said: "You never came to see me. Never once."

"Did you expect me to?"

"Was it expecting too much of you? I'm sorry." Contempt in her voice.

"Yes, it was expecting too much."

"I don't understand. I thought . . ." She stopped there. We were both trying to control ourselves.

"Yes, tell me," I said furiously. "Tell me just what you did think. I'd like to know."

Her eyes were startled out of their own hostility. She said: "When Tracey died—the way he did; when that happened, all my friends were so kind—and understanding, and tried to help me with their friendship . . . all except one. And I'd thought—expected—I'd expected . . ." She stopped and took a careful breath, avoiding my eyes now, struggling to get this out, what she'd come to say. "It's—all these months and you never even wrote. I tried not to come here this afternoon. I thought, if that's the way he feels . . . But I came because I had to. I had to make sure. I thought perhaps some sort of scruple, some feeling that you would be out of place, that——"

" 'Scruple' is the word," I said. "You said once we didn't speak the same language; but that should mean the same thing to us both."

"Why shouldn't it mean the same? What is the matter? If you feel as you do—apparently, for some reason . . ."

"Oh, what's the use," I said wearily. "That sort of blue-eyed innocence doesn't ring the bell any more."

She was staring at me. After a minute she said: "Go on. Don't stop there."

"What do you want me to say? What is there to say? That I've felt too *sick* about it all—sick to the stomach—to bother to see you or to be able to write. I found out the truth—quite by accident—just a few days before the fire. So you see it was . . . I went down to Lowis Manor, was there at the time of the fire, saw it all. I don't know what went wrong—something did—in a way just as much for you as for Tracey. But it didn't stop you from cashing in on the fraud right up to the limit. Did it? Well, I kept my mouth shut. What more was there you could have expected me to do?"

She got up. The colour had gone from her hair and from her face; she was like someone suddenly seen in black and white.

"Oliver, *what* are you saying?"

I couldn't stop now. "That Foster that was supposed to have been burnt in the first fire. The man who bought it from you didn't take it out of the country after all. It's still hanging in his

108

flat in Maida Vale. I saw it there and asked him about it. He described you and the story you'd told him. So I went down to Lowis Manor on the Saturday evening to see the other fakes for myself—found the fire had just been started."

I stopped there for a second, for breath. Her throat moved. Then she turned so quickly that her skirt swung in a fan.

I was just at the door in time to get in her way.

"You've got to listen to me now."

"I'll *not* listen!"

"You've no choice. . . . To begin with I hoped—I tried to believe—that you were only in it as an unwilling partner, playing Tracey's hand because you were his wife. Then when you said nothing, did nothing, played the innocent victim . . . It wasn't any good any longer. I'd been made a fool of by you both. There was no excuse for fooling myself."

"Please get out of my way!"

"Will you deny that you sold the Foster to an American called Croft in the first place—pretended it had been lost in the fire."

"*Deny*," she said. "Of course I deny it! I've never *heard* of a man called Croft. Our Foster was burnt! You've got fraud on the brain. And as for this—this later story it—it passes belief. If you think you've been withholding something for my sake, *please* don't withhold it for my sake any longer. Go to the police. Do what you like to smirch Tracey's memory. It's good enough to stand a few cheap smears!"

She pushed past me and out. There was a patter of footsteps and then they were gone. The slam of a car door, the rev. of an engine; then I rushed down the stairs after her. When I came out, the car was turning into Baker Street.

I got into my car and started it, threw in the gear; but, by the time I had turned round and reached the corner, she was out of sight.

Soon after five I drove up to Monk's Court, N.W.8. A pleasant-looking young woman, very tiny, with wide eyes, opened the door and I asked if Mr. Croft was in.

She smiled. "I'm expecting him back any minute. Can I help you?"

"My name's Branwell. I met your husband in the spring. It was something I wanted to see him about, rather urgently. . . ."

"Well, would you care to wait? He's only just gone taking some friends home."

I went in. Mrs. Croft excused herself, and I sat and read the *New Yorker* for seventeen minutes and never smiled once. I don't know how long it was after that. I was flipping the pages helplessly backwards and forwards when William Croft came in.

He said: "Oh, yes, of course I remember. You called about Charles Highbury. I haven't seen them since; but it wasn't a divorce after all. Some marriages are tough, aren't they? Let's see, you take Scotch. . . ."

"Not at the moment, thanks." We went into the big living room and the Myles Birket Foster looked across at me enigmatically. Croft followed my glance. "Is it something about the picture? I thought that first time you came it kind of upset you."

"It's not about the picture but about the person who sold you the picture. You told me, didn't you, that she was in her twenties, tallish and dark and pretty."

"Yes. Sure. That's the lady."

"With her hair curly, with a touch of bronze in it—her skin very clear . . . a—a quick-moving, vital sort of person; her eyes crinkle when she smiles and her brows straighten; her nose is straight and slim and fairly short; she sometimes catches up her bottom lip with her teeth."

He looked at me quizzically. "Yes, I think you might say that's fairly accurate."

"I don't mean *fairly* accurate. Does it describe her so there'd be no mistake?"

"Well, I couldn't say that. I only met her twice for two short interviews in a shop. And that's two years ago." He frowned and rubbed his chin with his thumb. "Yes, I'd say it was about right. The one thing I'd question is that she didn't seem specially *vital*. I thought she acted kind of tired, kind of bored. My impression was she was one of those women who put on a show of being aloof so you'll think they come out of a higher drawer than they really do. But maybe that was a mistaken view. Maybe it was because I wasn't her type. You'll have a Martini instead?"

"Wait." I fumbled in my pocket and took out a clipping from the *Daily Sketch*. "Was she like this?"

He took it and frowned at it and carried it nearer the light. Then he handed it back.

110

"No. She had more prominent cheekbones, the girl I met. Different shape of face. But I'll grant you she's rather like her."

When I got home I took down the telephone directory. There were two Darnleys with a G among their initials, but there was no mention of either being a doctor. But one lived in Leytonstone and the other at 21 Ponting Street, S.W.7. This sounded so much the more likely that it must be the first choice.

I took the road through Hyde Park and came out at Knightsbridge and turned down Sloane Street. I tried Pont Street, and then went on down Walton Street to the South Kensington tube and took the Old Brompton Road. Ponting Street is about a mile down on the right-hand side.

A short-haired fellow in a dark suit opened the door. I asked if this was Dr. Darnley's house. He said it was. So far so good.

"Is Mrs. Moreton at home, please?"

"I'll inquire," he said, and went off. I thought he walked like an old soldier. He came back to say she wasn't.

"When do you expect her?"

"Couldn't say, sir."

"Well, will you ask?"

"I expect it'll be late tonight. Usually is, sir."

Because I wasn't dead sure, I hesitated and he got the edge of me. In a minute I was looking at a closed door. I went down the steps and sat in the car. I looked up at the house but there was no sign of life about it. Nor was there any sign of the little car. I drove off along the main road till I found a shop that was open and sold cigarettes; then I reversed into another side street and came back. I stopped near the end of Ponting Street. It was just seven o'clock.

At seven-thirty the cockney manservant came out and stood on the steps and hailed a passing taxi. I got out and walked down.

After a minute or two the cockney came out again, but with him, leaning on his arm, was Dr. Darnley. He seemed to have a good deal of difficulty in getting into the taxi, and I thought: he's changed, too, since that night. I glanced up at the house and saw a hand let a curtain fall.

At a quarter to eight I rang the doorbell again. I had to ring three times before it opened.

The cockney said: "Sorry, Mrs. Moreton's phoned to say she won't be home tonight."

I said: "Forget it," and put my foot in the door.

" 'Ere," he said. "What the blazes d'you think——"

I was stronger than he was, or perhaps it was just the feelings behind it. I went in and he went back and sat down on a tiger rug in the middle of the narrow hall. He tried to grab me as I went past but I got to the stairs and went up them three at a time. I'd tried to work out where that hand was and I worked it out right. There were three doors and the extreme right one led into a bedroom. Sarah was sitting at a dressing table brushing her hair.

She dropped the brush and stood up, pulling her yellow house coat round her. Trixie began to bark from a corner.

"Matthews——"

I put my foot against the door. "If that's Matthews downstairs, tell him to lay off till I've finished. I *must* talk to you, Sarah."

She said furiously: "Get out of my room! How dare you force your way in here!"

I said: "I've been to see Croft. I took along a photo of you out of one of the papers. The girl who sold him the Foster wasn't you—although she was like you; closely enough for the mistake. But it *was* a mistake—so humiliatingly bad—so unspeakable. . . . There's nothing you can say bad enough, nothing I won't want to add to——"

Somebody knocked on the door and tried the handle.

"He's in here, Matthews!"

Matthews threw his weight against the door. It creaked and gave at the top, but my foot held firm.

"Listen, Sarah," I said desperately. "I mean to talk to you if I have to take this bloody house to pieces brick by brick. So call him off and give me a chance to work this out. Please."

"It's *worked* out," she said. "Finished. Done. I've nothing more to say to you—ever."

I put my weight against the door. Trixie had come out of her box and was sniffing at me in a friendly fashion. "I've made one terrible mistake. But they can't *all* be mistakes, all the things that prove the fraud. Croft's picture is the genuine Foster. He's had it verified twice. Foster's 'Mill and Spinney,' painted from just below that copse where we sat. The thing that was burned was a fake. So was the Lippi. The panel it was painted on was soft

112

wood; if it had been old it would have been hard. The Constable and the Watteau the same, I expect; but I never had the chance to find out. I don't know if the first fire was a put-up job but the second was. I was *there*, Sarah. I was there within a few minutes of it starting. The whole thing was planned. The paraffin—the candles—the shavings . . . Tracey never jumped to save himself from the fire. He was dead before it got going. I found him in the hall. God knows what had happened. I suppose he started it and then stayed on, making doubly sure. If he fell, then it was carrying the bed linen to pile in the hall, using the decorators' ladders as a frame. He didn't phone the police. *I* phoned the police after I'd tried to put out the fire. I've still got the scar of a burn on my arm. When the fire brigade came I slipped away, because I thought you were playing along with him. I was too knocked over to do what I should have done. Everything pointed to you being in it. The Foster, which I thought you'd sold—the fire started the way I'd told you of only the week before—things you said, things you had done and did do . . ." I stopped for breath. I'd moved a bit away from the door, but Matthews apparently had given up. She was listening to me at last, head up and listening.

I said: "I thought this was an idea of Tracey's. He'd gone out of his way to make a friend of me knowing that when the fire came I'd do what I could to ease through the claim. It had always puzzled me before. I've never been the sort of person people make a friend of. Perhaps he realized that, knew I should be flattered. Well, I was. Afterwards, when I found out, I thought, Sarah may be working with him out of a sense of loyalty. Now he's dead she'll be free to put the thing straight—if she wants to. Whatever she feels about me, she can at least refuse the insurance on the contents of a house that's been gradually stripped of its antiques and its Old Masters on the pretext that they were being taken away to be cleaned, restored. . . ."

Sarah said: "Stop. Wait a minute. Stop."

I waited. She went back slowly to the dressing table and sat down. Her hair was loose and she pushed it up with her hand. The sleeve of her coat slipped up to the elbow. I think she felt faint. I remember noticing she was wearing black patent-leather mules and no stockings.

I said: "But now . . . I'll never get straight with myself for thinking what I did about you."

"How d'you know you're completely wrong?"

"By your look. And because . . . well, I do."

"Tell me again," she said. "Everything that happened."

Standing there, I began trying to tell her. It was hard now—it had come easier with the anger. Part way through, there was the sound of double footsteps on the stairs. With a knock, the door opened and Matthews came in with a policeman behind him.

" 'Ere he is."

I still wasn't sure how I stood, didn't know what she would do. The policeman glanced from one to the other, as if he wasn't sure himself; as if this wasn't quite what he expected.

"Did this man break in here, Miss?"

Sarah got up. "I'm very sorry, Officer. I'm afraid I don't need you after all. I'm *sorry*, Matthews; you were quite right to go. It was—a misunderstanding."

Matthews' face was expressive. "Well, Ma'am, you did call. You did say——"

"I know. I'm very sorry. Mr. Branwell will be leaving in a few minutes."

"In that case," said the policeman, looking sourly at Matthews, "there's not much for me to do, is there, eh? I'll be getting back."

He turned and went out, and Matthews with an angry shrug did the same. I found a crumpled ten-shilling note in my pocket —change from the cigarettes—and followed the policeman out and tried to make him take it. He didn't want to, but before we got to the front door he gave way, and went out amiably enough. When the door was shut on him I gave Matthews a pound to try to ease the look on his face.

Her door was still open, and when I went in she was standing by the dressing table, with her hairbrush in her hands, turning it over and over.

I said: "Is there somewhere else we can talk?"

She put the brush down, turned away from me, fumbled in her pocket. "No. . . . Go on with what you were saying. I—before I do anything—I've got to hear."

I tried to go on. I groped through the rest of it, ashamed for the wrong reasons.

114

I'd seen before the interruption that I'd made the first hurdle. She was no longer chucking the story out emotionally—on sight. What I had to do now was put it over to her intellect—show her that there were no more bad guesses like the one that had tied it up with her. And I had to show myself too.

When I finished she didn't speak for a bit. Then she said: "Oh, God, this is awful. To think about it makes one . . . I've got to have *time*, Oliver. Time to work round it, see if there isn't some other . . . I'm supposed to be going out tonight. I was due at eight. I—don't feel . . ."

"Put it off. Come out with me. We can eat somewhere quietly —talk about it quietly. I won't press you in any way. But if a thing like this is on your mind . . . There's so much that *I* want to know too."

I was speaking gently, and you couldn't help but think of the sudden change—all the violence that had gone from between us these last minutes.

She looked at me doubtfully. "Give me a few minutes, will you? This afternoon has been . . . I'll change and come down—let you know then."

"All right," I said, and left her. She watched me go.

chapter 16

She said: "I knew, of course, about some of the furniture. There was a Sheraton desk, I remember. And a table. Those are closer, personal things, things you can't disguise. You know them by the grain of the wood, the way a drawer closes. It was never discussed between us; but—we were short of money; they were our own possessions; what we did with them was our own business; if there had ever been any occasion to lie about them, we'd have done so out of pride. The thought of insurance never entered my head because I never thought we should claim. But some of the things were genuinely restored—I'm sure of that—and I thought the pictures were. I didn't think he'd ever bear to part with them. He was very secretive about money. I never really knew what money we had. Sometimes he'd say we could afford nothing; another time he'd be generous."

We were sitting in one of those little restaurants that abound in London. An Italian or a Cypriot takes a shop, engages a black-chinned staff, and calls it the Something Grill.

"I've hardly seen the money yet," she said. "Victor has handled everything. I was surprised at the size of the insurance settlement —but it was a pleasant surprise, nothing more. Tracey had only a small insurance on his life—the company wouldn't increase it after the war. It didn't occur to me to consider the rights and wrongs of a few pieces of furniture. Would it have occurred to you?"

"Eat your dinner," I said gently.

"Even now it isn't really the proofs *you* have. . . . Perhaps you haven't told me them all. What were the other things you had against me?"

"Forget it. If you ever can."

"No. I want to know. First there was the picture."

"That damned picture set me off on the wrong foot. I don't know if you see—but once I'd accepted that . . ."

"Yes, I see."

"If I can possibly explain—the things that tied you in with it. Each by itself is nothing, but they came to mean what they did because they added up together. Perhaps it's partly something in me that was set off on the wrong foot—long ago. But I *liked* Tracey. Even with *him*, only considering him, there was such a ghastly sense of letdown. If——"

"Tell me what you thought," she said.

"Well, there was the way the fire was prepared. I'd explained that to you only the week before."

"Oh, but I knew about that before you told me. It was in a magazine last year sometime—about those fire-raisers before the war. Tracey probably read it too."

"But when I told you about it, why didn't you say you knew?"

"Well, I'm sorry. But don't you remember I'd been trying to get you to talk about yourself. It was always hard. You started telling me of your work. If I'd interrupted and said: 'Oh, yes, I read all about that last year' . . ."

The waiter came and served us with slivers of *filet mignon*, making a showoff of a simple job. That was what you paid for.

I said: "At the inquest, you said you left that morning for Yorkshire by yourself because Tracey wanted another injection. Knowing about the injections, I didn't believe it."

"Well, I had to say something. I couldn't very well tell them what had really happened. . . . It was very unusual for us to quarrel. I only remember three or four times. But we did that morning. I left Lewis not quite knowing—or caring—what Tracey intended to do. I went to London by bus and caught the one-forty from St. Pancras. I—was boiling; but when I got up to Yorkshire it all cooled off and I tried to phone him. I felt a bit guilty. You know how it is. When he didn't reply I thought he'd left. I didn't want to explain that at the inquest."

I nodded but didn't speak.

"But didn't you say there were things I'd said and done, other things?"

"Not that will bear mentioning now. There was the gatehouse —if that had been occupied. . . . You put the new tenants off for a week or two."

"That was Tracey's idea. I didn't see the point of it at the time. He was insistent. But he paid me the compliment of keeping his intentions to himself."

"I should have known."

"I don't see how."

"I do."

She took up a pat of butter, spread it slowly on her bread. "And the things I said?"

"Must I follow this out to the bitter end?"

"Of course."

"You said—when I asked you why you came out with me, knowing how I felt, you said there were reasons."

Her eyes flickered up to mine for a second and then went coolly past me, to fix on something out of range. "There were reasons. They were not those reasons."

Silence fell for a good time.

I said: "Do you see much of Clive Fisher these days?"

"Not a lot."

"I heard—you know how these rumours get about . . ."

"What?"

"I heard you were engaged."

Her lips moved. "No."

I said: "Is it likely to be true?"

"No."

I don't remember what came after the steak. We took an age finishing the meal. Since I knew she was not in the fraud, a great weight had gone from me, something that had been there ever since May; but there'd been too much anxiety and self-blame in these last hours to let me be properly aware of it. The news about Clive made me aware of it.

On the way home, we stopped for a few minutes on the Embankment watching the dark river.

She said: "Yes, it's been a shock, but it's some *particular* aspects that chiefly hurt. I didn't want ever to remember Tracey as . . . It isn't really the fact of the fraud. I'm not sure that he hadn't some excuses for that; they weren't good enough but they were better than most people's. You see, he felt that both he and his father had been crippled fighting for their country, and all his country had done was rob him of the means to live. It wasn't just a grudge—it was part of his illness. It's really the *personal* fraud that . . . On you in one way, if that was his reason. On me in another. I said just now he paid me the compliment of not telling me. But was it a compliment? D'you remember once I said to you that Tracey and I had a perfect understanding and trust? Well, it looks silly now, doesn't it? On the whole I should be less upset if I'd been in the fraud all through."

"Except that you never would have been."

"I never would have been in any fraud on you. But for the rest . . . If you cared for someone, wouldn't you rather help them to cheat than yourself be cheated?"

I didn't answer, and after a while she shivered.

"If you're cold, I'll——"

"No. . . . It isn't that. I've been thinking. . . . There's no proof, Oliver, is there; no absolute proof at all."

"Of what?"

"Of what you believe. We can't be positive that Tracey set fire to the house."

118

"For that matter," I said, "we can't be positive that he fell from the gallery."

"What time did you get to the house?"

"It would be about half past nine."

"And Elliott left at half past three. Tracey wouldn't be able to begin anything till then. It would need a lot of preparation, because there was nothing in the cellars. I expect he got most of his stuff from the stables and from the old hall. And with him not being well . . . But six hours."

"He may not have had six hours. He may have been dead two when I found him."

A tugboat with a couple of barges behind went chugging down the river. Its lights made silver snakes on the water.

She said: "How long should a candle burn if it was set to start a fire?"

"Oh, about four hours. But it was very windy that night and the cellars were draughty. The candle that hadn't burnt down was guttering all over the place. The other had gone quickly—perhaps an hour and a half—I don't know."

She didn't speak and I went on: "I've thought about it a lot; but there doesn't seem any other explanation. I can only think he set the fuses and then went upstairs for some last-minute job. And then he forgot about the balustrade being down. . . ."

She shivered again. "It never has made sense to me."

I started up the engine and drove her slowly home. I said: "I wonder how it got about that you might be going to marry Clive."

"He asked me."

I digested that. "When?"

"About a month ago. I haven't seen him since. I was as nice as I knew how—but I don't think he liked it much."

"Must you lose any sleep over that?"

"No; but he was an old friend of Tracey's. I've known him and Ambrosine since before I was married, and I don't want to cut all the connections. . . ."

We stopped outside her house, and there was a light in the front.

She said suddenly: "What can I do with this money? I can't touch it now."

"Have you spent much of it?"

"No. It's only just come to me. In any case, Tracey left about four thousand in cash. I suppose it was money from selling the pictures. . . . Then there were a few small investments. Can the insurance be paid back?"

"I imagine so, somehow. Let's see: Berkeley Reckitt were the underwriters. I don't know exactly how it will work out; but if you'd like me to, I'll put in a few inquiries to see if it can be done without publicity. There's no point in blackening Tracey's name unnecessarily."

"If it can possibly be avoided I wouldn't want to, Oliver. Not deliberately. He was . . . Besides, there's his mother. It would kill her if it ever came out." She paused. "But what will happen to the insurance on the house? That isn't mine to return."

"Oh, that's a fair settlement. In any case I think I'm right in saying that that money legally belongs to the trustees, and no insurance company could claim it back. The trustees didn't fire the place."

She fumbled with the door handle, and I got out and opened it for her.

"Will you come in for a minute?" she said.

I shook my head. "Thanks. The feeling dates back a bit, but I'm still scared of your father."

She smiled. "A bit hard to believe. Anyway it's rather difficult to be frightened of a man crippled with arthritis."

I said: "D'you think you can overlook all the shabby suspicions that have been festering inside me all these months?"

"Oh. . . . Yes. Were they shabby? I can't judge. If I'd been in your position . . ."

"Will you meet me tomorrow evening, then?"

She stood a minute on the pavement, looking up at the stars. "Yes," she said.

Next morning I phoned Henry Dane to see if I could make a date to talk the thing over with him. He said he was leaving town almost at once and wouldn't be back until Saturday, so I fixed to go and see him on the following Monday. There wasn't any hurry, and he, with the law under his fingers as well as insurance, would have the know-how if anybody had. I had lunch with Charles Robinson, and very nearly put the case to him. But hypothetical cases usually boil down to personal ones, and although Charles was as good a friend as I'd got, he was an underwriter by profes-

120

sion and I didn't know quite what his attitude might be. I wished it was his firm which had been involved.

In the evening I called for Sarah; and on the Tuesday it was the same, and on the Wednesday. Life suddenly began to have no recognizable identity with what it had been a week ago. Everything was newly significant. It's no good describing that feeling because those who've known it won't need the description and those who haven't won't recognize it as true.

We met and talked about the fire and the consequences of the fire; and the feeling of Tracey's death was never far from us; yet I hardly remember a thing we said because all that was only on the perimeter of my attention. She was the centre of it, and she knew it, and she still came out with me. I wondered if it was just admiration that she liked. God knows I gave it her. But I began to feel it was more than that. I began to know it was more than that, but sometimes you distrust your own instinct.

On the Wednesday we had dinner at one of the big hotels and danced afterwards. She'd been reluctant to come because she still had a feeling of not wanting to be seen out and about in quite this way by Tracey's friends. We sat and talked, as usual, and then danced.

She said: "I thought you *didn't* spend your youth socially."

"What? Oh, no. . . . This came later, such as it is. I haven't done much of it."

"Nor have I—for seven years. I used to like it."

"Used to?"

"Yes. Don't encourage me."

"But I want to."

"I know. Dangerous."

"Who for?"

"It could get out of hand. Sublimation of my old love for ballet . . ."

"Good. Let's help each other."

"How?"

"Well. . . . Sublimation of my old love for Sarah."

She didn't answer that. She was quite tall beside me. A maroon frock with a Medici collar. One pearl earring. Some women—a few women—when they're dancing seem to have a waist and no feet, a balance and no weight, so that a pleasant sensation gets

121

above itself and becomes an art, a form of sophisticated experience. She was one of them, and I told her so.

When we got back to the table she said: "Why do you say sometimes that you can't express yourself as you want to? Because it isn't true, is it?"

"It's—partly true. Half the trouble is I can't imagine other people are interested."

"But you think I am."

"Aren't you?"

"Yes. . . . That's what I mean." She smiled quickly at me and then away.

"It doesn't convince me of anything."

"That's the other half of the trouble. A—a lack of faith, is it? Or a lack of self-esteem. There's something in you, isn't there, that won't—believe. . . ."

I didn't speak.

"What's the matter with you, Oliver?" she asked quietly. "Did all your dreams fail?"

"I only ever had one—a grown-up one, I mean."

"What was that?"

I smiled at her. "I thought we'd got that clear."

After a while she said: "That's all very well, but . . . it isn't the grown-up ones that matter in this respect, is it? You've got a thing about yourself—dating back I don't know how long—and it isn't valid any longer—not any of it. How d'you suppose you've done what you have done, during and since the war? Just because you're a driver, a hard worker; is that what you think? Well, it isn't true. Tracey may have made a friend of you for his own reasons but—other people haven't."

"No. . . . I thought they had but they hadn't—thank God."

"I didn't mean just me. Forget me for a moment. There's Michael Abercrombie; and this Henry Dane you speak of. And in the Army too. There was a man I met the other week called John Graves. I expect there are lots of others. They don't speak well of you because of what they can get out of you."

"No, I didn't for a minute suppose they did. John——"

"So why not stop being like that? Why not let yourself be accepted as likable, direct, honest, kind; all the things you are but don't believe you are. I used to think—at one time I used to think you were intolerant towards other people. But now I know the only person you're really intolerant towards is yourself."

We danced again but talked very little. It didn't seem necessary. I couldn't believe that this time last week . . .

As we left the floor and sat down I said: "You know it's all very well to say those things about me. I like listening to it—and I'm grateful. . . ."

"I don't want you to be *grateful*. That——"

"Well, I am—whether they're really true or you only think they're true. But there's one thing. . . . You said, 'Forget me for a moment.' How can I do that when yours is the only approval or disapproval I really care about—and when everything else measures up to that? Maybe there's things the matter with me, as you say. Good stuff for the trick psychologist. But the chief thing wrong these last few years is that I've been in love with a woman who is—and always has been—out of my reach."

There was silence for a bit.

She said: "You think that's the chief thing wrong?"

"I'm sure it's the chief thing wrong."

She looked at me and smiled a bit doubtfully.

I added: "But of course I don't ask you to believe it."

"Perhaps you ought to. Perhaps it would be a worse thing if I was lacking in faith too."

My pulses began to beat faster. I said: "Darling Sarah, I don't know what you mean by that, but it seems an oncoming sort of remark."

She struck a match from the box in the middle of the table and watched the flame.

"Does it?"

"It's one that could be pretty easily mistaken by anyone with any belief in himself at all."

"D'you think," she said, "that anyone with any belief in himself at all would be likely to *mistake* it?"

The match went out. She looked up and met my look. And I knew then that she wasn't out of my reach any more.

I paid the bill somehow and we got out of the hotel. We'd come by taxi, and the commissionaire got one for us. As soon as he'd shut the door, before the driver had flicked down his flag, I said:

"Will you marry me?"

"Yes, Oliver."

"When?"

She hesitated. "I don't know."

"When?"

"When you say."

I couldn't believe it. "You mean that, Sarah?"

"Yes. If you want me to."

"Tomorrow? Saturday?"

The driver pushed open the partition. "Did you say 21 or 31 Ponting Street?"

"Either," I said. "You take *your* choice."

He shut the window, muttering, and the taxi lurched out into the traffic.

I didn't try to touch her. Her voice had been queer, uncertain. After a bit I said: "Saturday?"

"What—in three days?"

"Could you face it? Before anyone has time for wise advice or —or good intentions. A very quick matter-of-fact thing at a registry office, and then Paris or Rome or somewhere, by air—so that there's the absolute minimum of fuss. . . . I'm not afraid for myself but I am for you. If you let the light of too many cold mornings——"

"Please," she said softly. "I *want* you to believe. It won't make the slightest difference."

"Oh, yes, I'll try. But I know it's harder for you. I've no ties— or people to mourn—or anyone's feelings to consider. You see——"

"I've other people's feelings to consider. . . ."

"Your father——"

"And there's Mrs. Moreton. She always liked you—I don't think she would be upset after a time. But she'd think it far too soon. She . . . and Victor . . ."

"I'd be sorry to upset them. But wouldn't they get over it? Won't it seriously, really, have to be at once, almost before they know—or not for twelve months?"

"I don't know. It might be three."

"We've lost ten years already."

And it was in fact as if something had broken down between us, something that had been accumulating for years, perhaps unknown to me, certainly unknown to her. She'd drawn well back into the corner of the cab. I couldn't see her face. It was, as if in

124

spite of this sudden give-way of things, she was trying to keep her balance, trying to satisfy the critic, the reasonable mind within herself.

There wasn't anything more said until the taxi-driver, guessing right, drew up at No. 21. I got out and began to pay him. Sarah looked at me but didn't say anything. As we went up the steps and she took out her key I said:

"I must see your father tonight—try to explain to him . . ."

She said, "It's half past one. He'll have been in bed two hours."

"Oh, God, I'd forgotten. Can you break it to him?"

"If you could come round tomorrow. I'll phone you in the morning."

Somehow we were inside the house.

I said: "When I come, can I bring the air tickets for Saturday?"

She said: "Sometimes you frighten me, Oliver. There's no letup, is there? There's been no letup since Sunday afternoon."

"Sorry. I'm sorry."

"No, it isn't that. But some ways we're much alike. Headlong. Isn't that a risk? I'm trying to think for two."

When she got her mouth free I spoke just ahead of her. "Saturday?"

"Does it mean so much to you?"

"What can I say? It couldn't mean any more."

"It's impossible. Crazy. In a queer way I want to as much as you. To take this now. Now. It's—something stronger than either of us. . . . But I'd not even have time to *try* to explain. . . ."

"Saturday?" I said, and began to kiss round her mouth for a change.

She said: "Oh, darling, don't . . ." in such a drowning sort of voice that I stopped.

We clung to each other then in the darkness for a minute or two while I waited for her decision.

She said: "There's that money that doesn't belong to me. . . ."

"It won't hurt for a week or two. They won't expect interest on it."

"There's Tracey's memory. . . ."

My hands slackened. "I can't fight that."

After a pause she said: "But since Sunday I've had to revalue

125

everything. Do I owe him a lot or very little? I don't know. That's still a new thought."

chapter 17

I suppose it was asking for trouble rushing my fences like that. At any rate I got trouble. But when you've wanted something for ten or eleven years, at first subconsciously, but then very consciously, and for all except four days of that time . . .

And besides, when I was away from her I was never for an instant sure of her. Spectres that she would change her mind kept me company everywhere. I could see her swayed by other people's opinions; and no amount of conviction that she was not a person easily put off her course made any difference. I knew what I felt but I had no sureness how she felt. Perhaps it was that shortcoming in me. She'd called it a lack of faith.

I knew that she'd really cared for Tracey more than anyone, knew that she was suffering a temporary letdown in her feelings for him, feared that I was catching her on the rebound. There was such a difference between us, between him and me, in every way. Let her first impulses fail . . .

So among all the other sensations as the plane taxied along the runway and then took off lumpishly into the wind was one of *relief*. Whatever happened now, the thing was done. There was no going back. I looked down and thought: bits of paper scattering. . . . Oliver Branwell, the stoker, the hobo, the conscript, the officer, the adjuster, the partner; tear them up, let them blow.

I looked down at the small knot of figures. Michael would go back to the office. I remembered his startled face when I told him, the puzzled half-jesting way he took it; his tall stooping square-shouldered figure standing beside me in the church—Sarah had wanted it in church. Dr. Darnley would probably go back to his club. I'd had lunch with him there yesterday: a big early-Victorian place that looked as if it hadn't been decorated since Albert died; we sat opposite each other and sized each other up over the hors d'oeuvres and the roast pork, and he didn't know he'd ever seen me before. To me he was just as unrecognizable as the man who'd spoken brusquely to the tramp; too quiet and restrained—perhaps more than half the hostility had been in me that night. We talked about arthritis and the exploitation of Coca-Cola in Egypt and the origin of Lloyd's and the rise in the price of newsprint, and everything except Sarah. He was just finishing a book on the dialects of south India. I'd never known; I'd always thought him a doctor of medicine.

Neither Mrs. Moreton nor Victor had turned up. Mrs. Moreton was in the Isle of Wight, and Victor had been leaving for Scotland on the night train on Friday; Sarah had phoned him, and she said he had been quite nice about it.

I glanced at her sitting beside me. She had asked to have the gangway seat because she didn't like looking down. There was a lot we should have to talk of, lots of prosaic stuff; but at present that could slide. The old existence was still too near to start making arrangements for a new one. The only thing that mattered was Sarah's hand, which she'd not yet taken from my arm.

Very late that night as we lay together in the dark listening to the thinning traffic of the Rue de Rivoli, I told her a bit about the way it had been with me as a kid. I'd never told anyone before and she seemed to want to know.

I told her how, when I was seven, my father lost his job because the line laid up his ship, and how he never got any other proper work, and how we moved from a house to three rooms, and from there to two in a tenement, and how he rotted quicker than his ship.

I tried to tell her something of the sort of life it had been: the steamy pubs with their red blinds drawn, the tough kids, the fish-and-chip shops with greasy papers blowing down the street, the pawnbrokers and the touts, and the scores of idle men, like prisoners, the derelict sheds, the ships' sirens, and the muddy tide. And how my mother couldn't see that being out of work wasn't a personal disgrace, and how she never let my father forget how it was with him. There was never any repose in those two rooms; you couldn't come back to them—even I as a boy couldn't come back to them—with the right feeling at all. There was more sanctuary on the street corner.

I said: "Talking of it now, after so long, I get a bit ashamed of the way I've felt about her. You set up to judge a person, and then in a few years, when you get nearer their age, you wonder if you could have made out any better yourself. In many ways she was good: thrifty, handy with her needle, efficient, painfully clean. All the things that should have been helpful—that were. It's hard to explain, but, you see, he—he had different horizons —if he'd been allowed—if he'd not forever been dragged back to his own failure. He used to try to make me see. . . ."

"What happened?"

"Oh, nothing dramatic. At least, the end was; but that was only the last lap. The rest had happened before. It was only that last year or so that I was old enough to notice the way he was going downhill. He must have felt things just as much as my mother, but it was a different sort of pride. He kept it inside him. He wasn't a particularly easy man to know."

There was silence. Sarah said: "Was he like you to look at too?"

I didn't answer. Yet talking about it had loosened something, eased something that had been held in too long. I said: "For about three years he'd been promised the next job with his old company. It was something to hang on to—a sort of lifeline. Mother was always talking about it. 'When you go to sea again.' 'When your father gets that job back.' 'When my husband joins his ship.' It was a bit shopworn, but we all reckoned on it more or less. Then one day when my mother had gone to visit Marion, who was married to a clerk, Dad got a phone message asking him to go round to the offices at once. The vacancy'd come up. He went along full of hope, and they asked him his age and he said he was fifty last birthday, and they turned him down for a younger man—even though he'd been waiting since he was thirty-nine. He came back and shut the door and window and turned on the gas. I was working in a garage then, and I found him when I got back. He wasn't quite dead, and I might have been able to save him if I'd known what to do or we'd been able to get a doctor in time. But he passed out with his head on my knee without ever properly coming round. The only word he said was 'Dorothy.'"

128

Outside the traffic had almost stopped. Paris was asleep. Then a car with a noisy exhaust came from far in the distance racing at fifty or sixty along the length of the gardens. When it was past, Sarah said:

"He still thought a lot of your mother, didn't he?"

"Oh, yes . . . I suppose so. Otherwise she couldn't have touched him. And I used to think she felt the same for him. I used to think it was just her way of . . . But soon after his death I overheard her talking with Marion; and then I knew it wasn't so, just by the tone of her voice. Perhaps it was poverty that had killed it. . . ."

There was a longish silence. Sarah stirred against my arm. She said: "You can build yourself a protection, can't you—as high and as strong as you like—but there's no protection against those you love. That's the privilege and the responsibility of caring."

I thought she spoke from her own experience.

We had eight days, really. Eight days until the thing came. I'd never known Sarah until that week. Falling in love with someone the way I had with her is like seeing two or three colours and thinking you see the whole spectrum. I hadn't realized before—though I should have—how highly strung she was, how her vitality burned itself out at times, yet never left her empty and depressed. I hadn't realized what fun there was in her or how she could flare up in a sudden anger that never lasted. I hadn't known how easy she was to please or how hard she was to impress, or how sweet she could be in the most improbable and enchanting ways.

We didn't do many of the obvious things. Of course we went to the ballet. I could see more in it now, and of course I would have gone in any case to see her pleasure. We tried a play or two, but I couldn't follow them, and some of the night clubs. We dined at the most expensive restaurants and the cheapest. We shopped in the Faubourg St. Honoré and in the Boulevard de Clichy. We walked for miles, along the banks of the Seine, west to Trocadéro, east to Notre Dame and the Ile St. Louis, where the fishermen sit all day and watched the river creeping past. We travelled in the shabby old buses and the shakier tubes, north to the Sacré Coeur, south to Montparnasse. I don't remember what the weather was, but I suppose it must have been fine. I remember there was a shower once when we were near the Rond-Point, and we ducked into a café.

Above all we talked. I never knew there were so many subjects in the world or any of such passionate interest. We talked and argued and settled the world's problems and faced our own, made plans and then threw them over for something better. And often and often there was laughter—which had been so absent from her during the week in London. It sparkled and bubbled in her until I felt that perhaps she really was almost as happy as she seemed.

I've not been in Paris since, but the sight of a word like "Châtelet" or "Neuilly" brings back the time and the mood and the memory. . . .

The eighth morning we got up and had our breakfast at the table by the window as usual. After the first morning in bed, we did this because of the wonderful view. The Hotel Continentale overlooks the Tuileries, and from it you can see nearly all the beauty of Paris. On the extreme right we could see the Arc de Triomphe set at the tip of the glimmering sword that the moving cars and the morning sun made of the Champs-Elysées. Beyond it and south were the Eiffel Tower and the dome of Napoleon's Tomb. The government buildings and the Chamber of Deputies were directly across the gardens, and away to the left was the Louvre, backed by the twin towers of Notre Dame —all set in a semicircle for us to look at, over the tinted treetops.

I was lazily finishing my coffee when the post came, and Sarah took it from the boy and passed me my share, which I could see was a letter from Michael and a bill for new tyres that somebody had mistakenly sent on. She had two letters as well, and she read the first, from her father, with her bare elbows on the table. As her hair was quite loose, it kept falling forward, and she'd push it back with a slow movement of her fingers. I got something out of seeing her just do that, and for a bit I didn't read my letter. Then she looked up, met my look, and smiled with her eyes. I got up and went over to her chair.

She said against my face: "Daddy's having some of the second thoughts he hadn't breath for before we left."

"Decent of him to wait till now."

"We really are quite nice people, we Darnleys, in spite of what you once thought."

"I can't remember what I once thought. It belongs to somebody else's life. All I know is that if I'd been your father I should have made a lot of trouble about letting you go off with a man like me."

She said: "You're not going to be an easygoing husband, are you?"

I picked up the cigarettes from the dressing table and was back in my seat when she put a knife through the flap of the envelope. Absently she took a cigarette, and I flipped my lighter and leaned across, but she didn't take a light.

"Doesn't seem to be any letter in it," she said. "But there is something. Very exciting! Wedding present, I believe."

She unwrapped the bit of tissue paper and a ring fell out and rolled across the table. It rolled halfway across to me and then fell on its side.

I'd no difficulty in recognizing it as Tracey's signet ring.

chapter 18

I said: "Drink this: it'll make you feel better. No, take a gulp; sips won't help."

She coughed. "It's all right. I'm all right now." She slid her legs off the bed and put up the usual hand to her hair. "What a fool."

"I should like to get hold of the person who played this pretty little joke."

"I don't know how it could have happened."

"Never mind. Forget it. Look, the sun's coming out. Let's be honest tourists for one day and do something really dashing. Take a car out to Fontainebleau or somewhere."

She smiled and got up. "All right. Anything you say."

While she was finishing dressing I picked up the ring and put it in my pocket, and we didn't mention it again that morning, although it was so carefully ignored that it got more and more in the way. Over lunch she said again:

"I don't see how it can have happened."

"What does it matter? If we let it spoil our fun we're playing their game."

"Oh, yes . . . if it were only that. What I can't understand is how anyone—got it."

"I suppose sometimes he took it off?"

"Never, as far as I know."

"Then . . ."

"Yes, that's what I think."

"Who saw him—afterwards?"

"Only Victor. Mrs. Moreton wouldn't go in. I didn't."

"Maybe things like that are taken off the body before burial. But in that case they'd be returned to the next of kin, which was you. Victor . . ."

"He wouldn't do a thing like this. A barrister at the top of his profession. What has he to gain?"

"Mrs. Moreton—if she could have got it. But I can't somehow see her. . . ."

"In any case, they aren't the sort of people."

"Perhaps somebody at the fire—or after—found it on the ground —someone with a grudge against you."

"I don't know. It's possible. There's no one I can think of."

"I suppose it wouldn't be Clive Fisher?"

"Oh, *surely* not."

"Isn't he a man who could be catty in a womanish sort of way?"

She looked at me with her glinting little smile. "Not very complimentary to women, are you?"

"Well, men—ordinary men—usually have a reason for their misdeeds, don't you think? This is so pointlessly vindictive. No purpose except to give you an unpleasant shock."

After a while she said sombrely: "That row Tracey and I had on the Saturday morning, it was about you. Did I tell you that?"

"Me. Why?"

"On the Monday before, when we came back so late from the ballet, he seemed to make nothing of it, feel no resentment or suspicion at our lateness. Did you think so?"

"None at all."

"Well, I suppose it had meant something to him. Or he chose

to let it. I realize that now. He may have picked the quarrel deliberately to get me out of the house . . . as he did so many things deliberately that I didn't realize. He'd tried very hard to persuade me to go to Scarborough on the Friday without him. We almost squabbled over that. On the Saturday morning he . . . It made me so angry because there'd never been *anything* between us—except that one thing that seemed to happen unawares. And even that . . . In the end, after we'd both said a good many hot-tempered things, he said he was going to consult you next time you came, to see about taking out a policy against adultery."

I said: "That's just about as nasty as . . ." I was going to say as nasty as sending a signet ring, but stopped in time.

"Of course the result was what he expected."

I smiled rather tenderly at her profile. "Yes. I imagine so."

That other question that I'd wanted to ask before kept pushing itself to the front—yet I couldn't think how to put it in a casual way. At last it came out almost without meaning to.

"Did Victor say—did he mention if Tracey was badly burned?"

"I don't think he said. Obviously he wouldn't to me. Why?"

"I was only wondering."

"Yes, but why were you wondering?" It didn't do to give Sarah a lead.

"I don't know. It's not a pleasant subject. But I thought one of the salvage men perhaps . . ."

Fortunately the excuse seemed to satisfy her. But I wasn't satisfied or content any more. Once I'd almost told her of the breathing I'd imagined I'd heard in the house that night. Now I couldn't, not ever, because of what she might think. I realized that.

We had supper that night at a little place near the Rue Dauphine, in the artists' quarter just on the Left Bank. The meal took four hours, and all the diners talked to each other and shouted at each other and flirted with each other and pinched the waitresses; and people acted the fool and gave recitations in a variety of languages; not because they were drunk—there wasn't a drunk among them—but because they were full of high spirits and were out for an evening's fun.

The great advantage, of course, was that we couldn't talk here even if we wanted to, because there was far too much noise. Now and then, if I specially wanted to say something I had to put my lips against Sarah's ear.

About halfway through, I shouted to her:

"I should think we're the only English people in the place."

Some echo of this must have reached the stringy middle-aged man who, with a blond girl he'd obviously never seen till that evening, was sharing our table. Although he'd been chattering in French, he leaned across at me and shouted in English:

"No, sir. You're very much mistaken. Don't you recognize the old Royal Artillery tie?"

After a minute I got out: "No, really?"

"Yes. Was born in Hove. Have moved about a bit since then, of course. What part are you from?"

We both felt a bit silly, and I could feel Sarah fairly quivering with suppressed laughter at the way he'd enlightened us. But a man at the next table, a real poilu type with a blue beret, had also heard, and he immediately got up and did a dude English-officer act that nearly brought the house down. He used a silver five-franc piece for an eyeglass and a roll of bread for a cane, and the English he put on was an absolutely impeccable drawl.

When he sat down and the cheering was over, the Englishman opposite me got up and tried to tug something out of his pocket. There was more or less silence while he struggled, but a cheer went up as he got out a blue beret of his own and put it on his head. Then he did an imitation of a French pimp trying to persuade a tourist to come and sleep with his grandmother. It was rich, it was lewd, it was magnificent. You didn't need to know much French to tell that; but I could see Sarah, who did, getting rather pink. When it was over, the place fairly rocked, and the French poilu came across and kissed him on both cheeks.

About twelve I could see Sarah had had enough, and we managed to fight our way out, followed by the love-calls and adieus of our neighbours. When we got out she was trembling, and I hailed a cab and we drove quickly home. In the bedroom she was still full of laughter at the antics of the people in the café, but the laughter was a bit too near tears for my liking, and when she got in bed she couldn't stop trembling.

I held her close to me. I was overwhelmed with a feeling of

134

tenderness towards her. Her body was cold, as if she'd caught a chill; but I knew it wasn't that.

"Darling, don't. You've been overplaying your hand. Try to relax. Lie quiet; you'll be all right in a minute." I didn't know what to say or what to do; but perhaps I did the right thing after all, because she began slowly to get warm; and then after a bit she gave a deep sigh and the trembling quieted down.

I reached up with my free arm and plugged off the light, and we lay for a long time while her breathing steadied and deepened. I thought perhaps she'd gone to sleep; I couldn't see her face, and her hair lay in a cloud across the pillow. But after a long time she said:

"Breakdown in morale. Sorry."

"Nonsense. This morning was to blame."

"Oh, yes. When somebody puts a jinx on your mind . . ."

"Go on," I said when she stopped. "Talk. You can't rub a thing out of your thoughts but sometimes you can talk it out."

"What must I talk about?"

"The ring—and Tracey—and his death—and your life with him —and who can have sent the ring: on and on till you fall asleep."

"I shan't fall asleep that way."

"Well, I'm not your doctor but I should have thought it a good way. We've funked it today. Fatal. Face up. To begin with, tell me why it upset you so much."

"Isn't it obvious? Perhaps I've a sort of guilt complex."

"Guilt complex? What on earth do you mean?"

"Well, I don't know what else to call it." She was silent again for a minute. "Last week you said you were good material for a psychiatrist. Well, perhaps I am too. You remember that day we went riding . . . you told me I was frustrated."

"No, I didn't. I only said you hadn't done what you were capable of doing. It's a favourite opening of the professional seducer —didn't you know?"

She wouldn't rise to that. "At the time I pretended I didn't cotton on—had to. But it was absolutely true. I've been an absolute failure. Somehow you knew."

"Oh, nonsense! You've been true to yourself and the things you believe in——"

"It isn't nonsense, Oliver. And I *haven't* been true to myself. If I had I shouldn't have felt such a desperate sense these last years

135

of—of emptiness, of nonexistence—of the sort of failure when you owe something and can't *begin* to pay." She stirred restlessly. "Tracey's being ill made it worse. One felt so useless—incapable of helping to build anything, because there was nothing to build on. I shouldn't have minded what it was. . . . Something left from yesterday's efforts that could be used tomorrow."

"I know. I know the feeling exactly. But——"

"When the ring came I *had* a sense of guilt. Because since Tracey died there's been a *sort* of ease-up inside me that I haven't allowed myself to think was relief. Nor was it—exactly. Certainly not relief that he was dead but a release from the kind of life that . . ."

"I don't know if you're helping yourself by talking," I said, "but you're doing me a lot of good."

She said: "I think ever since I can remember I've wanted something I couldn't find. Not discontentedly—but to give point to being alive. Sometimes I've thought it was there—but it hasn't been, not really ever—always only the escape; the make do, the second best, the failure. . . ."

I said: "You've taken a risk, marrying me."

"Why?"

"Well . . ." I didn't know quite how to say what I wanted to say: that first she'd married a man who had become a victim of the postwar years; and now she'd married one with a hangover from the prewar years. A bad bargain in both cases. "If you need a meaning to your life——"

She said: "I don't want a meaning just to my life. I want it to be to *our* lives. I don't see why that can't be."

"It can be. I only hope one thing."

"What?"

"That you won't ever be content with second best between us —at least. . . ." I was going to say "at least unless everything between us is bound to be second best for you." But on the brink I funked it.

She said: "When that thing came this morning . . . You know those old melodramas that used to speak of 'a voice from the grave.' . . . Why does one *have* to be frightened?"

"Oh, darling, don't be that. The thing's over and done with. There's nothing more to come."

"Isn't there? How do we know?"

"Well, what can there be?"

She didn't answer, and I was glad. The fear in my own mind couldn't be rationalized out of existence because it didn't have the strength to stand and be examined. I hoped and prayed it never would.

We flew back from Paris on the Saturday because we wanted Sunday free to go prospecting for somewhere to live. It sounded a forlorn hope. We couldn't afford fancy prices and it wasn't specially encouraging to feel that about a thousand others had trod this way before. But I wasn't going to see Sarah start life afresh in my horrible flat. I had a bit of my gratuity left and had saved something over the last two years—more accidentally than by design—and the few hundred pounds might help to pay a premium or something. She wanted me to have some of the money she'd legitimately inherited from Tracey, but I couldn't stomach that.

Sarah had wanted us to go back to her father's house, but I jibbed at this also. Even at the speed things had moved, it would take me a month or two to get used to being Dr. Darnley's son-in-law. So we collected Trixie from Ponting Street and stayed at a hotel. Sunday we house- and flat-hunted. It wasn't quite as depressing as I'd expected: there were one or two just possible places; but we fixed on nothing. We might see something better in another week or so.

On the Monday, I went down to the office. Michael was out, but the Old Man had one or two fairly coy things to say and was really quite nice about it. I determined that when we had our house-warming he should get the first invitation.

During the morning, I rang Henry Dane and apologized for having had to put off the other appointment.

He said: "Well, I hope your problem's solved itself in the meantime."

"No, it hasn't. Nor will it till I make some move. I've a superstitious feeling that you're still the best person to advise me. Could we meet one day this week?"

"I shall be at the courts all today. How about lunch tomorrow? Red Boar at one?"

"Fine. Thank you."

I heard Michael's voice in the outer office and waited for him to come in to see me. But he didn't, and I concluded they'd not told him I was back. After a bit I went into his office and found him using the phone. He raised his eyebrows at me, and I sat on a corner of his desk until he finished.

"Well, old boy, welcome back. Had a good time?"

I replied in the usual way, but his voice sounded rather odd, and after we'd talked for a minute or two I said:

"Something the matter?"

"Matter? What could there be?"

"That's what I was asking."

He went and stood by the fireplace and hunched his shoulders till they looked squarer than ever. "No, I've been a bit worried about one or two jobs that have come up while you've been away. Did you manage on the currency all right?"

"It was a lifesaver. What are the jobs?"

"Oh, they're pretty well fixed now. Nothing very important really. How's . . . Sarah?"

This, too, was queer, this hedging, because nobody usually was more keen to share his problems than Michael. It was nearly a fault. However, I didn't say anything then.

At lunch he'd got an appointment, so I went to a local pub that specialized in business lunches and had it with three strangers. Charles Robinson was in the room at the other end, and he waved in a friendly way; but he didn't come across as he went out.

I stayed in the office all afternoon picking up the threads. I had to ring several people, and at least one of them, a man called Carey, cut me short, saying he'd got an appointment. Perhaps I was expecting too much. Red carpet for returning newlywed. I didn't see Michael again that day because he was on a case that took him out of London, and as I was anxious to get home I left fairly early.

Sarah was waiting for me in the foyer of the hotel, and sight of her threw out the minor doubts of the day. She'd found a flat, or thought she had, and we went that night and took it for three months. It was in Hallam Street and furnished, and was fairly expensive, but we reckoned that with Sarah earning as well as myself we could manage pretty well. Afterwards we went to see her father. Meeting him was still a bit of an ordeal to me. I always

138

felt as if my hands were too big, my collar crumpled, and my aitches as undependable as a comedian's trousers.

The next morning, business took me with Michael to Lloyd's. In the early days, when I saw it all with new eyes, I used to think you could explain quite convincingly to a man from Mars that this was the temple of a religious sect who came to worship here every day. The great glass dome, the painted ceiling, the bent heads, the hushed activity; and in the shrine in the middle the priest sat calling out the prayers and entering up the sins in the Judgment Book. And if by any chance the Lutine bell rang, it meant that the holy spirit was among them, and there was a great stirring and a commotion.

As it happened, it was Mr. Berkeley Reckitt that we had to see, about a report I'd sent in just before I went away; and Michael was anxious to get the thing settled; otherwise, I realized afterwards, he wouldn't have taken me. Reckitt was a thin chap with prematurely white hair and a dry cough. He'd never been a favourite of mine but his firm were our second-best friends so far as business was concerned.

Well, today he carried on a conversation with me, listening to what I had to say and putting the questions he wanted; but he never looked higher than my tie all through the interview. When it was over and we were outside, I said:

"What on earth was the matter with him?"

"Matter?" said Michael. "I don't know. What was the matter?"

"He looked as if I was something very decomposed that his dog had found."

Michael seemed to put on extra speed, shoving his way along. "I expect he was worried. They caught a packet over that fire in Singapore."

"Everybody's worried about something. But they don't need to take it out on me." I stopped, so that after a pace or two Michael had to stop too. "What *is* this, Michael? Is there something wrong that you don't want to tell me about?"

He frowned at me. You could see the indecision behind his scowl. "No, nothing. Come on. It's time I was back."

"Tell me what's the matter."

"Nothing. You're imagining things."

"If you don't tell me I shall go back and ask Reckitt."

"A lot of good that will do you. None of it will do you any good, making mountains out of molehills."

"I think I must be the judge of that."

He hesitated again. "You're asking me to repeat an unsavoury rumour that nobody at all believes in."

"Some people have a peculiar way of showing it."

We began to walk again. "Oh, it isn't that. But you know enough of the insurance world to know that it's worse than a village institute. A whisper starts—and in a few hours . . . People don't believe what they hear. But it's like being told that so-and-so is a smallpox contact. You look at him a bit anxiously next time you see him to make sure you can see no spots. Then in a week or two you forget all about it."

"Well, tell me what particular disease I'm supposed to be suffering from."

We crossed the road, and Michael nearly plunged under a bus. He said:

"You know the Lowis Manor fire. There's a rumour about that your car was seen outside Lowis Manor that night just before the fire started."

chapter 19

Sarah said: "What did you say?"

"Tried to sound like a badly injured man. What else could I do."

"What do you think Michael feels?"

"I think he's embarrassed and annoyed. Embarrassed because he'd got to make up his mind about something and annoyed that a situation has come about whereby anybody can point a finger at a member of his firm."

"You mean he hasn't made up his mind whether he believes you or not?"

140

"Oh, he believes me. It's not in his nature to give room to suspicion lightly. But he must remember that I did behave a bit peculiarly about the fire claim on Lowis."

"What will happen?"

"Nothing very much, I'm sure."

"No, don't put me off. Tell me what you think."

"Well, what can anybody do? If the story's accepted at all it will knock my good name for a bit. But there's no proof."

After a minute she said: "But this man who saw you get into the car. Might he have taken the number? And do you think he could recognize you?"

"Maybe. But if so, why didn't the police follow it up?"

Sarah got up. "I wish . . ." She didn't finish.

"What do you wish?"

She looked at me thoughtfully. "It's a fine marriage settlement I brought you, isn't it?"

"Any trouble is my own fault for not being willing to wait for you. If the money had been paid back first, it would have taken the curse off the thing."

"How did you put off Henry Dane?"

"Said I'd been called suddenly out of town. I confess I do feel a bit fussed about that. I don't see how I can say anything to him now. We're *saddled* with the money, Sarah; unless you decide to give it to a dogs' home. If the negotiations had been begun with Berkeley Reckitt before this rumour broke out . . . But we can't go now and say, 'Please, Mr. Reckitt, I know you're suspicious of us; may we give back the money before we get arrested for fraud?' "

She lit a cigarette. "What I can't understand is how the rumour has begun now. Surely if anything was known, it would have come out at the time, not now, not five months after."

I got up too. I was too jumpy and annoyed with myself to keep up the pretence of being neither; and I told her about McDonald. "I imagined the night of the dinner that he was a bit cagey; but I was upset myself at the time—thinking you were in it—and anyway I didn't much worry what he thought."

"But why should he think all that—just because you made an inquiry?"

"I don't know what he thought. But I've given him reason to dislike me and the thing may have rankled—not so much a

141

suspicion as a hunch. Then when I suddenly married you . . ."

She said: "Even then . . ."

"Perhaps I'm doing him an injustice and the rumour hasn't come from him at all. But who else? And once there's a suspicion there . . . Perhaps he thinks I not only set fire to the house but made you a widow as well."

Her back was to me and she didn't turn. All I could see was the hand on the cigarette. She didn't speak.

I went on awkwardly: "What puzzles me is this rumour about the car, where it originated, and what proof there is of it. Until I know what actual evidence——"

She said: "Don't say that again, Oliver, will you? It's—a rather poor joke. . . ."

I went to her and put my arm around her. "Sorry. Expunged from the records."

"I suppose it was meant as a joke."

"Well, of course. Even McDonald . . ."

She looked into my face. "But if one suspicion exists . . ."

I said: "The only practical thing we've got to worry about is this rumour. Heaven knows it's vague enough as Michael told it me. The question is whether there's sufficient presumptive evidence for people in the insurance world to take notice of it. That's really all that counts."

The next morning, I went into Michael's office and said:

"I've been thinking all round this business. In fact I've thought of nothing else since you told me. There's not a lot I can do unless I hear it, hear this story repeated myself——"

"You know what my feeling is." He chewed the end of his pencil. "Ignore it. Carry on as if nothing had happened. I'm sorry I had to tell you. It's a thousand pities we had to see Reckitt yesterday, otherwise you'd not have noticed."

"Oh, yes, I should. I noticed a change in most people—even in you."

"Did you?" He sounded a bit startled. "Well, you can understand how I feel. It's not because I give the thing a minute's credence. If I showed any sign of worry it was because of its existence. You know what our job is like: we don't carry a stock or a large capital. Our asset is reputation. It's Caesar's wife or you're out of business in a week."

142

"And you think——"

"No, I don't. I think it'll blow over. What you should try to do is keep out of people's way as much as possible for the next few weeks. And when you do meet them, however they behave, act just as if nothing had happened. Particularly to Reckitt, since it was his firm . . . The vast majority of people—if they hear it at all—will say: 'What? Branwell? Oh, nonsense; he's far too straightforward and decent a fellow for that.' And so will Reckitt, if he takes time to think it over."

I said: "Your father doesn't know about this yet?"

"I don't think so. I certainly haven't told him."

"Then keep it from him if you can, will you? I shouldn't want to be the cause of a lot of unnecessary worry."

Michael looked at me. "All right. I'll do my best."

I left then and went out on a job in Hammersmith. Of course it wasn't entirely that I wanted to save the Old Man the worry. I wanted to be saved the unpleasant job of lying to another man I respected. That sort of thing makes you feel guilty after a time even if in fact you're innocent of all the larger crimes.

The job in Hammersmith was to do with some fur robberies, and I plunged into it trying to forget all the rest. I soon suspected that there was an attempt being made by the furrier, a man called Collandi, to get more compensation for his furs than he was entitled to, and I spent most of the day on it. There was some trouble over the books, which he first said had been stolen and then said were at his accountants. He promised to produce them on the following day.

Back at the office I made a preliminary report and began to get busy putting through the usual inquiries about Collandi's past history and general reputation. I thought: this is right in my line of country; set a thief to catch a thief.

The next day no books were forthcoming, but an assessor called Abel had been engaged by Collandi to act for him. Abel was a type I didn't like, as sharp as a needle and a good deal tougher. But by now I was armed with the knowledge that Collandi's reputation was about as shaky as it could be and I said I wasn't recommending any settlement until the books were produced. There was a good deal of blustering and threats of legal action, but it didn't cut any ice, and I left them with the plain issue before them. Once again the underwriter was Berkeley Reckitt, and

143

I wondered if Mr. Reckitt would be able to overcome his repugnance at the sight of my signature and appreciate that I wasn't giving his money away easily.

I was a bit late home that night, and Sarah wasn't in the foyer as she had been before. It was her day for being at Delahaye's, and I thought she might not be back; but I found her upstairs.

Her face always changed, lit up when she saw me. Perhaps it did that for everyone she liked and not specially for me—but it was already becoming the best moment of my day.

Tonight, although the same thing happened, I could tell as soon as I kissed her that there was something wrong.

"You're late," she said. "Anything new?"

"No, thank God. I've hardly seen Michael, and the other people I've had dealings with behaved normally enough. Hello, old girl. . . ." I bent to return Trixie's welcome. "Is she settling down?"

"Grudgingly, yes. She's country bred, though, and doesn't approve of the town. It was the same at Ponting Street, except that she had the run of the house."

After a minute I said: "Was she really your dog, or was she Tracey's?"

"Mine. Tracey gave her to me as a birthday present. But I always used to feel—in a queer way—that her first allegiance was to him. . . ."

As she spoke, Sarah had gone to a cupboard and taken out a couple of bottles. I watched her carefully. I said: "I can't help feeling that Trixie isn't the worst thing on your mind."

She turned and gave me a very searching look: "Am I such a give-away?"

"Pretty well. Yes."

"It wouldn't be any use trying to hide something from you, would it?"

"Not much."

"No. . . ." She turned back to the bottles. "Well, would you like a gin-and-French or a gin-and-French? We have every known variety. Don't you think we might get really foxed tonight? Let's have a hangover from drink instead of a hangover from my first marriage. Then you won't have time to regret you haven't married a really *nice* girl with no past. . . ."

I took the glass out of her hand. "You know the answers to all

144

that. There's nothing I wouldn't have taken to get you. And there's nothing I won't take to keep you. So don't say that, will you? Don't ever talk that way."

She said in the same queer voice: "I got home at five. It's nice living so near. There was a man waiting for me in the lounge. Said he was a solicitor, called Mr. Jerome. Said he had business with me, so I ordered tea and we sat talking among the old ladies, sipping tea and talking blackmail. . . ."

"Look," I said. "Is this——"

She pulled some wrapping paper off the vermouth bottle, screwed it carefully into a ball.

"Mr. Jerome said he was acting for his client—wouldn't give him a name. His client, he said, was interested in the fate of certain monies—Mr. Jerome had the usual lovely way of putting things—of certain monies that had come to me as a result of the unfortunate fire in which my unfortunate husband met his death. Mr. Jerome said the fire was supposed to have happened accidentally; but of course 'among friends' that story just wouldn't wash. 'Among friends' one knew very well what it was all about. Twenty-eight thousand pounds after all was quite a fair sum of money, and his client realized I would like to keep it all. But that unfortunately wasn't possible. Even fourteen thousand——"

"Don't tell it me that way," I said. "I don't like it. What did he want and what did you say?"

She dropped the wrapping into a wastepaper basket. "He wanted fourteen thousand to keep quiet. Like someone saying that an investment in—in wool was a good thing. Stirring his tea and fiddling with his spectacles. And the old lady on the next settee complaining that her toast was burnt. He said he wouldn't have anything to eat because he was a diabetic. He said he had proof of the swindle, and if the police got it I should end in jail. He said the thing had been in preparation by Tracey for twelve months, and his client could show that it had, and his client could prove that I must have been in it as well. He said that this was a nice hotel and rather expensive, he supposed. He said that his client didn't want to be hard on me and that he'd undertaken to leave me in 'undisturbed enjoyment' of the other half. . . . Mr. Jerome went in about half an hour, after thanking me very courteously for the tea. . . ."

"What did you say? How did he leave you?"

"I said I didn't know what he was talking about. I said I couldn't believe there was a word of truth in what he said. In any case I'd have to have time to think it over."

"Good girl. And he . . ."

"I suggested he might come to the flat next Sunday, but he wouldn't do that. He said he'd call back here—tonight."

I drank the thing she had mixed, and thought it out. She poured another, not moving from the table, though once or twice she looked up into my face.

I said: "Did he mention me?"

"No."

"Did he give the impression that *we* had better pay the money, or that you had?"

"That I had."

"Do you feel like a criminal being overtaken by your crime?"

"Yes."

"It isn't hard, is it? You only need enough people to think you are and you start acting like one. If I'd allowed you to stay as innocent as you were a month ago you'd have gone straight out into the lobby and sent the porter for a policeman."

"I nearly did. But the rumour that you heard on Tuesday—I felt I couldn't do anything until I'd seen you."

"What time did he say he'd be back?"

"About nine." She stared at her glass.

"Can you eat any dinner?"

"Not much."

"Well, let's try. Perhaps this isn't such a bad thing after all. At least it's something we can fight. Perhaps we shall have the answer to quite a lot of our questions before tomorrow."

We toyed with the meal and were back upstairs again before eight-thirty. Sarah said Mr. Jerome had been quite definite that they must meet again in the public lounge; so I let her go down and then followed in a few minutes and took a seat in the extreme opposite corner and tried to read *Country Life*. I didn't want to scare him away if he was a timid bird.

The lounge was fairly empty at first, but it filled up towards nine, and I had quite a job to see Sarah's dark curly head across all the other odd-looking coiffures that sprouted between. I suppose the English aren't uglier or more eccentric than any other race; but the public lounge of a hotel makes you think so.

Quarter past nine came, and every time the revolving doors began to move I thought, this is it. Although Sarah had given me a fairly good idea, I saw him paunchy and shortsighted, black-haired and suave. At half past nine, Sarah got up and came towards me. She looked white and tired.

"Something's put him off. He may have seen you and thought it was a trap."

"Perhaps he's just unpunctual. Give him another fifteen minutes."

She said: "You stay here. I'll ask at the desk and then walk round the hotel."

I agreed to that and sat down again. *Country Life* was full of big places for sale—other Lowis Manors—whose owners were able to take the more conventional course. I threw it down and put my hand in my pocket and took out Tracey's ring and looked at it. So far, I'd carried it with me all the time, though I never let Sarah see it again. I felt pretty much on edge, and wondered what the fine would be if I kicked Mr. Jerome down the steps. I wondered what I should do if I had to give up the insurance game. It wouldn't be fair to stay if the rumour reflected on Michael and his father. In a way, with Sarah as my wife, the idea of starting absolutely afresh, perhaps in New Zealand, had a new and exciting appeal. I didn't know what she would think——

A page boy was coming across the lounge followed by a man in a dirty mackintosh. They came straight up to me.

"Mr. Branwell, sir? Gent to see you."

The man was a tall chap, with a thin rather ugly face and prominent teeth. He uncovered them at me as the page boy turned away and said:

"Mr. *Oliver* Branwell?"

"Yes." I got up. "Are you Mr. Jerome?"

He looked at me with a slight frown. "No, sir. I'm afraid not. My name is Barnes. Detective Sergeant Barnes. Is there anywhere do you think we could go for a little private chat?"

chapter 20

I was afraid Sarah would give something away when we met her on the stairs and I introduced him. But although she was under a big strain she was too finely tempered for that. She smiled at him slightly and her eyes flickered away to mine and then looked across the hall.

"Is it something to do with your work, darling?"

"Yes. We'll be about ten minutes. I'll find you in the lounge?"

"I expect so. You don't *want* me, I suppose?"

I looked at Barnes and he smiled deprecatingly.

"No," I said. "I'll be down in a jiffy."

Of course, it could have been something to do with my work. In our room I pushed a chair forward.

"Take your mack off if you're hot. What will you have to drink?"

"Thanks. Thank you; nothing on duty, you know." He folded up on the chair and looked rather apologetic. He wasn't any older than I was.

I offered the cigarette box. "So it's a duty call, is it? Well, what have I done, forgotten to take out a driving licence or something?"

"Thank you. . . . No, nothing like that. As a matter of fact, it's nothing you've *done*, Mr. Branwell. It's really rather a matter of routine, you know; just checking up on a case. It's an old case; one that we've been keeping an eye on, just in the ordinary course of business, as you might say. One or two new facts have come along, and I'm going round picking up a pointer here and there." He got out his lighter before me and stood up to hold it to my cigarette. "We thought you might be able to help us."

"Well. Anything I can do . . ."

Barnes drew on his cigarette and then looked round for an

148

ashtray. "It's that *fire,* you know. That fire at Lowis Manor, when Mr. Moreton lost his life. There are one or two things about it which we've always felt were ever so slightly unsatisfactory, and we wondered . . . I believe you were a friend of Mr. Moreton, visited there, et cetera; knew them all pretty well; at least I suppose that's not too much to assume in view of the fact . . ."

"In view of the fact that I married his widow."

He uncovered his teeth again. They were large and rather yellow. "I wasn't going to say that, but still . . . Oh, thanks." He tapped his cigarette. "When did you meet Mr. Moreton first, Mr. Branwell?"

"It'll be about two years ago. Two years this month. They had an outbreak of fire in his study at Lowis Manor, but they were able to put it out before it did much damage. I was sent down by my firm to assess the loss."

"I see. And was that also the first time you'd met Mrs. Moreton?"

I hesitated and knew the next moment that I was a fool to have done so.

"No. We met once before the war. Just for a few minutes. We'd completely forgotten each other."

"I suppose it was at a friend's house or something—before the war?"

"No. She had a puncture in her car. I happened to be passing and mended it for her."

He dug about in the pocket of his raincoat and took out a notebook.

"Did you—lose touch altogether—or write occasionally—or——"

"Lost touch. I forgot her existence. She forgot mine. She never even knew my name. But I thought you'd come to ask me about the fire."

He grinned apologetically. "Sorry. It's the old flatfoot coming out in me. But it really leads up to how you became a friend of Mr. Moreton's, instead of just a—just someone calling in the way of business, as you might say. . . ."

"I don't think it had anything to do with it. Moreton had been in the Desert War. So had I. We began to talk about it and he invited me to lunch."

Detective Sergeant Barnes made a note. "Pencils are cheap

149

muck these days, aren't they? It's practically impossible to get a decent one, and I can't get used to these ball-pointed pens. When you grew friendly, did he ever discuss the insurance of his house with you, Mr. Branwell?"

"No. Never." Then I remembered that excuse I'd made to McDonald. "Or I believe once I suggested the place was under-insured for present-day prices."

"You knew what it was insured for, then?"

"Well, of course. It's always given on the underwriter's slip when a claim is made."

"Oh, of course. Naturally. What would be the last time you saw Mr. Moreton before he died?"

"About a week before."

"You went down there?"

"Yes."

"On a visit?"

I said rather wearily: "We'd a long-standing date to go to the ballet together. In the end he couldn't make it and only his wife came. Afterwards I drove her home and went in and had a drink with them."

"Did he seem—quite happy then?"

"Happy isn't the word to use. He was always off colour—asthmatic; and he had a bit of a grudge against the way things had turned out for him. If anything, that night he was more cheerful and more talkative than usual."

"What did you talk about?"

"Chiefly about the repairs and decorations he was having done. Is this important?"

"Well, one likes to know; sometimes these little indications . . . Tell me, Mr. Branwell, did you ever see Mr. Moreton go off into a faint?"

"No, never."

"Or look like it?"

"No. Wouldn't his doctor be able to tell you about that?"

"Well, I'm just asking you to tell me about it, if you see what I mean."

"Frankly I don't."

Barnes put down his pencil and picked up his cigarette. He drew at it a minute. He didn't seem discouraged.

"You'll remember the night of the fire, I suppose, Mr. Branwell?

May the sixth. Do you remember what you were doing that evening, whether you were in London or . . ."

"I remember very well. I stood on a chair in my flat and slipped off it and sprained my ankle. I spent the next two days in bed."

"What time would it be when you had the accident?"

"Just about seven."

"You had a doctor, I suppose?"

Careful. "No. It didn't seem worth while. I was hobbling around by the Wednesday."

"So when was the first you heard of the fire?"

"My partner, Mr. Abercrombie, phoned me on Sunday morning and asked me to go down. I explained I couldn't; so he went instead."

"I suppose you—you phoned Mrs. Moreton, or got in touch with her somehow?"

"No."

He didn't speak, but waited with an inquiring look. "I felt there was very little I could do," I said. "Mr. Abercrombie was there to help in any way that was necessary."

"So when was the first time you communicated with Mrs. Moreton—after that?"

"I was at the inquest," I said. "Look, is this getting you anywhere; because it's not amusing me. Can we cut it short and come to the point?"

He looked apologetic for the last time and rubbed out his cigarette. "I don't think I can come to any *point*, Mr. Branwell. You can't, you know, on these sort of jobs. It's a question of accumulating all the material you can and then laboriously sifting it through at headquarters. You probably know that, being a sort of detective—an insurance detective—yourself." He uncovered his teeth again. I didn't smile back. "But if it would assist you in any way I can tell you one of the circumstances which left us a little dissatisfied as to the manner of Mr. Moreton's death. You remember the medical evidence?"

"Very vaguely."

"The pathologist said that Moreton had only about one per cent of carbon monoxide in his blood. You remember? Well, that's no more than you would expect to find in a smoker—herbal *or* tobacco, it's the burning *vegetable* matter that counts. So that left nothing at all for any other smoke he might have inhaled.

Now you remember Moreton is supposed to have telephoned the fire station, and the fire officer claimed they were on the scene within twelve minutes—so that he could only have sent the message when the house was well ablaze. I expect you know where the phone was?"

"I have a general idea."

"It was in a small cloakroom between the main kitchens and the baize door. There was only the one; no extensions. Well, we carefully worked it out. It seemed quite possible for Mr. Moreton to have stayed in one of the bedrooms and come out suddenly, have found the house on fire, and jumped to his death with no extra contamination of the blood stream. But it was impossible, we thought, for him to have telephoned from a room which must have been full of smoke, to have fought his way upstairs, and then to have died with no excess of carbon monoxide at all."

There was silence for a bit. I said: "And what do you deduce from that?"

"We think someone else may have been in the house and done the phoning, perhaps in order to confuse the issue or give the impression Moreton was alive a lot later than he really was."

I got up and strolled to the window. "You're assuming rather a lot. Fires are very capricious. I should hesitate to predict how one was going to burn or how one had burnt."

"It's a little speculative, of course. But it does give room for dissatisfaction. That and other circumstances." He got up too. "Well, thanks for your help, Mr. Branwell. I'll be getting along now. You're here to stay?"

"No. We're moving into a flat on Saturday. I'll give you the address."

"I expect the hotel will have it if I need it, won't they?" At the door he stopped. "Oh, there was one other thing. What make of a car have you got, Mr. Branwell?"

I said: "A Standard 16. The Council offices would tell you."

"Not a new model?"

"Oh, dear, no. Just prewar."

"Go all right?"

"Yes. Fine."

He nodded and went out. I stood and watched him down the corridor. I gave him three minutes before I went to rejoin Sarah.

Mr. Jerome didn't turn up.

152

Loving Sarah just then was like loving somebody under the shadow of a closing hand.

Perhaps I hadn't killed Tracey, with her knowing all about it and encouraging me; perhaps I hadn't set fire to the house to cover up what I'd done. But, like it or not, where the law's concerned it isn't what really happened that counts, it's what certain other people think happened.

In sensible moments I reasoned it out, and so did she. But it isn't always reason that has the last say. The hunch that you're being followed and watched and overtaken, that something is pending, that a sort of circumstantial evidence exists and is being gathered up and made ready for use, that a number of other people know more than you do and so you can't guard against any moves they may make—all these feelings get under your skin and under your good sense and make you jumpy and at stretch.

Yet in my marriage itself, which was something separate, something much more at the centre of things, I found only one flaw. It was that in spite of Sarah's apparent love and loyalty I couldn't rid myself of a sense of impermanence, as if she wasn't here to stay. . . .

The awful part of all this was that it made you feel you *could* have killed Tracey, if this sort of bewitched happiness could come of it and if by doing so it could be made to last. . . . You can't work it out on moral grounds.

On the Friday I met McDonald.

The Hammersmith fur claim hadn't got any further, but Abel, acting for Collandi, suddenly decided to push things along by making a formal protest to the brokers that I was obstructing the claim unfairly. The broker was McDonald, and he passed the matter to Berkeley Reckitt. While I was out on another thing, Reckitt rang through and asked to speak to Michael, though he knew darned well that I was on the assignment. I went out to lunch feeling ruffled and edgy, and knowing I ought to call in and see McDonald sometime during the afternoon. A broker's natural concern is for his client, and it was really up to me to go along and have a chat, explaining why I was holding things up. But I couldn't face the thought of seeing McDonald.

At lunch I met Charles Robinson again, and we carefully

153

talked about nothing but cars and motor-racing. After lunch I went into the men's lavatory with Charles and found McDonald there, in his shirt sleeves, wiping his hands on a towel.

His flabby face changed its shape when he saw me, and he just nodded frostily and went on using the towel. There was nobody else in the place except Charles. I thought now the opportunity was thrust at me I must take it; so much better than a phone call, and a third person present would make it easier.

I said: "I was coming to see you this afternoon."

Perhaps because I didn't feel friendly it didn't sound as friendly as I intended. He gave the towel an extra tug and carefully wiped between each finger. He stared at me and said: "What for?" and then before I could answer he turned back to the basin and picked up a comb and passed it once or twice through his hair.

"About Collandi. I really can't recommend a settlement yet. The whole claim is very unsatisfactory."

"Well, you've made your views perfectly plain in your report. I don't see what good will be served by coming to see me about it."

"I thought I could try to explain to you a bit more fully."

He looked at himself in the mirror. "What is there to explain? There's no doubt about the robbery, is there?"

The tone of his voice got me. "There's no doubt about the robbery. There's doubt as to what was stolen. I don't believe for a minute he ever had any kolinskies or sables."

"You think Collandi's a swindler?"

"I do."

"That's only your opinion, isn't it?"

"I'll change it when I see his invoices."

"Perhaps that won't be necessary."

It was plain what he meant. He was pressing Reckitt to have me withdrawn from the case. From the first words the meeting had gone racing downhill. Charles came across.

"Hullo, what's the matter with you two?"

McDonald put down the comb. "Branwell's suffering from an excess of zeal. Success must have gone to his head."

I said: "What the hell d'you mean by that?"

I heard two other men come into the place talking. Charles put a hand on my arm. "Gently, brothers, gently."

McDonald said: "I should have thought the answer obvious."

154

"I'd like to hear it."

"Well . . . I meant the success you've had in marrying money."

I hit him. I'd really lost my temper and put more weight behind it than I thought. He cannoned into one of the men who had just come in, took a couple more steps, and then sat down on the floor, holding his jaw.

"You damned fool," said Charles, grabbing my arm again.

I knew Marshall and Ainslie slightly. Marshall went over and helped McDonald to sit up. Ainslie, who'd nearly had his spectacles knocked off, jerked them back and made some protest.

I shook off Charles's arm and went over to McDonald. Marshall straightened up excitedly to fend me off, but I only wanted to help McDonald to his feet.

He wouldn't take my hand but went on dabbing at his mouth, which was trying to bleed. The other three seemed all to be talking at once.

McDonald said: "This all fits in with the rest. It's what I might have expected."

"It's what you asked for," I said. "Only I'm sorry because you're an older man."

He rolled over on his knees and got up. His mouth was puffing out but he was all right. He turned his back on me and got his handkerchief out and then began struggling into his coat. Marshall went to help him.

Ainslie said: "Well, I've heard of some peculiar places for a free fight . . ."

I turned then and went out, Charles Robinson following. I supposed I must have looked white or a bit peculiar, because people stared at me as I went through the restaurant. I got out on the pavement, and tried to remember what I'd intended doing after lunch.

Charles said: "If I were you I'd write him an apology. It's not very dignified but——"

"Apology be hanged. He's already had one."

"Well, you don't want more trouble on your hands—especially now."

I looked at Charles. "Do you believe it, this rumour that's going about?"

He flushed. "Should I be here with you if I did?"

I said: "He started it, didn't he, that rumour. I wish I'd broken his neck."

Charles said shortly: "This row won't help you if it gets out. It doesn't matter who provoked it. You're both hot-tempered devils. I'll go back now to see him, before he does anything silly. I'll do my best to keep him quiet."

I remembered where I'd been going then and caught a bus for Hammersmith.

chapter 21

*J*ust outside the Law Courts, Victor Moreton got on the same bus. Everything seemed to be crowding on me that day, and at first I was only aware that somebody had taken the opposite front corner seat and was shaking the rain off his umbrella. A lot of thoughts later, a heavy voice said:

"Good afternoon, Branwell."

I hadn't seen him since the inquest. He looked oversize in the bus, and the grey light made his skin look poor. I muttered some sort of reply.

He said: "Dreadful day. I don't know why all the taxis seem to go off the streets at the first hint of rain."

I put my hand up to my hair and found it wet. "Yes."

"Sorry I didn't write while you were away. Been very busy. I believe Mother wrote, didn't she?"

"Yes. It didn't matter. How is she?"

He frowned. "Not well. The shock . . . I mean to send you a wedding present as soon as I have time to look round." He went on twisting his umbrella round in his fat capable hands. "But this month . . . Of course one doesn't serve on Royal Commissions purely out of altruism; but if I'd known the work involved . . . Have you found a flat?"

I told him. I felt grateful to him just for behaving in a normal way, as if our marriage was a natural thing and not a plan to rob

156

the dead or steal the crown jewels. As the bus raced up Waterloo Place, I moved to share the seat with him. We talked, and I began some apology for not being at his brother's funeral, but he didn't seem to have thought anything of it. I felt much inclined to tell him the truth, to blurt it all out from beginning to end.

He said: "I get off at Hyde Park Corner. Sarah knows where I live. I hope you'll come round sometime."

"Thank you very much. We'd like to."

He made a note of our address, and I rubbed my knuckles, which were sore. "There's one thing I wanted to ask you," I said. "Was Tracey badly burnt when you saw him?"

He looked at me, and you could see the sharp legal mind taking over.

"Badly enough. Why?"

"How did you identify him? Was it quite a job?"

"Oh . . . not particularly. His clothes, his shoes, his figure. It couldn't have been anybody else. What are you suggesting?"

"Did you notice if his signet ring was still on his finger?"

There was a pause. "I'm not absolutely certain. May I ask again what your point is?"

"Would you recognize it if you saw it?"

"Of course."

"Is this it?" I asked, handing him the ring.

He took it and turned it over, looked inside. "Yes. I suppose Sarah had it." He passed it back to me as if he was glad to get it out of his hands.

"This is your stop," I said. "Do you mind if I don't explain now?"

Our eyes met as he got up. "If you want to see me at my chambers you'd better ring my clerk. Or my home address after seven."

"Thanks," I said.

As I watched him moving off across the pavement with his rather in-toed fastidious walk, I realized he was the third person I'd asked that question. Now I'd got the answer.

It was all I could do to think straight about ordinary things; but when I reached Hammersmith, there had been a new development. The thieves had been caught two hours before in actual possession of some of the furs. Abel was triumphant, and I had to share his car as far as the police station at Stepney; but when we went in we found that nothing had been recovered but the cheap skins, compensation for which I'd never been contesting. Abel worked up a good show of indignation when I pointed this out to him; but I felt at my most mulish and left him there no nearer settlement than before.

I got back to the hotel about five. It was early, but I felt too sore and ragged to face the office again that day. By now no doubt they'd have heard of the scuffle with McDonald. News of it would spread the rumour twice as fast.

I didn't really expect Sarah to be in when I got home—she'd said she would take the car and move some of her own personal belongings from her father's home to the new flat—and sure enough the room key was on its hook.

All the same it was the first time, and a feeling of flatness joined all the others as I walked towards the lift. Today of all days I needed her. There was a sheer physical void.

It was one of those self-operating lifts, and I'd just pressed the button to bring it down when a man came to me and said:

"Mr. Branwell?"

He was thin and grey-haired and wore rimless spectacles that clipped on his nose. He looked like a retired bank cashier.

"Yes," I said.

"I wonder if—perhaps a word or two . . . I don't know if your wife will have mentioned me. My name is Jerome."

chapter 22

I said: "You don't take sugar, do you? My wife told me that too."

He smiled, showing a gold tooth and a gap. "Very kind. I carry saccharine. Thank you, sir. Thank you."

I stirred my tea. McDonald had been the first tangible fact. This was the second. I was feeling wolfish.

"You're a solicitor, Mr. Jerome?"

"That is so." He fiddled in a waistcoat pocket and brought out a little round tablet.

"On or off the rolls?"

The tablet disappeared into the cup and left three small bubbles on the surface of the tea. "Off. A gross miscarriage of justice in March, 1931."

"You remember your dates but not your appointments."

He smiled again. "I never keep appointments, Mr. Branwell. I see my clients when the—the impulse takes me."

"You mean your victims?"

"Well . . . There isn't as much difference as you'd think. Terms aren't really important, are they? No, nothing to eat, thank you. I daren't touch it."

I said: "Do you jab yourself with a needle every morning?"

"Yes. One suffers a certain wastage of flesh. It's difficult to find a new place." He buttoned his coat, and the buttonhole needed stitching. "Now, having answered all your questions . . ."

"Not all. Who sent you?"

A page boy came in and walked across the room. "Calling Mr. Inglethorpe. Calling Mr. Inglethorpe." A fat man in a check suit got up as if something had pricked him, and went out with the boy.

Mr. Jerome said: "If I told you that, there'd be no point in my coming . . . would there? The purpose of a go-between . . . But you can negotiate with me in every good faith. I have full power."

"Full power of blackmail?"

He swallowed stringily and put his cup down. "I'm too long used to the wickedness of men, Mr. Branwell. Blackmail, arson, fraud, murder. People commit them whether one likes it or not . . . and we have to consider the consequences. One doesn't necessarily *condemn*."

"No. One makes a living."

"Precisely."

He thought he saw my eyes wandering and looked quickly round. But I was only looking for Sarah. He said with sudden energy: "I'm glad your wife has told you. In the first place we were anxious to save her any embarrassment if she had kept the guilty knowledge to herself. But of course one——"

"Why d'you suppose she had this knowledge and not me?"

"My instructions——"

"Or that either of us had any knowledge at all?"

"Oh, my dear sir . . ."

Four ladies came into the lounge, chattering about a film they'd seen, pulling off their gloves, piling their furs and their bags, talking too long and too loudly.

I said: "And now that she's told me I suppose you feel—quite safe and among friends."

He tightened his lips disapprovingly. "What I feel is a little beside the point."

"And what is the point?"

"Fourteen thousand pounds."

I drank my own tea. "I don't know what you take us for, Mr. Jerome; but you come here with some cock-and-bull story of an insurance fraud and, without any sort of proof either that there was such a fraud or that we were in it, you expect my wife to hand over this money as if you were picking up a guinea for the church funds. When was the last time it was as easy as that?"

He took off his glasses. The mark in his nose where they pinched looked sore. He put them back and refocussed, knowing well enough that my eyes hadn't moved off him.

He said: "My client has ample proof of the fraud. Details of how each of the paintings was disposed of and whose hands they passed through. He also has details of how the fire was prepared. Tracey Moreton was a common swindler. *And* his wife. You—at the very least—are an accessory after the fact."

"Tell your client to come round himself. There's always tea going."

Mr. Jerome got up. I saw he was sweating. "By Tuesday put a note in the Personal Column of the *Daily Telegraph*. Just, 'Accept, O.B.' We shall want the money in cash, but I'll communicate with you later about that."

"And if I don't play."

"It would be a very unhealthy situation. Can you afford to face a police inquiry?"

"Yes, there is that."

He glanced at me. "Don't underrate me, Mr. Branwell. Although I'm getting up in years—I'm well able to take care of myself."

"And if we paid—how long before your next visit?"

"There'll be no other demand. We are not greedy. . . . But in any case, if I may say so, you're not in a position to bargain. I should certainly settle and have done with it."

"You would?"

"Yes, I certainly would."

I watched him go. He walked on his toes, as if it had paid him all his life to tread quietly. His striped trousers were too narrow and a bit too long. As he reached the outer door of the hotel, I got up and followed him.

Dusk was just falling. The crowds were still thick. He walked briskly down Davies Street in the direction of Piccadilly, and when he reached it he crossed to the south side and turned in the Princes Arcade. At Jermyn Street he went east to Lower Regent Street, and walked down to Trafalgar Square.

I'd never done any shadowing before, and I don't know when he first saw me. I didn't much care. I fancy he was making for Charing Cross Station, but he changed his mind and walked down Whitehall. It was helpful of him not to take a taxi.

At Whitehall he bought an evening paper and crossed Westminster Bridge. The rain was coming on again, and halfway across he stopped to open his umbrella. I slowed but didn't stop because it was better to be nearer in the dark.

At the other side he continued along Westminster Bridge Road and then turned to the right. He was a pretty good walker for his age and I couldn't decide whether he was going somewhere or only trying to shake me off.

The streets were poor now, the way they are when you get off the main route, and the rain was trickling off my hair. Mr. Jerome stopped to let a van turn out, and I caught him up a bit more. Was I trying to catch him, I wondered, or was he trying to let me?

We came to a blitzed area where there was nothing but the street going between rubble, and weeds and a hoarding or two, and in the distance prefabs. I put on a spurt and caught up with him and took his arm.

"This isn't your line," I said. "Why didn't you stick to key-holes?"

He tried to pull his arm free. "You'll do no good by following me like this!"

I held him till he came to a stop. He glared at me, his face red and his pince-nez shaking.

"Tell me who you're working for——"

Luckily it was raining and I heard the rubber shoes on the pavement behind me. I must have ducked at just the right moment, because the blackjack followed my head down and I got a stinging thump on the back of the neck that made things blur. I turned and lashed out with my fist and caught somebody in the face. It was the hardest crack I'd ever given anyone, and he disappeared somewhere among the rubble. Then I took to my heels after Jerome.

I caught him under a lamp. By now I'd given up caring whether there was anyone else about, and I gave him a shove that sent him on his knees. Then as he sprawled I grabbed his collar and hauled him out of the lamplight among the weeds and the broken bottles.

By the time I'd come to the shelter of a bit of wall, he was sounding the worse for wear. I propped him up against the wall and took him by the collar and squeezed.

"Now. . . . The name of the man."

"Careful . . ." he got out. "My heart! Diabetic . . ."

"Come on! Tell me."

"Can't breathe. . . ."

"The name of the man."

He suddenly went limp on me and I let him slump. His face was the colour of the wall and I thought I'd gone too far. If he was dead I'd better go, and quickly.

Then a police whistle sounded. I got up, and at the same moment Jerome stirred. I knelt down again and grabbed him by the throat and shook him. His eyes rolled.

"The name of the man."

There were people in a knot under the furthest lamp where the buildings began again. One was a policeman, and he came along the blitzed street staring about him.

Mr. Jerome muttered: "No, my lord. No evidence at all. If we adjourn *sine die* . . ."

For a second his eyes seemed to focus then.

"I swear to God," I said, "that if you don't tell me the name of the man, I'll kill you now before help comes." I gave him another squeeze, and his eyes fairly popped. He said something that sounded like "Hush!"

"What?"

162

"Fish," he said.

"Tell me the name."

"Telling you . . . Fish. Fisher . . ."

"Clive Fisher?"

He nodded, and I let him drop. I took a deep breath and stood up. The policeman saw me. I turned and ran. He shouted and came after me.

I ran through the rubbish and the rubble, jumping and leaping across it; came up with the prefabs as he blew his whistle again; a man came out of a door in shirt sleeves: by the time he'd taken his pipe out of his mouth it was too late.

I was nearly garrotted on a clothesline, and I twisted among the shacks with their bits of gardens and their unseen booby traps. At the back of them was a nine-foot wall, part of the old buildings; I jumped at this but couldn't get a foothold. Run along it, a rat looking for a way out. Voices and footsteps behind; a light from an open door gleamed on a helmet.

A terrier shot like a rocket out of an open window, scuttling at me, barking as if I'd done him a personal injury; it was a pity to disappoint him, and he suddenly went off yelping. I found a lower place in the wall and got over. I ploughed up a steep incline, and then fell flat as a train came roaring along the rails.

As soon as it had gone I ducked gingerly across the rails, picking my steps, slid down the other side. Then I began to run along the edge of the embankment.

They'd lost me. After about five minutes I stopped for breath and the shouts were a long way off. I climbed a wire fence into a cul-de-sac street and walked up it. Two or three minutes later I caught a prowling taxi and directed it back to the hotel.

chapter 23

I'd been a normal person for so long that there was a sense of shock about today. It was suddenly as if all the years of conforming had never been. When I got back to the hotel I was very relieved to see our car parked outside, and I went in and inquired for Sarah. They said she was having dinner. I tried to tidy myself a bit, pushed a hand through my hair, and went straight in.

I must have still looked a sight, because the headwaiter raised his bald eyebrows and two or three other people forgot to be well bred. Sarah half got up when she saw me.

"*Oliver*, what's the matter!"

"I'm all right." I slumped down in my seat, still in a lather like a horse.

"You look frightful." Her eyes searched mine. "And rather frightening . . . What is it?"

I ordered soup. "Where does Clive Fisher live?"

"In Kent. About five miles from Lowis. Why?"

"We're going down to see him."

In between the little I ate, I told her. The only thing I didn't say was the questions I'd asked Victor Moreton earlier. Listening, *she* forgot to eat.

"So you were right," she said.

"Yes. I always felt Clive might have something to do with it, being an artist himself and a close friend of Tracey's. But you put me off. . . ."

"It wasn't because I didn't think the same as you."

I stared at her.

She looked upset. After a minute she said: "If you described Ambrosine Fisher, who would she sound like?"

"My God . . . I didn't think of that. But why on earth did you scout the idea when I put it up to you?"

Sarah stared at a corner of the table, straightened her brows. "Before all this trouble blew up—when you mentioned about Clive—it seemed better to head you off. We were *married*, that was all that mattered. There'd been a fraud, but it was over. Nobody'd benefited from it but me—and I was going to pay the money back. What was the use of making trouble between him and you?"

"Very considerate to him."

"It was meant to be considerate to you. Can't you see that?"

"So that when Mr. Jerome came along, you let me find out about him the hard way."

164

Her head came up. "Do you seriously think that?"

After a minute I said: "No. No, of course not."

"Heavens, I'd no idea Clive would mix himself up in *blackmail*. I've always thought him a lightweight—not above earning a few dishonest pounds, perhaps—but this . . . It's in another class. It's out of character. Or it's out of the character I gave him."

"And Ambrosine?"

"That was another reason. She'd always been in love with Tracey; and somehow, to her, selling the pictures couldn't have been more than a—an act of friendship . . . particularly if it excluded me." Sarah stirred. "At least that's what I thought. Now I don't know what to think."

"Well," I said. "We'll find out tonight."

"What are you going to do?"

"Call on him."

"What will you say?"

"Something lacking in culture. I haven't yet learned to meet my troubles with a stiff upper lip."

She said: "Oh, *don't*, darling, please."

The waiter came across, and we picked through the rest of the meal.

She said: "You make me feel that not only have I brought all this nastiness on you but that I've failed you in common loyalty."

"I didn't mean that. It's only that I'm a bit on edge. But things have somehow got out of hand today."

"I can't help thinking about it. I swear I never connected Clive with Mr. Jerome. Even now I wonder if there's someone behind Clive. It seems . . . You do believe me, don't you?"

Our eyes met. "Yes," I said.

"You see," she said carefully, "I feel if I did ever let you down it still wouldn't come as much of a surprise to you. Or to part of you, the part we were talking about not very long ago. And I should hate that more than anything at all."

She drove because she knew the way. I thought of that other time, years ago, when she had driven me through the dark. And the thought was comforting, because in the middle of all this mess she was beside me, and somehow we had come all this way together; and everything was changed from that other time and changed in a way I hadn't thought possible. But I was annoyed with myself for having let a shadow of that time creep back today—and, more important, come between us for a minute tonight. It was the one thing it mustn't ever do.

We didn't talk much. What we might have to say seemed unimportant until after this interview with Clive. It wasn't half past nine when she drew up near a biggish sort of cottage.

"There's no light in his studio. That's at the back. But I think that's some sort of light in the front, isn't it?"

"You stay here. I'll go along and have a chat."

"Oh, no." She opened her door. "I'll come with you."

There was no doubting what she felt, so I didn't argue. We walked through the drizzling rain up to the door and I lifted the knocker once or twice.

Sarah fidgeted with her gloves, and somewhere in the house a door banged. Then there were footsteps. The door came open and a woman with untidy grey hair looked out.

Sarah said: "Good evening, Mrs. Payne. Is Mr. Fisher in?"

The woman stared at her. "Oh, it's young Mrs. Moreton, isn't it? Good evening, Madam. I'm sorry, Mr. Fisher's gone abroad."

"Abroad? When did he go?"

"About a week ago. I think it was Madeira, on one of those cruises; but I couldn't be sure. He didn't leave an address."

Sarah glanced at me. "And Miss Fisher?"

"She's in Scotland, Ma'am, staying with the Dundonalds. She's been up there since August."

A black cat came round the door and rubbed itself against Sarah's legs.

I said: "Surely if Mr. Fisher was going away for some time he'd leave you word where to find him."

Mrs. Payne looked at me. "Mr. Fisher does what he pleases. I'm only the housekeeper, and it isn't for me to tell him what he should do."

"Where do you forward his letters?"

"They're all here." She made a backward movement with her hand. "Sorry. I can't help you."

I said: "I happen to know Mr. Fisher's in England."

"What you happen to know or don't happen to know is no concern of mine. I'm only telling you what he told me."

The door was beginning to close. I stopped it. "May we come in?"

"Here! . . . What's the idea! *Really*. . . . Mrs. Moreton, I never thought——"

We went in.

Sarah said: "His studio's at the back—up those stairs."

"Well, I've never been so insulted in my life! If you don't go at once I shall phone the police!"

On a brass tray on an antique chest was a pile of letters addressed to him. Three-quarters of them looked like bills. The dates on the stamps covered most of the last ten days.

The woman came up to me. "Get out of this house at once! D'you hear me? Get out!"

I looked over her head at Sarah. "Is there anywhere we can put her?"

"There's a cloakroom here," Sarah said. "It hasn't got an outside window."

"Lay a finger on me and I'll scream the place down," Mrs. Payne said, backing away.

"Open the door," I said to Sarah, and went after the woman.

The minute I laid a hand on her arm, she turned and slapped me hard in the face and let out the most piercing scream I've ever heard in my life. It just wasn't human. I dragged her, kicking at my shins, to the cloakroom and pushed her in. Sarah, who had taken the key from the inside, shut the door quickly and locked it.

I said: "Well done!"

She said: "I don't want to let you down again."

I stopped at the foot of the stairs and came back to her. "Look, darling: you've never let me down. I *know* that. Let's forget it."

I kissed her but she didn't smile.

The studio was a big new room with a glass roof and an Egyptian fresco scene on the walls more sharp-elbowed than anything at the Pyramids. A half-finished painting on the main easel wasn't recognizable. There were two or three steel chairs, an Indian circular table, canvases in a corner, and a few modellings of sub-human life in bronze. I put my finger on the table and it came away dusty.

I said: "Will anybody hear her? It sounds as if we're killing pigs."

"There's another cottage down the road. We'd better not be long."

There didn't seem to be anything in the room that was going to help, but I went across to the stacked canvases and looked through them. I suppose it was expecting too much that he should have left any sort of ready-made proof lying about. The only thing of any significance was a folder of photographs of paintings, presumably taken by himself or some other amateur, and among them was a photograph, exact size, of the small Watteau that had hung in the living room at Lowis. I detached it from the rest.

"There's this," said Sarah as I straightened up.

She'd been looking among a pile of books on a chair and the book she held out was titled "Art and the Cubists," by Valentine Roget. I didn't see the point until she showed me it was a Boots Library book and that it had been taken out under the subscription of Mrs. V. Litchen.

Outside the woman had gone quiet for a minute. I said: "Where's his bedroom?"

"Round the corner. I'll show you. I'm afraid we've drawn a blank."

She went to the door, and I was following her when I caught sight of something in an ashtray on the table. I glanced up quickly at Sarah, but she was already going out. I slipped the thing into my pocket and followed her.

His bedroom had striped yellow wallpaper and maroon silk curtains. It didn't look as if it had been used for a week or so, and it's hard to fake that feel of unoccupancy. There was a desk, and I fingered through some cheque stubs, but for me the zest had gone completely out of the search.

I said: "Did he ever speak of going abroad to you?"

"No. But he has done this before, when he's been short of money—left his house and gone where his creditors couldn't find him."

The woman began again. I said: "We'd better cut it and go. I don't want another brush with the police."

We went back into the hall. "You're not going to leave her locked in?"

"No. You go to the car and start it. When I hear the engine I'll turn the key and come."

168

"Right," she said, and went.

Mrs. Payne stopped as suddenly as she'd begun. It was queer standing there in the hall in the sudden silence. I thought of talking to her, trying to ask her about this thing that I'd found, but somehow I knew it was no use. She'd never open her mouth to me except to scream. I was glad when the hum of the car came and I could unlock the door and go.

The thing I'd found made me feel rather sick. It was a half-smoked herbal cigarette.

chapter 24

I felt ill that weekend. I felt as if I'd got an incurable disease. Sarah tried to persuade me out of it, but she thought I was only worrying about the row with McDonald and the visit of Detective Sergeant Barnes and the fact that we couldn't trace Clive. It was enough, but it wasn't what was upsetting me.

I didn't go down to the office on the Saturday morning. I helped Sarah move our belongings from the hotel and I brought my things along from the flat in George Street. In the ordinary way this would have been an exciting weekend; our first move into a place of our own. But now it all seemed perfunctory, as if it had no meaning at all. I went through it in a sort of bad dream.

All the troubles that had come on Sarah and me since our return from Paris had been outside us; except possibly for a minute or two on Friday evening, the danger of them, the worry of them had brought us closer together. But this was something quite different.

Sunday we spent mostly calling at people's houses, people Sarah knew who might know where Clive had gone; but we got no proof that he was not on his way to Madeira. One man said that he had definitely left on the last Tuesday in October. The first house we called at, of course, was Vere Litchen's, but the place was locked up and the curtains drawn. I wondered if she had gone with him. Sarah said she wasn't giving up but would carry on all through the week while I was at the office.

On the Monday there was a bit of an atmosphere at Abercrombie's, and in the afternoon the Old Man sent for me.

He was quite cordial, and we talked over the Collandi case to begin. Then after one or two throat-clearings he said:

"By the way, I believe there was some sort of fracas between yourself and Fred McDonald on Friday."

"Yes. . . . I knocked him down."

"It's all more than unfortunate, of course. McDonald's one of my oldest business friends."

"I'm very sorry. He made a damned unpleasant remark to me, and I lost my temper."

The Old Man got up and went to the window and polished his spectacles, but he didn't speak.

I said: "I suppose you'll have heard this rumour that's going around."

"I've heard something, yes. The implications naturally distressed me—as they would you. But unless there is something very much more concrete——"

"I hold McDonald responsible for starting it. That was why I cut up rough so quickly."

"Have you any reason to be certain that he did start it?"

"Not certain. I'm pretty sure."

The telephone rang, and Mr. Abercrombie got sidetracked for a minute or two. When he put the thing down, he picked up a pencil and twisted it round and round in his fingers.

I said: "I've been thinking seriously this weekend whether you'd like me to resign from the firm."

He didn't look up. "Don't be absurd, Oliver. We must keep this thing in its proper proportions. A malicious rumour—a hasty quarrel, they can't be allowed to ruin a man's career."

I thought he spoke just a bit too quickly, as if perhaps he'd used the arguments already, to himself. I said: "It won't exactly attract business if you employ a man who's under suspicion for fraud and then uses a thick-ear technique to defend himself."

"The thing will blow over. It must blow over. I'm going to see McDonald tomorrow morning to discuss it in a friendly way. The

170

first thing is to get him to withdraw this absurd charge. If we——"

"Charge?"

"Yes. . . . Haven't you seen Michael? Oh, dear. I thought that was what you were talking about. . . . McDonald has complained of your conduct to the council of the Fire Loss Adjusters."

In the main office a typewriter was clacking.

"What does that amount to? What's the complaint?"

"That you used insulting language to him and knocked him down. As I expect you know, a subcommittee exists to consider any breaches of the rules by members of the association; but of course its purpose isn't really to consider *this* sort of complaint at all, and he ought to have known it."

I said: "Probably he did; but he reasoned if an inquiry got started, all the rest of the dirty linen would come out too."

"I hoped there was no dirty linen to come out," Mr. Abercrombie said dryly. "Anyway we must put a stop to this business before it gets out of hand. I shall see McDonald and if necessary his general manager and make him see sense."

I got up to go. At the door I turned and said: "One thing I'd like to make clear. I'm not going to let Abercrombie's take the rap on my account. Any headaches that may be about are mine alone and I don't intend that any of my friends should share them."

The Old Man frowned. "That's all right, Oliver. I know how you feel. But I'm quite sure that you've done nothing to lower the standards of our profession, so we shall be behind you whether you want it or not."

"Thank you," I said, feeling about as uncomfortable as I'd ever done in my life, and went out.

I didn't do any more work that afternoon. I sat at my desk and drew squares and cubes on the blotter with my pencil. I broke the point and sharpened it, but it broke again, so I chucked it in the wastepaper basket. About five I went home and found Sarah in, and looking rather troubled.

"Any luck?"

"No," she said. "I went to his bank but they couldn't or wouldn't tell me anything. Then I went to the shop in Grafton Street where sometimes he has a picture on show, but they hadn't seen him for two months. After that I called at the London agents

171

of the *Venus*—you know, that motor ship that goes to Madeira—but he hadn't been on either of the last voyages, at least, not under his own name. The same at the Union Castle offices. I find you can go by air, so I'll try that tomorrow. On the way home I called at Vere Litchen's again, but there was no sign of life. I made one or two inquiries; nobody seems to know much about her. . . . Since I got home I've been looking for Trixie."

"Trixie?" I said. "Didn't you take her with you?"

"No. I wanted to get around quickly and so . . ."

There was a minute's silence. "Where did you leave her?"

"In here—as usual."

"You locked her in?"

"I thought I had, but when I came back, I found the catch hadn't clicked properly. At least, that was the way I found it, and I see now it does stick if you're not careful."

She was watching me, and I tried not to show how I felt.

"I expect the door blew open and she wandered out. Have you asked the porter?"

"Yes, but he says he was off part of the afternoon. In any case I can't understand Trixie going any distance by herself. She's absolutely terrified of traffic."

"Had he—I suppose he didn't see anyone come up?"

"No."

I said: "Well, she'll be in one of the other flats. Some old lady's found her wandering about and taken her in for a bone."

Sarah said: "The porter's been round to them all."

I felt suddenly as if I couldn't stand any more. "Look, Sarah, don't cook a meal for me tonight. I'm going out again and may be late. I'm going round to see Henry Dane."

"To tell him everything?"

"Yes. . . . At least I think so. It's getting completely out of my depth."

"I think you're right."

"It's a risk. If Dane thinks we're not on the level, he'll blow the story wide open. But that may come in any case." I told her about McDonald.

"Oh, Oliver. . . . Is there never going to be an end to this?"

"There's got to be—one way or another."

"I wish I was coming with you."

"I wish you were. You don't know how much I wish that. But it wouldn't do. I've got to see him on my own."

Dane was in. I thought I might catch him "between lights." He opened the door himself and said in his dry voice:

"Hullo, Oliver. How did you know I was back? Come in."

"Second sight. In fact I didn't know you'd been away."

"I'd a job in Scotland and stayed over the weekend. Gwyneth is still there."

"I suppose you're just off out to dinner or something."

"Not even something. I thought of poaching myself an egg and having an evening with a book. What will you drink?"

I looked at my watch. "You can give me half an hour?"

"Of course. All evening if you want it."

We sat down.

I said: "I've made two appointments with you and skipped both. This is the result."

"Well, you cancelled the original one to get married, didn't you? It struck me as being a very legitimate reason." He smiled his sardonic smile. "First things first. Cheers."

I drank with him. "That's exactly what I came to see you about, Henry. I'm in one hell of a mess—and partly at least because I didn't put first things first."

The smile faded as his eyes went over my face. Perhaps this week had left an impression.

"How big a mess?"

"Outsize."

"Well, go on."

So I told him.

He hadn't an easy face to read. He didn't interrupt me but stood there most of the time, first filling his pipe, ramming home his tobacco, then leaning with one arm on the mantelpiece, smoking and staring across the room. I thought once I saw his expression harden, but it may have been just the way his jaw set on the pipe. He smoked the way he did everything else, with terrific energy and determination, so that quite often his face was lost in a cloud of blue smoke.

I didn't make a good job of it. You never do when you need to most. And I couldn't put over to another man the sort of feelings I had for Sarah, which had really been at the root of my mistakes.

It took me a good time, and when at last I dried up, he bent and knocked out his pipe and started refilling it. I finished my drink.

He said coldly: "One thing: when you said you'd got in a mess you weren't exaggerating."

I didn't answer. I felt I'd done enough talking.

He relit his pipe. The light flickered over his deeply furrowed face, and I realized as I looked at him that I didn't know him very well after all. I hadn't an idea which way the cat was going to jump.

He said: "There are two possibilities, aren't there? And I suspect you haven't been thinking very clearly about either of them. In any case I suppose you realize that if this gets out—and you say it's getting out—you might as well take up market gardening right away. The insurance world won't have any further room for you."

"Yes, I know."

"We all make mistakes. Good God, I've made some woeful ones. But this lot . . . First you commit burglary. Then you fail to report death and arson. Then you compound a felony. And finally you commit a misdemeanour. It would be laughable if it weren't pathetic. How d'you suppose the business world would carry on if everyone started acting like you?"

"I don't suppose anything. I'm a misfit and I know it."

He gave me an unfriendly look through the smoke. "I'd like to meet your wife—get her story too."

"What d'you advise me to do?"

"There's only one thing to do. That's go straight to the police and tell them everything you've told me."

"I was afraid you might say that."

He said: "There's no need to register disgust. I'm the one who should be doing that. When you take up market gardening and find the bulbs interfering with your sex life I hope you'll let some other horticulturist into your confidence at an earlier stage."

"I'm sorry, Henry. Really I am. But as for the police—perhaps it's some sort of leftover from my youth—but I just can't see myself going to them and spilling all this."

He began to walk about the room. "You see, man, you bring this to me, but it's far out of my reach already. These two very different possibilities, for instance. In either case it's a matter for the police to investigate. Whether you stay in or out of the in-

174

surance world is small beer compared to the other things at issue. If Tracey Moreton is alive——"

I said: "Oh, for God's sake . . ."

"Well, that's what was in your mind, wasn't it?"

After a minute I said: "Yes. . . . I don't know. I suppose so."

"If he's alive, it's very much a police matter, and only they can handle it. If he's not, it's still a police matter because of the other suspicion that exists—though I don't know how seriously they hold it."

"I wonder what evidence the police have got."

"Against you? Very little, I should say, or they would have acted differently."

"So you suggest I should go and supply it."

"Not much harm ever came of telling the truth."

"Can you pick me a nice big sentimental sergeant?"

Dane frowned. "Oh, I know it won't be pleasant. But you've put over the story to me. And although you're a friend of mine, I'm not easy game."

I did a bit of room-pacing for a change. He poured himself a drink and put a perfunctory splash of soda in it.

I said: "No. I'm too much in the dark yet. You see I'm not only risking my own skin; there's Sarah to consider. It's possible that some sort of a charge of fraud or conspiracy could be pinned on her. Heaven knows what might not be pinned on her yet. That's what scares me stiff."

"And d'you think you're making her any safer by sitting on this thing until it blows up?"

"No. That's why I came to you."

"For advice? But you don't like my advice."

"I don't like it. I might take it."

He said: "Have another drink before you go."

"No, thanks."

"Do the Abercrombies know anything of this?"

"Nothing except the rumour."

"Which everyone within a half-mile radius of Leadenhall Street has heard."

"Apparently."

"I think you owe something to them."

"I'm *very* conscious of that."

We talked for a bit. I still didn't know quite what his feelings

175

were. I think all the time his brain was working over what he'd
been told.

After a long time he said: "When can I meet your wife?"

"Almost any time. Make a date and I'll fix it."

"No, give me your phone number. I'm not sure how things will
work out for me this week. Gwyneth said she'd be back on
Thursday, but when there's golf one never knows."

When I left, he stood at the door watching me till I got in
my car and started the engine. Then as I moved off he turned
and went in.

I felt disappointed, but I couldn't exactly have said why. Perhaps it was that he'd not made an offer of personal help. Nor had
he given me any crumb of comfort. I could have gone to the
police without his advice.

Perhaps I should have been relieved merely that he accepted
the story in its entirety and not quibbled over the details. But
when you feed something to a lion you expect it to roar.

chapter 25

*T*rixie didn't turn up. I could see it was worrying Sarah a lot
more than she would own, and it wasn't merely the loss of the
dog. She reported it to the police, and for the time being we
had to let it rest there.

I didn't see Mr. Abercrombie on the Tuesday. I saw Michael
two or three times but he didn't mention anything. Unlike his
father, he was a bit distant, didn't meet my eyes more than he
could help, kept his shoulders hunched and his brows vee'd in a
perpetual frown.

On the Wednesday I got a brief report through on Fisher, but
it told me nothing about his finances that I couldn't have guessed
myself, and it certainly gave me no clue as to where he might
be found.

Just before lunch the Old Man came in to see me. He said: "Oh, Oliver. . . . No, sit down, sit down. This will do me very well. I was just going out. . . ." He sat and crossed his long thin legs and stared over my head at the map on the wall.

"Have a cigarette," I said. "You remember we smoke the same brand."

He smiled as he took one, but I thought he looked old and tired. He said: "Well, I have some news for you. I saw McDonald yesterday and again this morning. He's agreed to withdraw the complaint he made to the council of the F.L.A.A."

"Oh," I said in surprise. "Well, I'm very glad. You—must have a lot of influence with him."

"No. . . . I made him see that there is no really appropriate body . . . I—put it to him that there was only one way of settling the matter, and that is as informally as possible."

"How?"

"He's agreed that there should be a meeting between you and him as soon as we can conveniently arrange it—to discuss outstanding differences."

I rubbed my chin. "Don't think I'm not very grateful; but it seems to me that the outstanding difference between us is that he thinks me a liar and a swindler and I resent it. How is that going to be bridged?"

"Well, it won't be *except* at a meeting, will it? Obviously, of course, not as a meeting between just the two of you. But I thought if I was there, and McDonald's boss, Rawson, as well, we might be able to see the thing through in a friendly way."

"I certainly can't say no to that. When is it to be and where?"

"My idea in the first place was over a meal, but after talking with McDonald I do feel that perhaps the *implications* of the quarrel are too serious for that. It's better that the thing should be thoroughly well aired." The Old Man uncrossed his legs and hesitated. "So we decided, provisionally, on Saturday morning. That's if it's agreeable to you. Mr. Reckitt has suggested that we meet in his office, which can be looked on, as it were, as neutral ground."

I began to see that there were strings to this arrangement. "Reckitt knows about it, then?"

"Yes. I was forced to discuss it with him. We thought it a good

177

idea to meet when there will be nobody else about and it will give rise to no further rumours——"

"Will he be there?"

"He may be. Though he may not consider it of sufficient importance to be worth his coming up from the country." I didn't believe that. Mr. Abercrombie studied my expression. "There is one other thing. In view of the fact that McDonald had already *made* his complaint to the F.L.A.A., I felt it my duty to invite a member of the council to come along. It'll be all quite informal, of course, but it won't be altogether a drawback to have somebody absolutely impartial on the scene and unknown to either of you."

"And have they accepted?"

"Yes. There's a Mr. Spenser, from Birmingham, happens to be in town this week. He's a past president of the association and a very *reasonable* man. I think you'll like him, and I think it will be for the best that way. It's to everybody's benefit that this unfortunate affair should be hushed up—but it would be to nobody's benefit to give the impression that we had anything to conceal."

About an hour later, Dane rang me up. "I've seen your wife," he said without preliminary.

"Oh? When?"

"I'd half an hour free so rang her, and she came round to my office. We had a long talk and she's just gone."

"Satisfied?"

"Quite reasonably."

I said: "I suppose you wanted her on her own."

"Well, naturally. I think we should meet again now, you and I. Are you free for lunch tomorrow?"

"Free enough. I haven't taken your advice."

"No, she said not. Well, we can discuss that. The Red Boar at one?"

"Thanks."

That night I was late, and Sarah had a meal ready. I thought that already in this short time the flat was showing signs of her occupancy. It wasn't just the pair of long black gloves on the bookcase, or the solitary carnation surviving from those I'd bought her the day we got back to England, cut down and down now till practically only its head stuck out of the wineglass

178

on the table. It was something much more subtle, an air of personality and possession that a gracious woman can give to a place just by being in it.

Of course the smart boys will say that was sentimental and commonplace; but I hadn't ever had it before. I'd not known what it was to be welcomed before, so it wasn't commonplace for me. Nor with Sarah did I think it ever would be.

She was holding my face in her hands, pushing it far enough away to see the expression. "What is it, Oliver? Something more?"

"No." I smiled at her. "Just a recap. Let's eat."

There was no report of Trixie, and, although Sarah had been out again today, she'd found nothing to help us in our search for Clive.

Over the meal we dropped it and talked about the things it would have been natural to talk about if all had been well. But it didn't really work.

At last I said: "So you went to see Henry Dane."

She was sitting on a stool before the fire, and she leaned forward and pushed a bit of coal further back where it would burn.

"Who told you?"

"He did. He phoned when you left."

"What did he say?"

"Nothing much. I'm lunching with him tomorrow."

"Oh."

I waited. "What did you think of him?"

She straightened her back and curled her hands round the edge of the stool.

"He seems all right."

"Did he ask you for your side of the story?"

"Oh, yes."

"And what didn't you like about him?"

She looked up briefly and smiled.

"Oh, I think he could be very nice. But we nearly came to blows."

I sat up. "*Why?*"

"Well, darling, if I ever have to stand trial for murder I shan't expect a much fiercer cross-examination than I got this afternoon."

"But what did he say? What did he ask you about?"

"Oh, he was polite enough in his own way. It seemed quite funny afterwards—this business of 'Where were you on the night of the fourteenth?' I never really quite believed they did it that way."

I got up. I felt dumfounded and furious. "Tell me what he said."

"Must I? It was the obvious sort of thing. When had I first met you? What were the state of my relations with Tracey at the time? Why did the first fire not come off and when had Tracey first told me of his intention to burn Lowis Manor? When did I tell you about it? When did the idea of double-crossing Tracey first occur to us? Did——"

"Good God," I said.

"How often had we met in London unknown to Tracey? How much was Tracey's life insured for? Why had I taken the trouble to create an obvious alibi in Yorkshire if I hadn't known Tracey's intentions and *also known yours?* Did I seriously expect him to believe that we'd not corresponded for four months after the fire? Why did we *suddenly* decide to get married, and what was the compulsion? How often had I put you off coming to see him? On and on and on, till I could hardly think straight."

For a bit there seemed to be nothing I could say. I made a movement towards her, but she got up and turned away.

"I came home feeling pretty limp. But afterwards, when I thought it over, I was glad it had happened."

"Glad?"

"Yes, I . . ." She stared at me with a queer dark sort of expression. "In a way, being cross-examined like that helps you to get your mind free of a lot of—of deadwood. It helps you to see and realize things you never have before—even if they're unpleasant things."

"Such as?"

She didn't answer.

I said: "I'm terribly sorry, Sarah. I'd no idea at all that he'd be like that."

"I know you hadn't. It doesn't matter. Perhaps it's all to the good. We've been shutting our eyes to some things too long."

Thursday morning I was busy because the Collandi fur case was being heard, and I didn't get away until nearly one. It was about twenty past when I entered the Red Boar and saw Henry Dane in his usual corner.

Before I left that morning, Sarah had made me promise to

180

keep the meeting civilized, and for my own sake I was going to do my best. She had been thoughtful and restrained all through the evening and I knew she hadn't slept well.

I said: "Sorry I'm late" as I sat down at the table. Dane was an ugly man in some lights.

He put down the *Times* and said: "Copper's up again. There seems to be no end to this stock-piling. What'll you drink?"

I suppose I must have ordered something, because the waitress came back with a glass. There was already quite a fug in the place and I didn't light a cigarette.

He stared at me keenly. "I hear you've got a date with Mc-Donald and others on Saturday morning. I asked you along today because I wanted to know if possible what line you intend to take when you meet him."

"I haven't decided yet."

"I suppose you know the whole thing's going to come out, do you?"

"Maybe."

"I don't think there's very much maybe about it."

I said: "You tell me."

He looked at me for a second, dispassionately. "They don't like to do things officially in the insurance world. Reputation means a lot. Black sheep are bad for business. So when one crops up he's put away as decently and as quietly as possible."

"And that's the blueprint for Saturday's meeting?"

"Not necessarily, of course. Its chief purpose is to compose a quarrel and to get at the truth. But if the truth has a nasty flavour to it . . ."

The waitress came up and we ordered some stuff.

He said: "I suppose you know that this man from the F.L.A.A. is going to be there on Mr. Abercrombie's insistence. I had a few words with him over the phone this morning."

"Abercrombie?"

"Yes. He has a very high standard of rectitude, you know, and I think that, although he's very much attached to you, he feels keenly his responsibility to the F.L.A.A. as one of its senior members."

"If he thinks that's his duty I wouldn't dispute it."

Although food was coming at any moment, Dane began to fill his pipe. "Your wife's told you about our talk yesterday?"

"She did," I said curtly.

"You did well for yourself when you married her, didn't you?"

"What the hell d'you mean?"

He stopped and looked at me over his pipe. "What a man you are for prickles. No wonder McDonald got in your hair."

"It's just a funny prejudice I have against my wife being treated like a jailbird."

Down went the old bullet on the tobacco. "My good fellow, you can't judge a woman by hearing about her from a man who's in love with her. I'd got to judge for myself. I've known decent worthy men in love with designing little bitches, but to hear the men talk about them you'd think they were all that was pure and holy."

"And what great thoughts did you have about Sarah?"

"She'll do."

"Thanks."

"In a way it would give me pleasure to prosecute her for something. Until she lost her temper yesterday, over some trivial thing I said about you, she was as cool as they come Even then she stood there answering me back as sharp as whipcord. Never a hesitation. Sign of a thoroughbred."

The waitress came just as he got his matches out. He put the pipe regretfully on the table and took up his soupspoon.

"You've a queer way of showing your approval," I said, but feeling a lot better

He finished his soup in about half a dozen mouthfuls. "You know, you've only yourself to blame for this mess. Your wife tried to take part of the blame but it didn't work. You're too hasty, Oliver. In everything. Sometimes it's a good way to be. But not always. You *jump* to the conclusion that a woman like your wife would connive in arson and fraud. Then when you find out that it isn't so, you turn on all your damned charm and *rush* her into marriage. You knock down a broker and nearly murder a blackmailer; and where does it get you? Why, one dip of the flag and you'd charge bullheaded at me this morning."

"No, I wouldn't. Your compliments have disarmed me."

He looked at his pipe but didn't pick it up. He smiled slightly, without showing his teeth.

"Nevertheless I'd like to help you both, because it grieves me to see a fundamentally honest person like yourself drifting on the

182

rocks when so many cheap-Jacks and shysters know just enough to get by. That's why I'd like to know just what way you intend to behave and what you intend to say to these men on Saturday morning."

"To tell you the truth it no longer seems as important as it did."

"That's only because you're out of focus."

"I don't know McDonald's case."

"Well, I do. Or part of it."

"Have you seen him?"

"No, but I know someone who has. It was your inquiry about the insurance on Lowis just before the fire that started it."

"I thought so."

"Then apparently he met you at a dinner a day or two after the fire and noticed you walked with a limp and that your eyebrows and eyelashes were singed. He mentioned that at the time, partly as a joke, to a friend of his. After that he says he more or less forgot all about it until last month when you married Sarah Moreton. Then he went to see Reckitt and discussed the whole thing with him, and they decided to employ a private snooper, who found the man who'd seen someone get into a black Standard 16. This fellow was a poacher, who wouldn't come forward to the police; but he didn't object to a pound or two on the quiet. He couldn't remember the number of the car but he remembered the letters, and when the detective took down photos of six men he picked out yours. Then the private snooper found a Mrs. Smith or Smyth, who had the flat above yours and admitted she dressed a bad burn on your arm the day after the fire. At this point apparently they decided they'd done enough so they called off the snooper and handed this information to the police."

"Very public-spirited of them."

"I think it explains the visit from your friend Barnes. It's highly probable you'll get another after Saturday's meeting. I shouldn't be surprised if everything that happens there gets to Barnes's ears. So if you haven't made up your mind what you're going to say on Saturday I suggest you don't leave this pub until you have."

chapter 26

*F*riday began quietly, and I thought it was going to be the calm day before the storm—not the storm itself. Perhaps something in Sarah should have warned me.

I left the flat about nine-thirty and got to the office just before ten. At lunch I saw Charles Robinson, and he said: "Mind if I come along in the morning?"

"Do you want to?"

He half smiled. "Material witness. . . . But seriously, I'd like to be there if you've no objection. Moral support, you know."

I said: "Of course I've no objection. Thank you."

In the afternoon things were slack, and I had a legitimate reason for knocking off early. I called in to see the Old Man and arranged to meet him and the others at eleven o'clock the following day, in Reckitt's office. I got home well before five, and let myself in. Sarah wasn't there, and I went into our bedroom because sometimes she left a note to say what time she'd be back. The note was there all right.

Dearest Oliver,

I think I've been terribly slow to understand what has happened. I am going off on my own to see if I can get things straightened out, for your sake and for mine—and for everyone's.

Darling, don't worry if I'm not back for a night or two, and please don't try to follow me. This is something I've got to do alone.

Your
Sarah.

I read the note twice and turned it over and examined the back and then read it twice more. Then I looked round the room and there was no one there. She's gone, I thought.

A tray was set for tea, but it would take too much thinking to make it. I poured myself a drink and picked up the note again. A night or two, I thought. And don't follow me. I went to a drawer and took out a new packet of cigarettes, but didn't light one. I stood in the middle of the room quite purposeless. I went in and washed my face and put cold water round the back of my neck. Then I came out with the towel in my hands and went to the telephone.

Dr. Darnley was in. I said: "Have you seen Sarah today, sir?"

"No, I haven't. Where are you speaking from?"

"The flat. It doesn't matter, but she said she'd be back early. I wondered if she'd taken her car."

"I don't know. You might find out at the garage."

"Thanks, I'll try there."

I tried the garage but there was no reply. Then I rang up Victor Moreton at his chambers. His man said he'd just left. He was going out of town for the weekend, but I might catch him at his home in about twenty minutes. I rang Henry Dane and found him in.

I said: "What did you tell Sarah the other day? Did you tell her my own doubts about Tracey's death?"

He said: "Certainly not. Why?"

"But from your questions, could she have got a pretty good idea?"

A pause. "Yes. Possibly that."

"I thought so. Have you seen Sarah since?"

"No. What's the matter?"

"Nothing." I rang off.

I rang Victor's flat but there was no reply, so I fetched my car and went round instead. He lived in Belgrave Place and I got there as he was going up the steps. We went up together. I thought he looked a bit peculiar when he saw me, a bit on the defensive.

"Have you seen Sarah today?"

"No."

"Or heard from her?"

"No, I haven't, Oliver."

He was the only one who hadn't asked why. "Have you seen her at all this week?" I asked.

He let himself in, and I followed.

"She called round at my chambers yesterday afternoon."

"What did she want?"

"She—wished to discuss certain problems with me. After all I'm still her brother-in-law and her trustee."

"Did she say what she was going to do today?"

He toed across in his dark suit and striped trousers, and opened a glass cocktail cabinet. It was a magnificent room, a little flamboyant for him.

"Drink?"

"No, thanks."

He poured himself a whisky-and-water. "She came to discuss certain—problems with me. She put forward some ideas of her own which frankly I considered—*monstrous,* untenable. She advanced what she considered were evidences that these ideas, these fears were not unsubstantial. I gave her my views and she went home—at least I suppose so."

"And did she say what she was going to do today?"

He looked at me as if the whisky didn't taste good. "She gave me some idea. . . . She also expressly asked me not to tell you."

"Look, Victor, this has gone beyond a joke."

"It has for all of us. I'm sorry."

In the light from the window, I could see that he looked worried and pasty. I said: "She's my wife. She's gone off like this, leaving just a note. I've no more idea than . . . And *you* know."

He put down his glass and met my stare. He looked bull-necked and fat. And formidable. "I can't help it. I'm *sorry,* but I can't help it. I've given her my word, Oliver. . . . And even if I hadn't I wouldn't tell you."

"Why not?"

"Because—until I hear more from her—or even then—I don't think it's a thing that ought to be told."

I didn't leave it at that, of course; I stayed and argued with him; but he gave nothing away. I felt pretty desperate, but he wasn't a man to be trapped into some admission that he didn't want to make. The only thing I got out of him was that he wasn't going off for the weekend as planned, and he promised to ring me if he heard again from Sarah.

Going back to our flat it wasn't really out of the way at all to turn up Prentiss Street, and I thought I might as well see if there was any sign of life from Vere Litchen. I didn't really expect anything, having drawn blank so many times over so many things, and I could hardly believe my eyes when I saw a light in the house. I stopped suddenly, and a taxi-driver shouted at me as he passed. There was just room by the curb between two other cars.

Nobody answered when I knocked. I wondered if it was just Dolores back, or perhaps burglars again. I knocked a second time and louder, and then a third. Almost before I'd let the knocker go, the door opened and a small red-faced, fair-haired man looked out.

We stared at each other. I said: "Are you Mr. Litchen?"

He blew out a breath of relief.

"No. . . . I thought you were. What do you want?"

"I wanted to see Mrs. Litchen."

"Well, she . . ."

"It's very urgent."

"What name is it?"

I told him and he went doubtfully in, leaving the door ajar. I pushed it open far enough to step into the little grained-oak-and-chromium hall. I thought, I'm always pushing my way into people's houses: it's becoming a technique. And what good does it do me, as Henry would say. Music came from the living room; it sounded like jive; I heard Vere Litchen's voice.

He came out, and his face twitched when he saw me in the hall. "Sorry. Mrs. Litchen can't see anyone tonight."

"I'm sorry," I said, and went past him into the living room.

She was in a sort of green thing, long and soft and flowing, like a house coat only more so; it didn't leave a lot to be puzzled out. She had her back to the door, was turning over the record.

"Has he gone?" she asked.

"No," I said.

"Look," said the man nervously, "what's the big idea? I told you she wasn't seeing anyone. . . ."

She turned, and her painted little face was as hard as wood.

"The man from the Prudential. I'm sorry, we're not interested in insurance tonight."

"Nor am I especially. I want to know if you can do me a favour."

She stared at me, turned back to the gramophone. In a second

187

or two, a piano, artificially deepened in the bass, began to beat out a jungle rhythm.

"I told you she wasn't seeing anyone," said the man, fingering his collar.

I went over to her. "This is pretty important to me. Do you think we could possibly skip the old grudges?"

"What do you want?"

"I want to get in touch with Clive Fisher."

She leaned back against the gramophone and whistled soundlessly. "Why should I know? I'm not his keeper."

"You're a friend of his. I'm very anxious to find him."

"You're spoiling this piece. Roger, show the—gentleman out."

Roger put a hand on my arm. "Come along, old man. She's told you she doesn't know. . . ."

I looked at him. "Go away."

He went away.

I said: "Where can I find Clive?"

"Try the lost-property office. Or the seamen's home."

"When did you see him last?"

She yawned. "About a month ago, if you must know. We saw each other at a party. Roger was there, weren't you, Roger?"

"Yes."

"You've seen him since then."

"What makes you think that?"

"There was a library book of yours at his cottage last Friday. The subscription had only been renewed the week before."

"That doesn't tell you where you can find him now, does it?"

Something began to go queer inside me. I said: "I've only one advantage in this argument, and that is I wasn't brought up the nice way."

Red spots began to burn in her cheeks. "Roger, my little mouse, have you any guts at all?"

"None that would help you," I said.

The record came to a stop and clicked off.

"Why don't you tell him and have done with it," Roger snapped. "I'm not a prize fighter."

"If you touch me," she said, "I'll scratch the skin off your face."

I said: "I'm about at the end of my tether. I've *got* to force this out of one of you. I don't want to break up your room. . . ."

188

Roger blurted out: "He's at the Fin de Siècle nearly every night."

"You fool."

"Well, I'm not getting in a roughhouse just to cover up for Clive! You told me you'd finished with him—months ago—— And all the time, I suppose——"

"You fool, d'you believe everything *he* tells you——"

"What's the Fin de Siècle?" I said.

"It's an artists' club in Chelsea. It's a sort of dining club where people meet."

She said: "So you got away with your clumsy bluff."

I didn't answer, but went to the phone in the corner and opened a book beside it. The number of the Fin de Siècle was there, and I dialled it. Roger plucked at his bottom lip and stared with doubtful jealous eyes at Vere, who took a cigarette out of a jade box and lit it. I watched them as I waited.

"Fin de Siècle." It was a man's voice.

"Is Mr. Clive Fisher there, please?"

"I don't know, sir. I'll just see." After a minute, Vere put on another record and turned up the volume, so that the room was bursting with the wails of a tenor saxophone. "No, sir, he's not here yet."

"Are you expecting him?"

"Well, he's here most nights."

"Thanks." I hung up and stared at Vere. Then I got hold of the phone wires and pulled at them till they broke. I walked towards her. She backed away and snatched up a brass ornament. But I only put the receiver down on top of the gramophone.

When I got out in the street and into my car I found I was soaked in sweat. Perhaps being like that didn't come natural to me after all.

chapter 27

*T*he Fin de Siècle wasn't far off Pimlico Road, an oldish Victorian house, and the only thing that made it different from the rest was a monogrammed "F/S" over the fanlight. When you got inside, there were a couple of uniformed men to take your coat, and upstairs was the main eating part, which was two rooms with a connecting corridor and a snack bar at either end.

To get in you had to be a member, but I asked for Clive Fisher and when they said he wasn't there I said I'd an appointment with him. They asked me my name; I said Victor Moreton, so one of them took me upstairs and I sat in a corner of the dining room and waited.

There was hardly an inch of wall in the club not hung with sketches and pastels and portraits; I wondered if some of the members paid for their meals that way. It was a quarter to eight now and the place was nearly full. There was a good bit of corduroy and dandruff about. Yet most of the members seemed to have plenty of money to spend on drink, and I guessed some of them got their livings in plebeian ways and worked off their artistic leanings after hours.

At eight o'clock a decadent-looking youth sat down at the grand piano in the further room and began to pick out self-conscious tunes on it. The music came through into this room by way of a loud-speaker. At five past eight, Clive Fisher came in.

They led him straight over to my corner, and half the people evidently knew him because he had to talk and joke on the way. So he was nearly at the table before he saw me and I got up to greet him. He gave a jump of surprise, and I suppose that was the moment when he could have disowned me and got me turned out. But he'd been in too many shady deals to be able to assume innocence without a second thought. And while he hesitated, the attendant moved away.

190

I said: "I wasn't sure what time you usually got here."

He glanced round the room, I think just to make sure Victor Moreton wasn't there. Then he said in his high nasal voice: "What a coincidence. I was only thinking of you the other day."

He looked just the same as ever: healthy and pink-faced and rather womanish and bold.

I said: "I've been thinking of you a lot. Join me at a meal."

He hesitated again, and then sat down uneasily. "How's Sarah? I suppose you're settling down now?"

"Not as quickly as we hoped. Have you been out to your cottage since last week?"

"No. . . . Why?"

"We called there last Friday."

"Oh . . ." He glanced at me sulkily as the waiter came up.

I said: "You order, I'll pay." And when he'd done so: "We went straight along there after Mr. Jerome called."

"I don't know what you're talking about."

"You should. He told me you sent him."

He knew then that the fences were down: up to then he'd been wary, hoping. There was hardly a movement in his face, yet his whole expression changed.

I said: "What *made* you send him? It was a pretty bad mistake, wasn't it?"

Clive picked up a roll and buttered it and ate it, greedily as if he was hungry. After he'd swallowed it he said vindictively: "Jerome's still in hospital. You'll be lucky to get away with that."

"So will you."

He eyed me: "If you're thinking of some of your strong-arm stuff here it won't wash, Branwell. You've chosen the wrong place."

"I can always wait for you."

"I'll take care to leave with friends."

At the table next to us two people were arguing about Salvador Dali.

I said: "You must have been pretty hard up to show your hand this way."

"So what? What are you going to do about it?"

"That depends on you. I suppose you realize I know all about you?"

He hesitated, picking up another roll; glanced at the people nearest; you could see the indecision crawling across the face. "Well, why should I be done out of my share?" he said suddenly. "I worked for it."

"Your share being fourteen thousand pounds?"

"Why not?—now."

"You were only a helper—like Ambrosine. You got paid for your work."

"Helper be damned! I was—well, never mind. . . ."

"Probably you suggested it," I said. "It seems more in your line than his."

He didn't speak.

I said: "I can imagine Tracey sometime saying, 'I'd burn the place down before I'd sell those pictures.' And you saying, 'Why not do both?'"

He shrugged uncomfortably. "I'm not ashamed of anything I did. We live as we must. Before you throw stones at me, think about yourself and Sarah. It's perfectly obvious . . ."

"What's perfectly obvious?"

"Well, I was fool enough to believe Sarah knew nothing, that Tracey had kept it from her, as he said he had. Then when she married you it began to look different, didn't it? I sent Jerome along that first time just to see the lie of the land, to *tell* her about Tracey if necessary, to point out what might happen—the disgrace, the loss of *all* the insurance money, the mud that would stick to her and to you. But she didn't need any telling. . . ."

The meal came but we didn't begin to eat.

I said: "When you set fire to the place, why didn't you clear out at once?"

He looked at me and laughed shortly. "Oh, no, you don't get that dog to bark. I was in London."

"Any proof?"

"You bet."

"And what went wrong?"

"You're the insurance hound. You tell me."

I said: "I suppose you know I was there that night."

He looked up, really startled. After a minute he said: "What are you trying to sell me?"

"Probably a ticket to Madeira—if you can get one before the police catch up with you."

His hand fumbled on his knife. His fingers were long and flat with the nails cut close. "Don't talk to me about the police. Any minute I like, I can put you on the run, Branwell. You're in this, both of you, up to the eyes. Why shouldn't you pay me half the money? It's better than having to part with it all and having to face the police yourselves."

I said: "Isn't it about time you stopped telling yourself fairy tales? The police know all about this. I'd spoken to them before ever Jerome turned up."

I said: "What happened to the originals of the paintings you copied for Tracey?"

I don't think Clive had enjoyed his meal. I think it had stuck in his chest.

"They're far away—where you can't reach them."

"One isn't."

He looked up at me. "The Foster?"

"It was a mistake to sell it in England, wasn't it?"

"You seem to know all about it."

"Well, there's such a thing as export licences, if the owner wants to take it home. Was that first fire a rehearsal or did it go wrong?"

"What do you think?"

"I think it was a bit of both, just to see if it was as easy as you thought—but chiefly that it went wrong. What made you go in for this sort of thing—an artist like you?"

The place had emptied rather quickly. The pianist in the next room was ambling his fingers over the piano like a sleepwalker.

"Have you tried to live on what a painter can make? You get kicked around in the gutter for forty years—when you're dead somebody discovers you and the dealers make a packet."

"You must have had a good many profitable lines before this."

He said: "I don't believe you were really there that night. I don't see how you can have been—unless . . ."

"Yes, I was there. So don't you think it's about time you told me the rest?"

He sat for a minute uneasily stirring his coffee. "I don't know what you mean——"

"Did you start this blackmail racket all by yourself, or is there someone else in it?"

"Why should there be? Anyway, what difference does it make?"

"It could make a lot——"

I hadn't heard the man come up behind me. "Beg your pardon, Mr. Fisher; you're wanted on the phone."

It was one of the attendants from downstairs, a big chap, not the one who had shown me in here. I looked up and saw that the other one was just inside the door.

Clive said: "Who wants me?" I could see a sudden glint in his eye.

"Mrs. Litchen. She asked me if . . ."

Clive began to get up. I said: "Vere Litchen hasn't got anything that'll help us. Send word you'll phone her later."

Clive sat down again, but he, too, glanced towards the door. It's queer how quickly the feel of a place can change. There were only six other diners in this room now; two in a corner and four at the bar.

The other attendant must have had a signal because he came in and up to the table. The big attendant said: "Mrs. Litchen sent word, sir, that this—guest you've got . . . wasn't invited by you."

"Nor was he," said Clive petulantly. "He's come here—throwing his weight about."

"She said we was to see the manager about it, but just at the moment Mr. Browning's out." The big man turned and looked at me. "This is a private club, you know. You've no right in here except on the invitation of one of the members. That's the law."

I said: "Mr. Fisher and I have had a meal together. It's a bit late for him to complain."

"But I *do* complain," Clive said quickly. "This man came here under a wrong name and forced himself on me. He thinks he can get away with anything."

"That's what Mrs. Litchen said. She said he'd been——"

"Well, what are you going to do about it?" I asked.

The piano had stopped in the other room. The youth who'd been playing came through into our room and ordered a drink at the bar. He sat on one of the stools and combed his fair hair back with a hand.

The big man said: "I'm afraid we shall have to ask you to leave."

"And if I don't?"

"Then we'll have to take steps, like."

Two more of the diners were going. The youth stared across at our table curiously and made some remark to the man at the bar. I took my time and thought things out. A roughhouse here wouldn't hurt Clive. I'd learned a good bit. But there was still one thing, and the most important.

I said to the big man: "Perhaps we can make a deal."

He didn't budge. "That's up to you, sir."

I said to Fisher: "There's one question I'd like you to answer me. If you did I might call it quits—for the time being."

You could see he was very uneasy. He'd taken the chance Vere Litchen had given him; but he was afraid of what I'd say in front of the attendants. In the end he decided to risk it.

"There's no harm in asking."

I said: "Who comes to your cottage now and smokes asthma cigarettes?"

He turned his coffee cup round but didn't pick it up. A very peculiar expression crept over his face.

"Tracey—*did*, of course."

"And does he occasionally get up out of Lowis churchyard and smoke one with you still?"

He parted his lips in a humourless grin. After a minute he said: "What's it worth to you to know?"

"Whatever it's worth to you to get rid of me."

His eyes went round the room but he didn't look at me. There was a spurt of talk from the people at the bar.

Fisher said: "Why don't you go down and see?"

"Where? To your house again?"

"No. . . . To Lowis Manor."

"You seem to forget it was burnt down."

He pushed back his chair.

"Not all of it," he said.

chapter 28

A clock was striking nine as I left the Fin de Siècle. There was only one obvious thing to do and I did it.

A light fog had come down while I was indoors, but in Kent it was no more than wet roads and a drizzle. There was a moon somewhere, for the night was not really dark. Traffic lights and traffic were with me, and I made good time; but it seemed a week, a nightmare when you *must* open a door and are afraid of what's beyond.

I felt cold and curiously alone. If Sarah had been with me it would have been different. But she'd gone. I felt as if something had happened to her, so that already, instead of my having seen her twelve hours ago, days had passed. Still more, that days would pass before I saw her again—that our marriage and our life together were a sort of delusion which had only a few thin strands binding it to reality—no root, no foundation that would last. And part of the fault was in me, but most of it was in circumstances that, as always, operated outside our control. And the bitterest trick of all was still to be turned. And it was my privilege now to turn it.

As I came through Sladen and turned up the lane to Lowis, my heart began to thump. It was the first time I'd been to the manor since. "There's the old stone-built hall," Michael had said, "and of course the stables. And part of the kitchens were saved."

For some reason, I hadn't counted on the gatehouse. It was a shock, like seeing something you never expected to see again. I drove past the lighted windows and stopped the car exactly where I'd put it in May. I got out and my hand fumbled with the keys and nearly dropped them. The trees were dripping. I climbed the hedge in the same place and made a stumbling way round to the drive. It was all the *same:* that was what surprised me, the holly hedge, the garden. As I turned the corner of the drive, I could see a light. . . .

Just for a second I got the feeling that the fire, too, and everything that came after it was a sort of confidence trick and that I could make out the low straggling shape of the house, the tall grouped chimneys and the timbered walls, the overgrown yew and the irregular windows with their leaded panes; and that when I went up to the door, Trixie and her owner would be waiting to greet me. Then the feeling passed and I blinked my eyes and could see that where the house should have been was a great gap. A tooth had been pulled out of the countryside. Nothing else was marred, but all else was marred because of it. A sharp wall or two made edges in the dark that the trees couldn't copy. The stables were unlighted and the old hall: the light came from the back of the house.

I went slowly across the gravel drive and came to the place where the front door had been. It was like some of the houses I'd seen in the Falaise pocket. A wind blew where no wind should have been. I stepped over the threshold among the rubble and the weeds. There were bits of flooring, treacherous, pot-holed; planks across a crater which must have been part of the cellars. You could just pick out the design, the layout as it had once been. The body had been here, and the broken balustrade . . . across there the stairs and the door to the kitchens. . . . It was rooms at the back, attached to the old hall at the back, that had escaped. The light was in an upstairs room.

Staring at it, I nearly fell, groped my way to a solid wall, an unlighted window. This was new. Something had been bricked in to make a solid front. I traced it with my hands and then with my eyes. There seemed to be no door here. The light was nearly above me. My hands were sticky with sweat.

Not far from where I was standing, a big piece of charred timber reared itself like the muzzle of a gun. There seemed to be no door anywhere along the front. This was the no man's land, left to the grass and the weeds to cover over the worst scars.

I tried the window. It was a sash window and slithered up without much sound. As I put my foot over the sill, a dog began to bark. It was Trixie.

I waited a bit to see if she would quiet down, but she went on.

I slid my leg over and climbed in. Immediately, all around me in the indoor air, was the heavy smell of herbal cigarettes. I stood there and straightened up. I wasn't in a room but in a passage. At the end of it were stairs leading up, and at the top was a door with a crack of light underneath. My own breathing didn't seem to be working properly.

Trixie wasn't upstairs. Trixie was downstairs somewhere, shut in a room. You could tell that by the tone of the bark. Suddenly she stopped. The place was suddenly quiet. It was far more silent than the damp night outside. I went up the stairs, climbing the stairs leaden-footed, like a deep-sea diver. I put my hand on the door handle, but for a second couldn't turn it. I was more frightened than I'd ever been in my life before.

Something worked in me at last, and the handle turned. I went in.

It was part of the old house, you could tell by the beams, the window; used as a living room now; fire burned in the hearth; a radio; papers and a cushion on the floor; it was empty. There was another room beyond, half lit, the door open; you could see a chair, the corner of a bed.

I thought at first there was complete silence except for the crackling of the fire, but then it wasn't so. I heard it. I heard his breathing again.

I shut the door behind me. There was a stick behind the door. I picked it up in my sweaty hands, went across the room. I don't think it was for attack. I needed defence, just as I'd needed it once before, to fend off the unnamable.

A voice said: "Who is it?"

Sarah's voice.

So she had faced it. Gladly, perhaps; welcoming; off with the new love. . . . I'd known it. Somewhere, some deep-laid doubt had known it all the time.

I went in, stood by the door, holding it and the stick. Sarah was standing beside the bed. In an armchair was an old woman. Dim light from a shaded bulb. The furniture made gaunt shadows. With sudden panic I swung to look behind the door. No one.

Sarah said: "Oliver! How did you . . . We didn't know. . . ."

The old woman said: "You're just in time."

It was Mrs. Moreton.

198

I said: "Where's——" And stopped as Sarah raised a sharp hand.

Mrs. Moreton said: "Your—wife . . . your wife has been here two hours persuading me, insisting, dictating terms."

Sarah said gently: "Oh, my dear, you mustn't say that. Persuading, perhaps. . . . It couldn't be more than that, because I knew in the end you would see it as I see it. It's as much a duty that you have now as ever in the past. Loyalty isn't something only within a family. . . ."

It was Mrs. Moreton breathing like that. I stared at her and *stared* at her and then stared at Sarah. I'd never seen Sarah look so tired, so drawn. Her hair was lank, perspiration on her forehead. . . .

"Loyalty," said Mrs. Moreton, and coughed, and took a minute to snatch her breath. "Loyalty should be in thought as well as in act. Ever since you met this man, ever since he first came to the house, your—your allegiance was divided. You let Tracey down when he *most* needed help—not in a common way—oh, I know there was no misconduct. But the betrayal of sympathy, of understanding. If he'd had it from you—wholeheartedly—the worst calamity . . ."

"My understanding," said Sarah. "Where was his before ever Oliver came to the house? You woke and discovered the first fire and suspected it, quarrelled with him about it, lied to me about the quarrel, made an excuse. Where was *his* trust in me, preparing that fire, making me a dupe; or *yours*, discovering it and then helping to hide the truth. That was before I ever saw Oliver. And——"

"I hoped it would stop there. He was my *son*, Sarah. *I* couldn't tell you, and I didn't press him to tell you; hoping as I did . . ." Mrs. Moreton stopped and sighed, got slowly to her feet. "Oh, well. We have been over this before. I'm ready to go. . . ."

It was then I truly saw the ruin that she was. Her hair was colourless, smoky white, like in people of great age. She'd fallen away to bone: cheekbone and wristbone and long jointed fingers. She struggled for every breath.

"Mrs. Moreton . . ."

Sarah made a quick gesture to stop me, but Mrs. Moreton turned. "You've come at the end of a battle, Mr. Branwell. Sarah has been fighting hard for you—and only for you. She's had no one else in mind. I'm tired of fighting, and—so I have lost."

199

Vast relief was creeping into me. Like blood coming back. Like hope. I gave room to it reluctantly, scared of being wrong; watching Sarah, trying to get ahead of all that had happened in two hours, to take my cue. My knees felt like jelly.

Sarah said: "I've been trying to tell Mrs. Moreton how it has been with us ever since she sent Tracey's ring, how one thing has piled on another, so that now you're likely to be ruined and perhaps arrested too. I've been—trying so hard to convince her that I played fair with Tracey and that we'd both do *anything* to save his good name if it can possibly be done. As she did. As she has done all along."

I said: "*You* were in the house that night?"

Mrs. Moreton met my look without a flicker. "It was my responsibility—all of it."

"Oh, *no*," said Sarah impatiently. "It's *not* true, and you know it. And the end—that was an accident. The purest misfortune."

"What happened?" I said. "Why were you here? Good *God*, I can't believe it!"

The fact that I was really upset may have touched her some way. Her gaunt face looked a bit softer. "You can tell him about it, Sarah, when this is all over."

"No," said Sarah. "You tell him now—as you told me."

Mrs. Moreton put her hand on the bed. "You've gained your point. What more is there you must insist on?"

"No. . . . It's because he's come," said Sarah. "You've said you like him. Really, at heart. *Tell* him."

"He'll hear it. He knows all that it's necessary to know. I'll trouble you for my stick, Mr. Branwell."

I held it out to her, still stupefied. "Where are you going?"

"To London. Sarah wishes me to make a statement to the police."

The old lady went out. As Sarah came up to me she stumbled and I caught her arm. "Oh, darling . . ."

She shook her head. "Not now. I'm all right."

At the second door, Mrs. Moreton was waiting for us. "What else is it you want him to know?"

Sarah said: "That it was my letter that brought you back before the fire. I'd written to her, Oliver, on the Thursday saying we were going away for a holiday. I thought nothing of it; I didn't know Tracey hadn't told her. It made her suspect. . . . Ever since that first fire she'd been anxious, watching him, afraid he might attempt it again. So she came back on the Saturday, got here about seven, found Tracey here, just leaving."

There was a short silence. The bones in Mrs. Moreton's face were so strong they might have been a man's. Her face had a kind of nobility, a hard unattached look, like a death mask.

She said: "When I got here, he had his coat on, was going to the stables for the car. I almost knew then by his face when he saw me. I told him I had come back for the weekend. He said it was impossible, there was no staff, no food in. I said I could quite easily get Elliott back—he lives only four miles away. Tracey stayed on with me, trying to hide his impatience, thinking perhaps I could still be persuaded to go. He pretended to phone Elliott and then came back and said he couldn't come. I know that wasn't true; Elliott has never refused me anything. We were here more than an hour. I went upstairs to my room. Tracey followed me, wanted me to go to Yorkshire with him. I refused. By then my asthma was coming on. He said I must be—out of my mind to risk my health for a silly fad. I said my fad was my suspicion of what he intended to do. . . . Then he—lost his temper, said—unforgivable things and shouted at me that he had already done it, that the fuses were already lit when I came in; in another hour. . . . I think he thought I might give way then, but I didn't believe him. I didn't understand. I thought he was trying to frighten me. Still in anger he went into his own bedroom, began dragging out some curtains which had been in a drawer. I followed him, almost as angry as he—in the end I caught his arm— I'm strong . . . *was* strong and have a strong will. We struggled and fell. We both fell. Tracey underneath." She stopped for breath. She was telling it as if it didn't any longer belong to her, was something held at arm's length in her memory, beyond emotion. "I think I fainted. . . . At least when I could move it was nearly dark. The lights wouldn't work. I'd hurt my arm. I— struggled into the kitchen to try and find the main switch. Then you rang the bell. My only regret since is that I didn't stay in the house with the fire. . . ."

I cleared my throat. "And after?"

"Does that matter?"

"You'd hurt your arm."

"I walked over to Elliott's cottage. He dressed it for me. I spent the night there."

"What did you tell him?"

"I told him the truth. . . ."

We stood in complete silence for a minute. I looked at Sarah. You could see the strength in *her* tonight.

I said to Mrs. Moreton: "I wish it had been almost anyone else."

She didn't speak but turned and went slowly down the stairs.

chapter 29

I got the car somehow, brought it round to where the front of the house had been.

Thinking of it, I suppose I should have realized it couldn't be as easy as that. I should have taken charge, have done it my own way. Then perhaps we might have avoided the rest. But I didn't have time to query the play; the pieces had been set for me when I walked in. And just at that moment I felt as if nothing mattered except that the thing I feared was not true. I felt as if I'd come from some Harley Street physician with a new life in my pocket.

They were waiting for me in the fine drizzle. Trixie yelped and wagged her tail. In the half light, Mrs. Moreton was gaunter than ever—a curious look of fatality about her—as if she was going to the gallows. I opened the door for her, but for a minute she didn't move, grasping her stick and looking at me.

She said: "We're an old family, Mr. Branwell. In six hundred years we were not distinguished except in a certain standard of behaviour, something handed down, grown with us. We've kept to that standard—with surprising fidelity. Such a family is like an old tree—it has, I believe, a—a value, inherent, that's always greater than its parts. Its honour is worth something by any assessment—even today. I tried to preserve it. If you think badly of me, try to remember that."

She got in. Sarah made a move to follow, but Mrs. Moreton waved her to sit in front. Trixie scrambled in at the back.

For a second when I got in, I didn't start the engine. Sarah looked at me. I said in a low voice: "How did you work it out?"

"Henry Dane mentioned the breathing. You should have *told* me. Please start."

As we turned out of the gatehouse, I saw her put her hand to her face. "What's the matter?"

"Nothing. I'm about all in."

"Shall we stop?"

"*No.*"

"Can't we go to Tonbridge or even Sladen?"

"No. Mrs. Moreton—it was the only condition, that it shouldn't be anywhere local."

We came out at Sladen. Through the moving screen wipers our headlights made the houses moon-faced, peering. In the mirror I could see the tall quiet figure in the corner of the back seat. I didn't know how much she could hear or what she thought. Especially what she thought.

"This asthma. She never had it before. . . ."

"Oh, yes, if she was in Kent in the pollen season. May and June. Not otherwise. But now it's been like this ever since, she says. The shock, I suppose. Her father had it all his life."

On the better road I put my foot on the accelerator. Sarah's sense of urgency had passed itself on to me. Sarah turned. "Is your breathing better?"

Mrs. Moreton said: "It will do."

I suppose that was the moment when I should have had some hunch, should have realized and foreseen.

Sarah said to me in the same undertone: "I went to Shanklin first. She left Victor's on Monday. I suppose she called at our flat then, took Trixie. Victor thought she'd gone to the Isle of Wight. Coming here afterwards was a guess. I only got here at seven. I knew the one chance—the only chance was to get her alone."

"I still don't know how . . ."

"At first she denied everything. But I knew *her*. I knew that if she could be made to understand . . . fully—all that I felt, that we felt, all that was at stake. She and I had been very *fond* of

203

each other until this happened. I'd never seen her since my marriage to you, to explain, to put things straight in her mind. She'd got it all so twisted. There's no evil in her, Oliver. She sent the ring, I know; that was the one thing done in bitterness and resentment. But that was Clive's fault. She's often visited him since Tracey's death, and after we were married he tried to put all sorts of suspicions into her head. She'd no idea of *his* part in the fraud, or he of her presence at the fire. But I think he got to know there was something wrong and played on that. It's been *her* tragedy more than anyone else's. . . . The one thing I didn't count on was Victor."

"Victor?"

"He was always her favourite. She says that if this comes out it will affect his career—in Parliament—or his chances of becoming a judge. All along her greatest anxiety has been for him, to protect him. I thought I'd lost. I thought I couldn't move her."

"How did you in the end?"

"I knew too much. So much fitted. I threatened that if she didn't go to the police and tell the truth I'd make a statement myself—to the papers as well as to the police. I said that if you were going down she would as well—and Tracey's memory and Victor's good name. I'm not very proud of what I said."

I put my hand over hers for a moment.

She said: "I made her see that this way would mean the least publicity. I promised her that this way *we'd* do all we could. Need it be made public, Oliver?"

"It's a police matter. But I don't see why it should. They can hardly prosecute her. If I make a statement as well, I don't see what more need be done."

We turned out into the main London road. There was silence then for a while, except for the hum of the car and the hiss of the tyres on the wet road. It was a strange drive, the strangest I've known. I was uncomfortable, ill-at-ease. It came in my head then to query whether this was the safest way or the only way to have done it; but I decided it was all right. Sarah knew what she was about. And she knew Mrs. Moreton better than I did, sensed perhaps that her victory might not last.

In the back, Trixie began to whine. I looked in the mirror and saw that Mrs. Moreton had moved to the other corner.

I said: "Sarah . . . that note you left."

204

"I'm sorry. It wasn't—explicit. But it couldn't be. I couldn't be sure then. This was something I had to face alone."

"I thought . . ."

"What? That I'd let you down?"

"No."

"Won't you ever feel sure about that? Have I failed you in some other way?"

"*No.* Good God, no. I was afraid—that Tracey was alive. . . ."

"Oh, *Oliver*. . . . I thought when you——'

"That was the chief thing—like a nightmare Now that hasn't happened nothing else seems to matter. So long as I haven't lost you."

After a minute she said: "In no possible case would you have lost me. That's what I want you to know."

I looked at her. "I think I realize that. For the first time. Sometimes it's fantastically hard to believe what you most want to believe. Well, there're no doubts any more—and there never will be, Sarah. Can I promise you that? Can I try to—tell you about it later?"

I saw her face. "There's no need."

There wasn't much traffic about, and I know it happened just above Farningham. The rain had stopped and the road was straight and wide, and I suppose we were doing about fifty. Some flicker of light from a cottage made me glance in the mirror to see if it was a car behind. Then I saw that Mrs. Moreton was no longer in her corner. I shifted my head to see the other. As I did so, there was a violent gust of wind, a scared yelp from Trixie; a cry—and then a cry from Sarah—the car swerved even before I braked, the open door like a sail; braking skid and scream of tyres; let off brake, too late; we'd spun right round, were going off the road. Hedges and a tree rushed madly at us; through them and over; something smashed into the engine and the night turned in a somersault of flying fields; then crash.

I'd got out of the car somehow, and what I heard was Trixie barking. I got up on my hands and knees and saw the bulk of the car lying on its side—and the dog barking. The grass in the field was heavy with rain, and I know I wanted to lie down in it to stop my head from throbbing. I crawled to the car and it was all dark. Trixie was still inside.

"Sarah!" I said.

The wing had been wrenched off, and the front wheel looked like the wheel of a racing car. I pulled myself up by it, and it turned in my hands. I moved round the front of the car. Through the starred windscreen I could see Sarah's face. I had a sudden impulse to be sick.

I crawled round to her side, but there seemed no way to get at her because her door was now undermost. Trixie was scuffling in the back, and I saw her lick Sarah's face. The sunshine roof. I groped about and found a big stone and began blindly to hack at the roof. After a couple of minutes, I'd made a big dent but no break in the metal. I hadn't got the strength. I was struggling under some weakness that seemed a part of the fatality of the moment. Events had come full circle. I'd first met her in a car and was to lose her in a car—in darkness and futility and pain. This, and not Tracey, was to separate us; a blind accident, frustration at the last. Something was running down my face and I didn't know if it was sweat or tears.

I got another stone, sharper, and tried again. The metal split: I could see the wood strips of the frame. I pushed my hand in and wormed my fingers round, but couldn't reach the catch. I hacked at the wood but could not budge it, attacked the roof in a new place, made a second hole.

Even then it wasn't easy. The catch was rigid, as if jammed; my wet fingers slipped on it. At last it turned; but then the roof had to be lifted before it would slide back. I couldn't get the right leverage. Somebody was panting in the darkness. I pushed my other hand through and pulled with all my strength and the thing moved. Then it slowly slid open, and in another second my hands were on Sarah's hair. Not dead. In fact she stirred as my fingers touched her face.

In a queer way that shook me out of my own shock, I knew then there was everything still to lose. In a panic I began to talk to her, stroke her face, try to revive her; shouted angrily at Trixie because she wanted to wriggle through, at last got my hands under Sarah's armpits, tried to drag her out. She wouldn't come. The second time I pulled at her, she groaned.

It seemed to be one of her feet that was stuck, or at least somewhere below the knee. Then I heard voices and shouted back.

It was somebody out of one of the cottages, a young man with spectacles. He came slithering down through the broken hedge, stopped a minute staring, came on and saw me.

"I say, there. Are you all right?"

"My wife," I said. "She's hurt and I can't get her out! Can you fetch a doctor—and an ambulance—at once?"

It was at that moment I caught the glint of Sarah's eyes.

She said: "Hullo . . ."

"Sarah . . . Are you . . ."

"I'm all right, Oliver."

"Any—pain?"

"My legs feel a bit queer."

"Oh, Christ, darling, it was my fault: I didn't realize, and she jumped and the car skidded and—and . . ."

"Yes, I know. What happened to her?"

I thought the young man had gone, but he'd come round to the other side of the car and swung himself up on to the top. The door was free, and he shone a light through it down into the car upon Sarah. After a minute he said in a different voice: "It's the dashboard—been crushed right down. But I think we can manage it. I'll nip home for a crowbar."

I said: "Get a doctor. Are you on the phone?"

"No," he said. "But the place next door is. Don't worry. I've sent my brother to do that. . . ."

chapter 30

I was twenty minutes late for the meeting. They were all there waiting for me, and it was pretty clear some of them weren't too pleased at having to wait. Reckitt had turned up, and Rawson, McDonald's boss, and the two Abercrombies, and Charles Robinson and Spenser, the F.L.A.A. man from Birmingham. Spenser was a red-faced chap of about sixty with a way of closing his eyes unexpectedly in the middle of a sentence. Reckitt had sent out for coffee, and everyone was standing round drinking it and chatting. Michael came straight across to me, and asked me if I was all right. I said yes, I was all right.

I don't remember much about the way the thing began because other thoughts were in my head, and I was still feeling queer at times. I remember taking a seat just by one corner of a desk and seeing McDonald at the opposite corner and Spenser behind it, where I suppose Reckitt usually sat. The others had settled as they pleased, and Spenser had set the ball rolling by saying something about family squabbles being no excuse for rather solemn meetings like this; but he understood the case raised far more important issues than a scuffle in a lavatory—then there was a disturbance and Henry Dane came in. Apparently nobody expected him and there wasn't a chair for him, but he wouldn't have one brought and stood by the fireplace leaning against the mantelpiece and filling his pipe and scowling.

They started talking about the brawl, and I know Charles Robinson joined in; but all the time I was thinking about last night when I had my arm round Sarah and we couldn't get her out, and the man came back with the crowbar and at first I wouldn't let him use it because I was afraid of injuring Sarah's legs more. And Sarah kept asking about Mrs. Moreton, as if she was important; and then someone came along and shouted that there was a woman dead on the road half a mile back.

McDonald was saying: "If Branwell thinks I've some axe to grind or old score to pay off he's mistaken. Perhaps it's unusual for a—a broker to concern himself closely with investigating a possible fraud; but in the circumstances it seemed my duty to go on with it. The suspicious facts had come only to my notice. Either I did something about them—personally—or I ignored them, in which case I was surely letting down the things we stand for as a special business community, whichever branch of it we happen to be in. As for the rumours—if they got out they were not of my deliberate spreading. He surely has only himself to blame."

So then he began to speak about how he had felt and what he had done.

. . . When the ambulance came, they decided the easiest way to get Sarah out was to put the car on its four wheels again. They did it as gently as they knew how, six of them altogether; my heart and my stomach went with it as the car moved. There was a little jolt at the end. The morphia hadn't had time to work. Then they got her door open and prised the dashboard up. As they lifted her out she said: "Our proof's gone, darling. What we wanted so much."

. . . Spenser had asked me something. "I'm sorry," I said.

"As I mentioned when we began, Mr. Branwell, the only purpose of this meeting is to try to clear up these points as they are raised. Could you help us now by letting us have your view on them?"

Everybody was waiting. The cold coffee had stuck in my chest, and I felt sick again. I avoided Henry Dane's stare. (And I'd said: "What does that matter? Oh, darling, what the hell does that matter?")

"My view on them. . . . McDonald's got his facts right but his inferences wrong."

Spenser shut his eyes. "D'you mean you don't deny that you were on the scene of the fire that night?"

"No. I don't deny it. . . ." I made an effort to concentrate, trying to forget last night and think of today, trying to think of the effect that admission was likely to have.

Then, abruptly, I went on to tell them the rest, disjointedly, just as it came into my head.

It was queer, saying it out baldly like that. None of my reasons for doing anything seemed quite right, although they'd seemed logical enough at the time. For the first time, I realized what a mess people must get in in a court of law. Perhaps the law is wrong altogether, basing itself on the idea that people are reasonable human beings. Reason's only a thread in the warp and woof of conduct.

At least, feeling as I did that morning, there was no temptation to justify myself. I knew I'd made a muck of things, but I didn't know until I told it just how bad it was. But I didn't care any more.

I got through it somehow but stopped short at last night. I wanted to keep Mrs. Moreton out of it. It was my behaviour they were interested in, not hers. Besides, if I started talking about the accident it somehow seemed to be demanding sympathy, and that was putting the wrong slant on it. That was why I'd told Michael he mustn't say anything to the others.

When I finished as far as I was going, I got out a cigarette and lit it and snapped the lighter shut and stared at the glowing end. Nobody spoke. There would have to be an inquest. Suicide while the balance of her mind was disturbed. . . . The usual easy getout. She'd been perfectly balanced till the end—had carefully tied Trixie in the car before opening the door. . . . It had been a quite deliberate choice. "Its honour is worth something. I tried to preserve it."

I heard Spenser say: "Well, you've certainly given us a lot to think about, Mr. Branwell. I confess your story has surprised me in some of its aspects."

Reckitt coughed dryly and put a finger inside his collar. "Surprising is hardly the word, is it? On your own admission—and accepting this story at its face value—you stumbled upon the fraud, were actually at the scene of it, and yet did nothing at all about it for many months. Your own firm represented us—dealt with the claim, yet you didn't raise a finger to prevent the payment of a large sum of money in settlement. That's a very peculiar admission, Mr. Branwell."

When we got to the hospital, I'd gone a bit queer. Somehow it had all got tied up with my father, he'd come back and shut the door and turned on the gas, I'd found him there. . . . "Yes," I said.

"And then—four months later—after marrying the widow of this Tracey Moreton, and laying your hands on twenty-eight thousand pounds fraudulently come by—you ask us to believe that you intended to pay this money back, even though you've so far made no attempt to do so. Is that what you say?"

"I don't ask you to believe it. It happens to be the truth."

"Well, frankly. . . ." Reckitt looked across at the Abercrombies. "I was doubtful whether this meeting would be justified, but . . ."

Mr. Abercrombie was rather white. He said: "These—er—pictures, Branwell. Did you try to trace any of the other originals; did you tell the police or the customs about them?"

"No. I believe they've all gone out of the country."

"You *believe* so!" said Reckitt.

Rawson, McDonald's boss, fiddled with his glasses and said: "I'm still not altogether clear about this. Mr. Branwell admits that he failed in his duty to the insurance world. But there was surely a—a wider duty, as a citizen, to give evidence at an inquest, to tell the police of his finding the body of this man Moreton. How does Branwell explain his failure to do that?"

I put the cigarette down. My hands were still not quite steady. "It may look as if there are two issues now; but there was only one then. I thought Moreton's wife was involved in the fraud and I wasn't ready to denounce her. That's all there is to it. . . . But I'm not here this morning to excuse myself. I'm here to explain. My—failure as an ordinary person is something I've already acknowledged, in the proper quarter. I'm here now to talk about my failure as an insurance adjuster. I should think that's fairly clear to you all." I looked at McDonald, but he wasn't looking my way. "I've given the matter a good bit of thought during the—before coming here this morning; and it seemed to me there was only one very obvious thing to do. So I phoned Michael Abercrombie a couple of hours ago and asked him to accept my resignation from the firm."

A clock outside was striking twelve. It reminded me of the hospital clock I'd heard every hour through the night. I felt as if I shouldn't ever drive a car again. One goes on for years without ever realizing what speed means in terms of impact. If I had nightmares in the future it would be of finding myself alone on the wet grass and hearing Trixie bark and knowing Sarah was inside the broken car. . . .

They were talking about me; there was a general murmur of voices; and Michael was explaining something, and Reckitt was nodding his head in agreement; it was the only possible thing to do.

"Just a minute," said Henry Dane and bent to knock out his pipe. I think it was quite accidental; but it was just like a judge's gavel bringing the court to order. "Aren't we going a bit fast? And being very one-sided. It's partly Branwell's fault for giving such a lame-duck account of himself; but even in the police courts we try to make allowances for a bad witness. Now——"

"Even in a police court," said Reckitt, "one does not ignore the facts."

"No, but one tries to get them all before passing judgment. What was that you were muttering a minute ago, Oliver? Something about having made your apologies elsewhere?"

"Not apologies," I said. "I made a full statement to the police."

"When?"

"About two hours ago. That was what made me late getting here."

"Why this morning? Why nine o'clock in the morning? Has there been some other development?"

I stared at him, feeling irritated with him for forcing this out of me. But perhaps it didn't matter. Perhaps in any event it would all have to come out, and it was better these men should know. Anyhow I'd postponed it until they'd had an opportunity of considering the case without it.

So I told them all about Sarah's visit to Lowis Manor last night, and what Mrs. Moreton had said and how it fitted in with what I knew and made an understandable whole. I told them about her jumping out of the car on the way back, and the car crash that followed. I explained I'd spent the night in hospital and come straight on here.

Afterwards there was an uncomfortable silence for a minute or so. Nobody knew quite what to say; and that was why I hadn't wanted to tell them.

Mr. Abercrombie said: "But why didn't you explain this when you came in? How is your wife?"

"She's got a broken leg and concussion. They say—the house surgeon says she'll be all right. I—shall feel surer about it in a day or two."

Dane said: "And Mrs. Moreton is dead?"

"Yes." Trust him to see the point.

"Did she give you any corroborative evidence of what she said?"

"The servant, Elliott, can confirm a good bit—if he will. She stayed with him that night of the fire."

"Were there any witnesses of the car accident?"

"A man on a bicycle saw Mrs. Moreton fall out."

"Thank God for that."

"You think of everything," I said.

"Well, it's a good job someone thinks for you," he answered vigorously. "Because you seem devoid of the ordinary instincts of self-preservation. What did the police say? Did you see Detective Sergeant Barnes?"

"Yes. I made the statement to him. He didn't say a lot, of

course, but he seemed fairly satisfied. He said things were looking a lot tidier now."

"You see, it wasn't so difficult after all."

"It isn't so difficult when you have to."

Spenser coughed. "Have you had something to do with this case before today, Mr. Dane?"

"Yes, of course I have. That's why I was advising you not to jump to conclusions. Branwell's acted like a damned fool, but never like a rogue."

Mr. Abercrombie said: "D'you mean he's consulted you on this?" There was a curious quickening in his voice that I liked and was grateful for.

"Almost from the beginning."

"And acted on your advice?" asked Reckitt.

"Certainly not. If he had he wouldn't be in quite such a mess."

They waited while he lit his pipe again. He didn't hurry. "Branwell came to me first a couple of days before the fire—about the time he called on you, McDonald—and told me all about his suspicions and I told him where to go to get advice on detecting fake pictures and furniture. He put it as a hypothetical case, of course, and we talked it over pretty thoroughly. But I'd no reason to connect what he said with Lowis Manor—either then or later. Nor had I any reason to suppose he contemplated anything so silly as housebreaking." Dane blew out a stream of smoke and watched it break up and drift away. "After the fire . . . Well, after the fire he didn't tell me as much as he might have done, but during the several months that followed we had various conversations, and I gave him advice which I later saw was relative to this case. You blame him for not immediately telling the police of his discovery of the dead body and that the fire was planned. Well, so do I; but it isn't such an open-and-shut issue as you seem to think. When he discovered the fire—if you accept his word for it—he did all he could. Then when the brigade came at his call, he'd to make a split-second decision whether to stay on or whether to go. He went, and after that it was too late."

"Too late for what?" said McDonald, breaking his long silence.

"Too late to do any of the orthodox things. Because once he'd left the scene of the fire he'd no proof that he'd ever *been* there. What sort of evidence could he produce that the fire was deliberately planned? He could talk and ruin himself, and make a

213

lot of trouble; but he hadn't any sort of factual proof—at least not the sort that *I* have to produce to persuade an underwriter to contest a settlement."

I saw Charles Robinson smile.

Spenser said: "Yes, but——"

"But never mind that. After some months he discovered quite suddenly that Mrs. Tracey Moreton had no hand in it. They met, and he told her what had happened, and without hesitation she agreed the money must be paid back. He came at once to see me——"

"*Before* their wedding?" asked Mr. Abercrombie.

"Well, of course . . ."

That's a lie, I wanted to say; but I couldn't without letting Dane down; and anyway it wasn't quite a lie; he was like a man walking carelessly across stepping stones; you thought every minute he was going to fall in, but he didn't even get his feet wet. He explained about the claims on his time, the case in Liverpool, which had prevented him from giving his full attention to my problem until I came back from my honeymoon, how by then the rumour had spread, making it impossible to put the thing in hand. He made it sound as if the rumourmongers were alone to blame for Mr. Reckitt not having his £28,000 back in his pocket before now. He told of his advice to me to go to the police and my refusal until I could see my own inquiries through. He ended by saying that I and my wife had succeeded in clearing the mystery up at last, to the satisfaction of the police, and it seemed a poor reward to him that as a result one of us should be in hospital seriously injured and the other out of a job.

When he finished, his pipe had gone out again and he began to unscrew the thread. Spenser's cigarette had smouldered away unsmoked.

I thought Reckitt would be the one to speak. "You've certainly shown us another side of the picture, Dane. Obliged to you for that, of course. It transforms Branwell's case. All the same I'm a little surprised that a man of your wide experience should go out of his way to excuse what are after all still very grave irregularities. We may well acquit a person of dishonesty and still consider him guilty of negligence, bad judgment, and a failure to see where his first duty lies. Now——"

"Oh, I know that," said Dane. "I told you. He acted like a fool.

214

But that's all. And what you don't realize, any of you, is that Branwell is still a newcomer to this sort of job. I've been in the law and in insurance thirty years. Some of you here more than forty. Branwell came into it untrained less than five years ago. If I was ever in an emergency like his—which God forbid—I wouldn't have to reason anything out; I'd *know* what to do by instinct. He wouldn't. That's the difference. What sort of a reputation has he made for himself in these few years? Ask the Abercrombies. Ask yourselves, or any of the other underwriters." Dane stopped and made a nasty juicy noise blowing through his pipestem. "He's earned a first-rate name, for integrity, guts, judgment—and if he hadn't I wouldn't be here talking about him. He's the sort of man we *need* in the insurance world; not the sort to kick out in disgrace for one black mark. And I tell you another thing: if he went out today he could get a job with a claims assessor tomorrow, black mark or no black mark, and earn just as much money as the Abercrombies pay him, working for the other side. It's a sobering thought and worth taking time to consider."

"I beg your pardon," said Reckitt, going a bit pinched round the nostrils. "So far as I know there's been no question of his being kicked out in disgrace, as you call it. This informal meeting hasn't authority to do anything at all. It was arranged, largely at Mr. Abercrombie's request and chiefly——"

"Yes, I know all that," said Dane. "But in effect its authority is final enough, just because its findings will never be promulgated and therefore there can never be any appeal against them. If the general opinion of this room is that Branwell has acted badly, he's no choice but to offer his resignation and the Abercrombies have no choice but to accept it."

In some ways, I wished Dane hadn't spoken for me. In the night I'd had hours to think; and I'd come to this meeting quite decided; but he was such a persuasive beggar that he was making even me see the other side of the picture. In spite of early doubts, I'd *enjoyed* my job with the Abercrombies. It did suit me, temperamentally. Or it had suited me until the Lowis Manor fire.

Thinking this, I'd lost track of the conversation again. I was suddenly aware that McDonald was speaking. He'd slumped in his chair, and his double chin looked heavy and gross.

". . . since my inquiries began it. What Henry Dane has said —and what Branwell said before him—has cleared up a lot of the

215

perplexities in my mind, and I've certainly no wish to be vindictive. Obviously there are plenty of people senior to me here, but if it helps any way I'm prepared to say I'm entirely satisfied with what I've heard, and I suggest we forget all about this meeting and consider it as never having happened."

It was very handsome of him. It staggered me a bit, and I think some of the others too. At least nobody spoke for quite a while. Eventually, Spenser began to say something, but just at that moment I realized that this was the third time I must speak, if I was ever going to speak at all.

"No," I said. "I'm—very grateful to McDonald for saying that. I'm very grateful indeed. . . . But it won't *do*. Ever since May, since the fire, I've been thinking about this; but it's only recently that it's come clear in my own mind. And it was really while I was awake last night that I finally saw the thing as it really is. I don't know whether the rest of you agree with McDonald or not—and perhaps it's better if I don't know—but, if you'll forgive me, I don't want to leave the decision to you. That's not egoism or old buck: if I thought I came out of this well. . . . But, whatever Henry Dane says, I don't come out of it well—at least that's my opinion, and, ultimately, it's your opinion of yourself that counts. So I *want* to resign, to get things straight with myself again."

Traffic was rumbling outside. Even the Saturday workers were beginning to go.

"When I came out of the Army," I said, "I got a chance to go and settle in New Zealand. It's an offer that still stands and I . . . and my wife and I want to accept it. It'll be a different life from this—perhaps not better, I don't know, but it'll be something different and quite new. I think that'll suit me. I think it'll suit her. Of course I shouldn't have thought of making the change if this hadn't happened, but perhaps in the long run it will be for the best." I stopped for a minute to find the few remaining words. Spenser was fiddling with his pencil, turning it end to end. The only one who was looking at me was Charles Robinson.

Mr. Abercrombie said: "The point is, Oliver——"

"I don't know what the Abercrombies think about it," I ploughed on, "except that they're the people I'll most regret leaving in this—because they've trained me and backed me and I've become a part of their firm and a part of their connection; and I shall always be grateful for their—trust and friendship. But so far

216

as I'm concerned myself, I don't feel that anything in these last five years has been wasted. Perhaps some of the stuff I know about insurance won't be any more use; but all the rest will be good to have wherever I go. Some people end their education fairly early; mine started differently and has gone on late. If this, this Lowis Manor business, means that I go out under a bit of a cloud, it's a pity. But it isn't so much a pity as if I didn't know when to go."

Spencer opened his eyes and looked at Reckitt. But Reckitt was staring out of the window. Spencer said: "Well, I don't know what the feeling is, but it doesn't seem to me there's a lot more we can usefully do this morning. Branwell's decision is something he must discuss with Mr. Abercrombie. If he's quite made up his mind to go, as I think he has, well, then it becomes a private matter which is no longer any concern of ours. But even in that case —still *more* in that case—there's a great deal to be said for Mc-Donald's generous suggestion. It seems to me that the purpose of this meeting has been fully achieved—not by forcing Branwell's resignation but by healing a quarrel and by eliciting the full facts of the situation. Personally, speaking as an observer in this, I'd like to say that Mr. Branwell's attitude this morning has left me with the highest opinion of his general integrity, and I'm sure there's no one here who doesn't wish him every possible success in the new life he has chosen."

Well, that was it. I stood on the corner of Lime Street and Leadenhall Street and watched the thinning trickle of traffic. In another hour, the City would be dead. As I would soon be dead, so far as the City was concerned.

It was all very well to talk about the new life I had chosen, but in fact I'd talked a lot more surely than I knew. I didn't know what Sarah would feel about it, because I'd not really seriously discussed it with her. I didn't even know if Roy Marshall's offer was still open. Not that I seriously doubted that Sarah would like the idea or that she would be entirely loyal to my decision —I knew that now—but the expenditure of nervous energy this morning, following last night, had left me empty and tired and depressed. I didn't regret what I'd done; but it suddenly seemed so much less straightforward than it had in Reckitt's room, and

217

fraught with difficulties and all the trials and errors of a new beginning.

Also, although it had seemed at the time, shaking hands with them all and meeting their eyes, that I'd come out of the business with credit and advantage after all, I knew that in the future the failure would look large again, that I should always feel I'd left under a cloud. And there would be times when that knowledge wouldn't be an easy thing to live with.

It was always an unnatural quiet, this, that fell on the City at a weekend; not so much restful as secret, not so much empty as watchful. It didn't seem very long since all this had been strange to me, foreign territory.

I hadn't even had the opportunity to say the things I wanted to say to the people who had stood by me. True, I'd seen Michael and his father alone at the end and tried to tell them how I felt, but, as usual, the things I said didn't sound right to me.

I turned up towards the Bank, where there would be a better chance of a taxi, and someone took my arm. It was Henry Dane.

He said: "Well, my friend, are you satisfied with the morning's work?"

I said grimly: "Are you?"

"No. If I knew you were bent on hara-kiri I shouldn't have wasted my morning's golf."

"Or one of your best defence speeches. Sorry."

"Can I drop you somewhere?"

"No." We walked a few paces and then I stopped, determined to say it to him. "Look, Henry, I want to *thank* you. I don't know why the hell you did it. I don't know why you went to all that trouble and sailed near the wind for the sake of——"

"My dear fellow——"

"No," I said, "there's no getting out of it. I shall never forget the way you . . . everything. . . . But it wasn't useless because I did have a chance of abandoning ship in good order instead of being torpedoed from all sides."

"Why abandon ship at all?"

"I *feel* it's right. Or I felt so. Now—just at this moment—I'm not sure of anything at all."

"The fact of your leaving while this rumour's still about——"

"I'm not. I've agreed to stay on for a bit—just while things

218

straighten themselves out. I don't care about the rumour but I do about the Abercrombies, and they put it to me. . . ."

"I'm glad."

We walked on in silence to the corner of Gracechurch Street. I said: "You think I'm making a mistake, then, in going to New Zealand."

"I think you're making a mistake in not fighting it out here. There are all sorts of obstacles, I know, but none that you can't surmount. You don't really solve any difficulty by avoiding it, especially when some of the difficulties are within yourself. England made you, Oliver, and it should take the credit—or the consequences. And so should you. This is where you began; and it's where you should work out your own solution. *Then* go, if you want to, but not before. You've integrity and courage, and a wife who's your equal in both. With her to help you, you can still do practically anything. But not if you scuttle now."

I stared at his lined vigorous face. "Scuttle's not a word I'm very fond of."

"I didn't suppose it would be. That's why I used it. . . . My car's down here. I'll say goodbye."

We shook hands, and I said: "In any case thanks again—for *everything*—for your help and for your advice. There's a lot about the police side I'd like you to know. I'll see you again."

He smiled. "I think you will. Ask Sarah's opinion on it all. You might even go by that."

"I might even go by that."

As we crossed the empty street and were about to separate he said: "I hope you find her better. Her well-being is all you *really* care about, isn't it?"

And when I had left him and walked on a bit further towards the Bank I knew that what he said was absolutely true.